The Dream Walker

Books by S. J. Scofield

The Fire Lord series
THE KEY BEARER
THE MOON SINGER
THE MIDWINTER KING
THE DREAM WALKER
THE FIRE LORD

THE MOON GLASS

The Dream Walker

S. J. Scofield

St Ursin Press

First published in Great Britain in 2024
by St Ursin Press, 3 Broadfield Court,
1-3 Broadfield Road, Folkestone, Kent CT20 2JT,
United Kingdom

ISBN 978-1-7384026-4-9

St Ursin Press is an imprint of Trencavel Press
www.trencavel.co.uk/St Ursin.html

Chapter 1

THUD.

Owen hit the rocky floor of the Earth Temple like a sack of potatoes. He was never going to get the hang of these Gateway tunnels, he thought ruefully, as he rubbed his bruised elbow.

"Look out!" Finn's warning cry came just a moment too late for him to get out of the way.

The Earth Temple was empty – fortunately! Owen hadn't even considered the possibility that Sir Dennis' people might be there when he stepped through the Gateway from Assyah with the Earth Sath in his rucksack.

The Earth Sath… His fingers tightened guiltily round the dragon's tooth in his hand. It should have been the Sath that he had kept firm hold of. Swiftly, before anyone had a chance to see what he was doing, he stashed the tooth in the pouch hanging round his neck.

"Let's get out of here!" Raya had already set off across the cave towards the dark passageway that led to the iron rungs. "What are you waiting for? Someone could come down at any moment."

She was right. There was no point staying here any longer than necessary, only more risk of being found. But his gaze was drawn to the cave walls, their contour lines of copper-green, ochre-yellow, russet and blue gleaming beneath the flames of the Everburners, and he felt a sharp stab of regret that he didn't have more time to examine the patterns carved into those walls – the spiralling labyrinthine coils, bunches of grapes and sheaves of wheat. There was so much more to learn in this temple of the Earth Element.

He started as behind him the millstone let out a grating, grinding groan. The Gateway was closing, the wide central hole shrinking back to the size of a normal millstone eye. His hand reached up for the key tucked into his pouch with the tooth and just for a moment he felt a deep, thudding pulse reverberate through his body – the heart of the stone.

"Come on!" Raya called to him again, a note of impatience in her voice.

With one last glance back at the millstone, he made his way across to his waiting friends. His shadow shivered in the flickering torchlight as he walked, reminding him uncomfortably of Aralu.

It must be night by now, he realized, and with only a small, crescent moon to light their way, they were going to have to get through the woods of Bale Castle in the dark. He tried to push the thought away. Their immediate problem was getting out of the underground bunker without being caught.

He followed Arin up the iron rungs in silence, feeling more confident about the ascent than the last time they had climbed up out of the cave, even if he was less confident about what lay beyond.

A pale light suddenly flooded down into the shaft, silhouetting Arin above him.

"Wait!" he called up. He wasn't even halfway up yet and didn't want Finn or Raya rushing straight out into the corridor. He was in charge, wasn't he?

"We are waiting," Finn replied in a loud whisper. "It's just a glow ball."

A glow ball... An idea popped into Owen's head as he clambered up on to the ledge at the top of the shaft.

"Finn," he whispered, not trusting the solid oak door to totally muffle the sound of their voices. "You know when we got away from those Eddleshi, we did a camouflage spell."

"It won't work here." Finn stopped him, guessing correctly his thought. "There's nothing *Woody* to work with – not living wood anyway," he added, running his hand over the carved oak, "and even if there was, what would Raya and Arin do?"

He nodded slowly. It was a good point. His friends didn't seem able to feel any magic other than that of their own Element. Raya and Arin would be no more able to work a Wood magic spell than Finn would a Water one. They would just have to take their chance and hope that there wouldn't be anyone down in the bunker at this time of night.

2

Cautiously he edged open the oak door, just enough to be able to get one eye to the narrow crack of light. He blinked as the harsh unnatural glare of electric strip lighting hit his eyes, reflecting off cold, clinical white walls. There was no sign of anyone out there. He waited, listening. No voices echoed along the corridor.

"It looks OK," he whispered back over his shoulder.

Very slowly he pushed the door open a little wider. Still there was no sound other than the constant droning hum of the electric lights. He hesitated. He had been here before, in the heart of his enemy's domain, with a Sath in his rucksack. But last time he hadn't known that the bunker lay below Bale Castle until they were out in the open. This time he knew exactly where he was. What's more, his enemy, the Fire Lord, was almost certainly now aware of the fact that they had at least one of the Sath and would be hunting for the others.

He took a deep breath. They had to get out now. Going back and waiting in Assyah until daylight would be too dangerous. Once the Baarash who had caught them on Mount Meru discovered that he had been tricked, he would set out to find them, and if the news of their presence in Assyah reached the Fire Lord himself... How long would it be before the great fiery eye that had been watching the Wood Gateway, came to watch over this one?

He glanced back at his friends waiting behind him, their faces pale and ghostly in the darkness, then stepped out into the corridor. At least they knew the way out this time. He hurried past the door to the library and map room, conscious of the sound of his feet on the concrete floor. But it was more important to get out as quickly as possible than to make no noise. However, just as they passed a second white painted door and the final corner of the corridor came into sight, just as it seemed that they would get out undetected, there was a loud clank. He stopped in his tracks, for an instant frozen like a rabbit in headlights. Someone was opening the heavy iron door, the door that he had thought was about to let them out of the bunker into the relative safety of the graveyard above.

Finn's reaction was quicker.

"In here." He opened the white door and pulled Owen into the darkness beyond. Raya and Arin hurried in after them, just in the nick of time.

There was nothing in the darkness that gave any clue to the nature of the room in which they were now hiding. He didn't dare move, let alone try to find a light switch. Outside the door he could hear voices approaching. If they were heading for this room... a knot of fear tightened in his stomach.

"The old lady must know where they are." A woman's voice with a foreign accent rang out harshly beyond the door. "I do not understand why Dennis wants us to wait."

"It doesn't matter." This time it was a man who spoke. "He'll be back in a couple of days."

"Yes," the woman cut in. "Exactly. They will all be here and it will be taken out of our hands. We will get no...what is the word?"

"Credit?" The man suggested with a heavy sigh. "No. But I'm not about to disobey a direct order, and anyway she doesn't..."

Owen strained to pick up what he was saying, but the speakers had continued along the corridor and were out of earshot.

He waited, motionless, in case there were more people following behind, but eventually, very cautiously, he edged the door open again and peered out.

"All clear," he whispered back. Then with one last check back along the corridor, he was out, running towards the iron door, then up the three worn, grey steps and along the grassy path through the dark graveyard, too anxious to be out of the bunker for caution. It was only as he reached the gnarled stump of the old yew tree beside the churchyard wall, that he slowed down and at the last moment ducked off the main path behind a thick clump of brambles.

"Over here" he hissed, as the shadowy figures of his friends hurried along the path towards him.

Despite the unsettling presence of broken, mouldering tombstones, reaching like stubby fingers through the tangled weeds, a great wave of relief swept over him. At least here, hidden in the darkness behind the bramble thicket, they wouldn't be seen. He let out a deep breath. After all he had been through in Assyah, he had no intention of being caught and losing the Sath the moment he arrived back in his world.

"We could wait here," Arin said, looking warily over the brambles towards the sinister looking wood that lay beyond the wall. "We'd be safe enough, wouldn't we? I mean no one is going to be looking for us

4

here and we could leave first thing in the morning, when we can see where we're going."

Owen considered the idea. It might be better to face the woods with a bit more light...

"Hissssss. HISSSSSSSSSSSSSSSSSSSSS." A pair of blood red, slanting eyes flashed open in the blackness, like a flame sparking to life.

And in an instant all thoughts of staying were extinguished. He scrambled out through the tangled undergrowth back on to the path and ran full pelt out past the yew tree stump and into the looming, shadowy ranks of Supertrees, only to trip moments later and crash heavily to the ground.

"Are you alright?" A glow ball flared alight beside him, and Finn's face peered down at him.

"I'm OK. Did you see it?" He stood up rather shakily.

"I heard it." It was Raya who answered. "What was it? It sounded like a snake... sort of."

He shook his head. "Not a snake. It..." He stopped. "Finn, can you make that a bit bigger?" He squinted into the darkness beyond. Something wasn't right.

Finn's glow ball expanded, opening a wider window of light in the dark wood.

"There must have been a storm," Finn said, staring wide eyed out along the previously clear path. "A big one."

That was an understatement. Owen had never seen anything like it, except on TV, on reports he had watched about natural disasters in far off places.

Finn's glow ball grew bigger. "At least they're not proper trees," he said, but he couldn't disguise the dismay in his voice.

The path ahead was blocked by fallen trees, lying prostrate like the bodies of soldiers laid out on a battlefield, their gigantic trunks snapped as easily as if they were matchsticks.

An awful thought suddenly struck Owen. The Old Mill couldn't have escaped a storm like this unscathed. What if something had happened to Nana?

The previously regimented rows of Supertrees looked less sinister now, defeated by nature, and as he concentrated on battling his way through the chaotic jumble of fallen wood Owen almost succeeded in forgetting about the snaggly toothed, scaly creatures which might be lurking in the darkness – almost…

By the time he reached the outer wall of the castle grounds and the gate through which they had entered a few days earlier, his lungs felt like they were about to burst. It was one thing running through the wood by day on a clear path, quite another doing it with fallen trees as obstacles in the dark.

He pulled open the gate, stumbling over yet more fallen debris in his hurry to get out, finally stopping to get his breath back only when he was safely under the cover of the reassuringly normal trees on the far side of the road.

"We did it!" Raya exclaimed, gasping for breath, as she joined Owen.

They *had* done it. Raya was right. But as he surveyed the scene of devastation illuminated by Finn's glow ball, it felt like a very hollow victory.

It looked as though a tornado had ripped through the woods. Some trees lay roots reaching skywards in a grotesque parody of branches, others appeared to have been hacked down by a giant axe, leaving only a ragged stump. And hanging heavy in the air was the overpowering smell of sap, a scent which before had made him think of Dayah, and of Beith laughing as she ran through the sunlit forest, but now seemed more like the pungent tang of blood – tree blood, soaking into the earth.

The road beyond lay silent as the grave.

"We might as well go back along the road." He turned to his friends, trying to sound calmer than he felt. Both Raya and Arin looked unhappy about the carnage around them, but Finn was distraught.

"These *are* proper trees." He placed his hand gently on the trunk of a fallen oak. "It must have been awful." His voice was thick with emotion.

"They'll grow back," Raya said, trying to cheer him up. "They're only trees!"

"Only trees!" Finn was appalled. "How can you say that!?"

"Raya!" Arin glared at his sister. "That's like Finn saying a dolphin is just a fish!"

Owen was suddenly reminded of Darius. He had called dolphins fish on that visit to the Dolphinarium.

"That's totally different," Raya began, but Owen interrupted her.

"Let's just get back now and make sure Nana is alright. Anything could have happened to her on her own in a huge storm." Finn was right, they weren't *only* trees, but right now finding Nana was more important than any argument about Wood and Water energy.

"If you hear a car coming, just get off the road and hide," he called back over his shoulder, as he set off. But as he picked his way through the fallen branches littering the tarmac, he realised that the chances of that happening were zero. The storm must only just have hit, and no one had tried to clear a route through the debris.

Even when they turned off the small lane on to the main road, it was no better. No car was getting through this, he thought grimly, and that meant that if Nana had been in the Mill when the storm struck, and had needed help, no one would have been able to get to her. He stepped carefully over a broken telegraph pole. There would have been no phone either.

"She'll be all right." Finn came up alongside him. "She's pretty tough, I reckon. Anyway, I bet she's been through worse storms than this in her life."

As they continued along the road, he tried to convince himself that Finn was right. Nana must have survived all sorts of natural and unnatural disasters over the course of her extremely long life. But his heart sank like a stone as he rounded the last corner before the Mill to be met by ominous darkness. Where was the lantern that always lit the kitchen by night? Nana left it burning as a beacon for travellers, and even if the electricity was down, that wouldn't have stopped her lighting the lantern.

He raced across the garden towards the kitchen and threw open the door. "Nana?" he shouted. "Nana!"

Silence.

He fumbled for the light switch and predictably it clicked uselessly, but Finn's glow ball was already spreading light into the shadowy room, a room which was almost unrecognisable. Nana's kitchen had always been cluttered and higgledy-piggledy, but there had been method in the apparent chaos – everything had its place. Now though, it looked as if the room had been hit by a tornado.

Jars and pots were smashed to smithereens, their contents scattered across the floor, and a huge oak cupboard, which held crockery, lay on its front, as though pushed from behind by a giant hand. He stepped over a fallen chair, trying to avoid treading on broken shards of pottery and glass. It didn't make any sense. The kitchen window had shattered, but even with a gale howling through the gaping hole, surely it couldn't have blown over the cupboard?

"It looks like a tidal wave," Raya said. "Except, nothing's wet." She ran her hand over the top of the table.

Owen picked up a big copper pan from the floor. A black, sticky goo coated the inside. It looked as though whatever had been in there had boiled dry. Surely if a storm had knocked the pan off the range, the contents would have spilled out all over the floor. He made his way across to the door to the hall with a rising sense of dread. Something very bad had happened here.

Chapter 2

A brief search of the Mill had been enough to reassure Owen that at least Nana wasn't lying crushed under fallen furniture. But beyond that there was little more he could do to find her that night. A wave of exhaustion swept over him. It had been a very long day. Despite having eaten next to nothing since the previous day, no one had much of an appetite, and though Finn found some recently cooked, sticky-bark flapjacks in a wooden box, Owen only managed a few mouthfuls. He could barely keep his eyes open and fell asleep the moment his head hit the pillow.

He woke with a start. He had been dreaming about Olafssey Island – a strange, confused dream, in which he and his father were climbing the volcano to find a dragon, but then inexplicably were jumping off a tower together. He yawned and rubbed his eyes. The remnants of the dream were already fading from his memory. He rubbed his eyes again. Was he still asleep? This wasn't right. He was in his bedroom at the Mill, that much was clear, but even at its messiest it had never looked like the mayhem that lay before him. Then everything came flooding back. He sat up, suddenly wide awake. Light was streaming in through the window, and he automatically looked over to where his clock should have been. An empty wall faced him. He clambered over a pile of books, which had fallen from the bookcase, and picked up the broken clock from the floor. Quarter to nine. He stared at the frozen hands for a few moments. Which quarter to nine? Morning or night? Where would Nana have been at that time? Out in the garden perhaps...

"Morning," Finn mumbled through a mouthful of flapjack as Owen burst into the kitchen. He, Raya and Arin were sitting round the table in a remarkably tidy kitchen. The broken pottery and glass had been swept up, chairs righted and only the heavy oak cupboard still lay flat on its front.

"Nana might have been in the garden when the storm came," he said, as he made straight for the door. "She could be under a tree or..."

"She won't be," Finn interrupted him. "Storms don't start that quickly. And anyway, she'd have known it was coming."

Owen stopped. "What do you mean?"

"Well... she's... er..." Finn hesitated a moment. "I reckon she's a Sylvan," he declared, a note of challenge in his voice.

Owen nodded. He had already come to the same conclusion himself a while ago. "I know. I think she is too. But what's that got to do with knowing the storm was coming?"

"She would have read the signs, wouldn't she?" Finn stopped. "How long have you known about her?"

"What signs?" Owen ignored his question.

"Well, the way the birds and animals behave," he replied. "Unless none of it works properly here in your world..." A frown crossed his face. "But people do still dream, don't they?" he asked a moment later.

"Yes, of course they do." Owen was lost.

"Then Finn's right," Arin said. "It's the same in Bryah. It's not magic or anything, just reading the signs around you – especially when you're asleep and dreaming," he added.

"So she would have known the storm was coming and wouldn't have just stood outside waiting for a tree to fall on her head," Finn concluded.

He nodded slowly. It made sense. Nana would have sheltered in the house – unless she hadn't been there at all.

"She could have gone to Aggie's. If she knew a huge storm was coming, I reckon that's what she would have done!" A wave of relief swept over him. That would also explain why the potion had boiled dry. She must have left it simmering, expecting to be back soon.

Feeling much better now, he made his way back to the table. That was surely the answer. Nana would have been fine with Aggie. He couldn't imagine any storm, no matter how bad it was, damaging Aggies's solid granite house. They could head into the village after breakfast to find out exactly what had happened. He suddenly felt ravenous.

A search of the cupboards fortunately revealed yet more sticky- bark flapjacks and an intact jar of still fresh mushroom and elderberry cakes.

The sunlight poured in through the broken window, dancing off shards of glass that had been missed by whoever had cleared up. Nana wasn't going to be happy when she got back and saw the damage, he thought, as he sat down to eat. He wondered how bad the garden was. At first sight it looked to have escaped the worst, but as he gazed out of the window a nasty thought struck him: what if something had befallen the two Sath he had hidden? One had been dangling on a flimsy piece of string in the well, and the other was at the bottom of a mine shaft! Before going to the village he should check on them – at least on the Wood Sath in the garden. And he ought to hide the Earth Sath too. He had been so distracted by what had happened to Nana that he had momentarily forgotten about it, lying at the bottom of his rucksack.

"You probably should hide that Sath," Arin suggested.

Owen nearly choked on his mouthful of cake. It was almost like having Eggo back!

"Yes," Finn agreed. "That Fire Spirit Baarash thing will know we tricked him by now. I reckon our descriptions will be all over Assyah as well as Dayah and Bryah – and probably everywhere before long."

If they weren't already, Owen thought grimly.

He headed out to the well a few minutes later, leaving his friends with strict instructions not to follow him.

"It's better only I know where the Sath are," he had explained. "This way, if you get caught and a Baarash tries to get you to talk, like on Mount Meru, then it would be the truth that you didn't know where they were."

In reality, he knew it was unlikely to save them if they were caught again, but despite no one looking very pleased about it, not even Raya had attempted to argue with him. What he didn't tell them was that Io's warnings about the Sath still rang loud in his ears. He trusted his friends implicitly, but if they had to choose between him and Dayah or him and Bryah…? There was no point in taking the risk.

The tall birch tree that stood just beyond the nettle patch where he had met Urti, rustled softly as he passed. He reached up and stroked the smooth bark.

"Hello Beith."

He hesitated a moment, wondering if he should try to talk to the Eddra as he had done before. Above him, the silver-green leaves shivered in the gentle summer breeze.

"Beith?" He pressed his cheek against the cool trunk and breathed in the musty honey scent of birch bark... No. He stepped back. There would be time to talk to Beith later. For now there were more urgent things to do.

A honeybee darted past, heading for the honeysuckle near his tree house, but he turned in the opposite direction. Despite some fallen branches, his first impression had been right, and the garden was remarkably unharmed by the storm. You could almost believe it was just another warm summer's day and nothing had happened.

The well too looked undamaged, and sure enough, the string was still attached firmly to the metal winch. He leant over and peered down into the cool darkness below, then gave the string a tentative tug. It was reassuringly heavy. The plastic box holding the little wooden apple was still there.

The next problem though, wasn't so easily resolved.

The Earth Sath had been hidden in Fire before, so it made sense to hide it there again. But how could he do that? He wondered briefly about asking his friends for ideas. None of them was a Boryad after all. The Earth Sath was no good to them. But having spun the line about it being safer for them not to know where the Sath were, he had backed himself into a corner.

There was the charcoal burner's kiln, of course. How long did the fire keep burning in there? He frowned. What he really needed was something like an Everburner, the torches which continued burning indefinitely with a slow, steady flame. He wished he knew more about Fire magic. He closed his eyes, letting the low droning hum of the bees fill his head.

There had been bees there that day, he remembered, the day his brother Dar had got so angry because he just couldn't get the flames of the fire to do what he willed them to do. Dar had not been good at Fire magic. Everything else had come so easily to his brother, or rather Tamus's brother, he corrected himself quickly. But the one talent he had wanted above all others, the one he had been convinced was superior to all other Elemental magics – mastery of Fire, had eluded him.

"Don't you see?" Dar had shouted, his face flushed, eyes shining with excitement. "You could burn the whole Earth from one tiny spark!"

A chill ran down Owen's spine at the memory, and he forced his thoughts back to the present. Where else could he find a fire that wouldn't go out? He frowned. The nearest thing he could think of was the great cast iron range in Nana's kitchen. Nana kept that alight all year round, feeding in a constant supply of firewood. It would have to do, he decided.

"Oak logs will warm you well,
That are old and dry.
Logs of pine will sweetly smell,
But the sparks will fly."

He tried to recall the words of the song Nana had sung as she built up the fire. Was there a wood mentioned which would burn a long time? He needed the fire to stay alight as long as possible just in case Nana wasn't going to return straight away to the Mill.

"Birch logs will burn too fast,
Chestnut scarce at all.
Hawthorn logs are good to last,
Cut them in the fall."

That was it: Hawthorn – Huathe. That was the name Nana had given it and he was certain there were hawthorn logs in the woodshed somewhere. He made his way round to the side of the Mill where the woodshed stood. He would rather it had been a more familiar wood, like apple, oak or beech. Hawthorn made him a little uneasy for some reason and he would have felt far more comfortable working with the wood if he had met a hawthorn Eddra in Dayah.

He ducked under the low lintel of the woodshed doorway. It had obviously been designed for Nana, and already, at only twelve, he was taller than her. His eyes took a few moments to adjust to the darkness inside, before a chaotic jumble of logs began to emerge from the shadows – not the usual neatly stacked piles. It might take some time to find the hawthorn!

Ten minutes later, with several splinters in his hands and knees, he had found enough hawthorn logs to fill the wood burner. He loaded up the wood barrow and made his way back to the house.

Finn, Arin and Raya were still at the table waiting for him.

"You took a long time!" Raya said. "We thought something might have happened." She sounded rather put out.

"Sorry." He felt a little sheepish. He suspected his friends didn't entirely buy his excuse for keeping them in the dark. "Look, I've got to hide this one too." He rummaged in his rucksack and pulled out the little dark grey disc. "So, er, maybe you could all, um."

"Close our eyes?" Raya suggested.

"No." This was getting embarrassing. "Why don't you go down to the tree house? I'll meet you there."

Raya raised her eyebrows but said nothing.

Once they had left the kitchen, he set to work building the hawthorn fire. There were still some blackened lumps of whatever wood Nana had been burning, smouldering in the ash at the bottom of the stove and it was beneath one of these that he hid the Sath, carefully pushing it in with the end of the poker. Then one by one he placed the hawthorn logs on top. He stood back once five logs were in, expecting them to catch light as they did when Nana fed the fire, but nothing happened. He frowned and reached up for the bellows but stopped as a thought struck him. Why was he putting his trust in an old folk song? What if it was wrong about hawthorn, and, anyway, no matter how slowly it burnt, it would go out eventually – unless...

He picked up a twig of hawthorn that had broken off one of the logs and rolled it lightly between his fingers. "Huathe," he whispered the word. "A fairy tree, a Fiery tree."

He stared for a moment at the little twig, then pointed it directly at the unlit logs.

"Bitom." The word rang from his mouth, loud and resonant, and a jolt of energy shot down his arm and out along the hawthorn stick. He held his arm steady, his eyes fixed now, unblinking, on the furnace in front of him. "Oip Teah Pdoke." It rolled easily off his tongue, and he felt a surge of excitement pump through his body as the hawthorn logs flared alight as if a gas jet had just been ignited.

He was transfixed. He had never felt so alive. Every cell of his body felt as if it was glowing with heat, like millions of tiny suns inside him. Very gently he sent another spear of Fire energy out along the little twig and the flames of the burning logs danced to his command. This was as different from the hot, prickling sensation that he had come to associate with Fire magic, as night was from day. This was how it felt when instead of being burned by fire, destroyed by fire, you became the fire – like being the Sun, he thought, as he watched the dancing flames. Then slowly, carefully, he shrank them, as though he was turning down a thermostat, down and down until they were barely more than a halo of light shimmering over the logs. He stopped. Was that enough? He thought of the Everburners. What was different about them? He stared harder into the flickering tongues of flame. Too fast! That was it – like when he ran and burnt up too much energy. "Slow." This time no strange foreign words came from his mouth. He was in total control of the fire. The Spirits of the flames, the tiny suns inside each spark, were his brothers and understood what he willed them to do.

He stood back. It was done. The wood-burner would stay alight now. Not forever, but long enough. Outside in the garden, a woodpecker had begun drumming busily. He laid down the hawthorn twig and closed the range door, feeling slightly dazed. It had all been so extraordinarily easy. Far, far easier than any Elemental magic he had learnt so far. And yet it hadn't been Tamus doing it. Tamus had never been especially good at Fire magic – only marginally better than Dar, he realized, as Tamus' memory popped into his head. It had been Owen doing it all. Owen Shepherd, who had never even dreamt of trying Fire magic before today.

He made his way across the garden to the tree house, unable to quite get his head around what had just happened. The memory of how to do Fire magic must have belonged to Tamus, but it had felt very different from the other times he had tapped into Tamus' memory to work magic. This time it had felt like Owen. How was that possible? Did it mean he was really a 'baddie' if he could do Fire magic so easily? The sound of his friends' voices rang across the garden, and he tried to push thoughts of Fire out of his mind. The Earth Sath was hidden – that was what mattered, and probably hidden better than the first two.

As he climbed up on to the wooden platform of the tree house, he was relieved to see that it had survived the storm intact.

"Done," he said, in answer to the quizzical looks. "It's safe."

"Two more to find." Finn sounded quite cheerful about it.

Owen nodded. Two more. But one of those was the Fire Sath.

He changed the subject. "I think we should go into the village and find Nana before anything else." At least that seemed like an achievable target. There was nothing more to be done at the Mill for now anyway. With no electricity, he couldn't even check the TV to find out any more about the storm.

With everyone back in 'normal' clothes, he hoped they wouldn't attract too much attention as they picked their way through the debris of fallen branches covering the road. It seemed there was no risk of meeting a car, but as they approached the village, he heard the unmistakeable sound of an engine interrupting the chorus of birdsong that had accompanied their journey from the Mill. Only then did he realize how wonderfully peaceful it had been before – almost like Dayah.

He had expected to see fallen trees and tiles blown off roofs, but not the scene of devastation that faced them when they reached the village. It was like one of the TV reports that he had seen about natural disasters.

"It does look like a tidal wave just hit it," Raya said grimly.

Barely a house was intact and where some of the newer ones had stood there were now just piles of rubble. He struggled to understand how a storm could have wreaked such havoc. Things like this didn't happen in Devon. It was as though he had stepped through the Gateway from Assyah into a totally different world from the one he had lived in before.

Across the village green two bulldozers were working where previously the village shop had stood, clearing a jumble of bricks and concrete dust. Everywhere he looked, he could see yellow jackets and hard hats, but no sign of any of the villagers. They had probably been evacuated. He had seen enough reports about disasters to know that that was what usually happened. Maybe Aggie had gone too.

"What are you doing here?"

Owen nearly jumped out of his skin, as one of the workmen came up behind him.

"Nothing," he stuttered. "We er..."

"It's not safe. Some of these buildings could come down at any moment. You shouldn't be here." The man sounded tired and not best pleased at finding four children wandering around.

"I'm looking for my Nana," Owen said. "I think she's with a friend here."

"Oh." The man's voice softened. "Go and talk to the policeman over there." He indicated over towards the bulldozers. "He's got a list of all the people who were here. He'll be able to help you."

'Were here'. That sounded ominous.

"Thanks." Owen hesitated. "Er...isn't anyone left here? I mean, in their houses still?"

The man frowned. "Yes. There's a few oldies refused to leave. Always are. Go and ask the policeman. He'll know."

Owen had no intention of speaking to the policeman but nodded his head obediently. He set off across the green in the direction he had been sent, but the moment the yellow jacketed man had disappeared from view, he turned in the opposite direction, away from the bulldozers and towards Aggie's house. He was certain that Aggie would be one of the 'oldies' who had refused to leave. She was inordinately fond of her little house and garden and Torquay was as far as she was willing to travel.

"Best corner of the Earth this is," she had told him on countless occasions. "I don't understand why you young people are so keen on travelling, moving around for the sake of it. No. Not for me. I have my piece of land, and this is where I belong."

He had been right about Aggie's house. It stood resolute and defiant, with not even a tile out of place. It would take a lot more than a storm to knock down those solid granite walls. They had been built to last.

He hurried up the path and knocked on the door. To one side a curtain twitched, then a moment later the door swung open.

"Owen! Come in, come in! And you must be the friends Nana has told me all about!" She beamed at Finn, Arin and Raya, as they followed Owen into the cool hallway.

"Is she here?" The mention of Nana had raised his hopes. But Aggie shook her head.

"We've not seen her in three days now."

"What?!" Owen was aghast. "I thought... Three days?"

"She's all right. Don't worry," Aggie reassured him. "We just don't know where she is."

Owen didn't understand. How could Aggie know Nana was all right, and who was the 'we' she was referring to?

"How do you know she's not buried under a tree or something?" A knot of fear gripped him.

"She *is* all right," Aggie repeated, "and she disappeared before the earthquake."

"Earthquake?" he exclaimed. "I thought..." He trailed off. That explained the fallen cupboard, the logs in the woodshed and the devastation in the village.

"Two days ago. A huge earthquake," Aggie replied.

He was so stunned by the fact that there had been an earthquake in Devon, that he didn't register Aggie's lack of surprise that he hadn't known about it.

"The epicentre was just off Torquay," she continued. "Awful. Over two thousand dead. Mostly in the town." She paused. "It shouldn't happen here, not in Devon. The Earth here, it's settled, peaceful. These rocks have lain tranquil for aeons. It's not like where you used to live – Olafssey. Those are young, restless lands. The rocks, the earth there, they are Fiery. Here, they are earth of Earth, old as time itself." She stopped. "Sorry. You're worried about Nana and I'm going on about the rocks. I promise she is alive and well... somewhere."

"Oh no!" Owen gasped, as an awful thought suddenly struck him. He turned to his friends, ashen faced. "What did that woman say? The one with the funny accent. You know, when we were down in... that place." He glanced quickly at Aggie. "It was something about an old lady, wasn't it?"

"The old lady must know where they are." Arin spoke slowly. "That's what she said."

"And something about someone being back in a couple of days and it being out of their hands." Raya said. "You think that's Nana, don't you, the old lady?"

"I think someone had better explain." Aggie looked straight at Owen. "Where exactly do you think Nana is?" She spoke calmly, her voice softer than usual, but her eyes bored into him with an intensity he had never seen before.

He didn't know what to do. Aggie was Nana's best friend and more importantly, he was as sure that she was a Boryad as he was that

Nana was a Sylvan, but that didn't mean that he could trust her.

"Where do you think she is?" Aggie repeated the question.

He hesitated a moment, then replied. "Bale Castle." Whatever else Aggie was or wasn't, he was sure she would never have harmed Nana. He had to trust her.

Aggie nodded slowly. "We feared as much."

"*We*? Who's we? I don't understand."

Chapter 3

'RAP. RAP. RAP'.

Owen jumped at the unwelcome sound of the door knocker and Aggie raised a finger to her lips, "Shh." She moved over to the curtained window.

"It's all right." She let out a huff of relief. "Wait here," she instructed as she went to open the door. Owen glanced at his friends. Despite Aggie's reassurance, no one moved a muscle. From the hall he could hear low voices, one of which was definitely male. He held his breath as he tried to make out what they were saying, but in vain.

"Who is it?" Raya whispered.

Owen shook his head. "I can't quite hear, but..." He stopped midsentence, his hopes suddenly soaring. Captain Sigursson! Of course! But just a few moments later, Aggie reappeared in the doorway, followed by the male speaker, and Raya's question was answered. It wasn't Captain Sigursson. Owen couldn't hide his dismay. It wasn't Sir Dennis or the Baron, but in his mind, someone not a lot better – Professor Vishnami.

He felt like a rabbit caught in headlights. If Aggie had invited the Professor in, that must surely mean she intended to include him in the conversation about Nana. He knew he was being irrational, knew that he had no good reason not to trust him, but those strange yellow eyes made him feel distinctly uncomfortable, as though the Professor was able to see inside his head and read his thoughts – not to mention the peculiar noises that had been emanating from the cellar on the two occasions he had been inside his house.

The Professor walked across the room and sat down in a big armchair, only acknowledging the four children with a grunt and a slight nod of the head.

"Sit down, sit down!" Aggie gestured to Owen and his friends, as she took the second chair, leaving them to squash up together on the sofa. Owen felt as though he was about to face an interrogation.

"So you think Nana is in Bale Castle?" The Professor launched straight in.

Owen turned to Aggie accusingly. "Why did you tell *him?*" He didn't care how rude it sounded. She might have just put them all in even more danger.

"Oh for goodness' sake!" Professor Vishnami exclaimed. "Just tell them and be done with it!" He gave an irritated snort and turned his glare from Owen to Aggie.

Aggie hesitated a moment. "We're not really meant to, are we? I mean... it was an oath."

"Oath?" The Professor practically spat the word out. "Didn't that oath include something about protecting them? Hmm?"

When Aggie didn't reply, he continued. "In my interpretation of that rather outdated and in many ways defunct oath, the greater need far outweighs something which was surely no more than a temporary expedient – appropriate at the time, but now inapposite!"

Owen hadn't a clue what the Professor was talking about. He might as well have been speaking Chinese for all the sense it made to him.

"If you don't tell them, I shall," Professor Vishnami said bluntly.

"No, no." Aggie was clearly not happy with this idea.

"Tell us what?" Owen was getting fed up with this. Aggie and the Professor could argue all they liked about oaths, but it wasn't going to help him rescue Nana.

"I told Professor Vishnami what you said about Bale Castle, because... er..." Aggie looked uncomfortable, "he's one of us – a friend."

"One of us?" He repeated her words. "What do you mean?"

She hesitated again, then made her mind up. "A Watcher." She stopped, expecting a reaction from him, but when he said nothing, she continued speaking, very slowly and deliberately, choosing her words carefully. "The Watchers – that's who we are. Me, Nana, Captain Sigursson, Professor Vishnami. You may well have guessed by now that we're not from er... 'here'." She paused again. "You do understand what I'm saying, don't you?"

21

Owen nodded slowly. "Nana's a Sylvan, you're a Boryad and Captain Sigursson is a Delfan." He glanced at Raya and Arin as he spoke.

"And I am an Aevyan," Professor Vishnami interjected. "Though you wouldn't know that since you appear not to have found the Gateway to Yezirah yet."

Yezirah! Owen was all ears.

"The Air Realm." Aggie explained unnecessarily. "One from each Element. Our job is to watch over the Key-Bearer, to keep you safe."

"Not that we did a very good job of keeping young Ned safe." Professor Vishnami shook his head. "Silly boy. What was he thinking?"

"I thought I was meant to be doing the telling!" Aggie glared at the Professor. "That is another story entirely."

And one Owen wanted to hear. But it would have to wait for now.

"So, where was I?" Aggie frowned. "Oh yes, the Watchers. Ever since before Time..." The Professor tutted disapprovingly at this phrase, but Aggie continued. "Ever since before Time, one has been chosen from each Realm to come through to this World to protect the Key-Bearer. The role of Watcher has been passed down throughout history. When one Watcher's time is drawing to a close, another is summoned to pass through the Gateway. The highest honour!"

"Hmm." Professor Vishnami didn't sound so sure.

"So you know all about the key and everything?" Owen was struggling to get his head around this. All these people whose role was to protect him!

"We know that the key is connected to the Gateways and our World." Aggie hesitated a moment. "We know too that the Key-Bearers have always been exceptionally magically talented." She exchanged a look with the Professor which Owen didn't understand. "And we know that keeping the key safe and the Key-Bearer safe, teaching you what you need in order to protect yourself, is our task."

"But you can't go back, can you?" Raya blurted out. "That's what Owen told us – that you forget where the Gateways are, and they're locked anyway."

Aggie nodded. "We can't go back. It's not an easy path." She looked pensively at Professor Vishnami. "The choosing is not done lightly."

Finn, Arin and Raya all wore identical, grave expressions and

Owen remembered how desperate Finn had been to get back to Dayah the first time he had come through the Gateway, and his fear when he had thought he might be trapped in Owen's world.

"It is the supreme sacrifice." Professor Vishnami put heavy emphasis on the words, and Owen got the distinct impression that it was one he wasn't entirely convinced was worth it. He shifted uncomfortably in his seat, under the unyielding stare of those strange yellow eyes.

"That's all you know? I mean..." He wasn't sure how best to put it. "You don't know what I'm meant to do with the key or anything?"

"We know you have used it." Professor Vishnami sounded irritated. "Why you, and not more appropriate Key-Bearers in the past, I can't imagine," he added.

"The Professor has seen you," Aggie began.

"Seen me?" He didn't understand.

"Air magic." Aggie tried to explain. "He..."

"I am a Dream Walker," the Professor cut in. "A very skilled one, as it happens. That means I am able to enter your dream-space and look out through your sleeping eyes, if I so wish."

"You what?!" Owen was appalled.

"Dreamwalking," Vishnami continued, ignoring Owen's look of horror, "is a highly specialized branch of Air magic. It has many different subdivisions. These include the entry into the dream-space of a third party, via the Universal Dream Cloud."

Owen was totally lost.

"It means that when you haven't slept inside a protective circle, when you have forgotten to cast one," Aggie gave Owen a stern look, "he has been able to see what you would have seen if you had opened your eyes."

"I saw a cave a few weeks ago – one which most certainly did not belong in Devon," the Professor said rather smugly. "And a boat. Bryah, if I had to guess. Recently, a rather claustrophobic little bedroom, with no windows, that can only have been Assyah."

"So Nana knew where I was too." Owen said slowly. He had thought she was just extremely laid back about his disappearances, but now her unconcerned attitude was more understandable. She would have known that he was at least alive. "Oh!" He suddenly understood. "That's how you know Nana is alive."

Aggie nodded. "He has seen her the last two nights. She hasn't put up any protection – deliberately I hope."

"What did you see?" he asked, heart in mouth.

"A bare, white room." Vishnami closed his eyes, as he recalled the details. "And one of those nasty strip lights. No window. Nothing else. It could have been anywhere."

But it wasn't anywhere. Owen was now certain he was right.

"It *is* Bale Castle, I'm sure," he said. "Or rather, it's in the grounds." He paused. To go on would mean revealing to Professor Vishnami that they had been down in the bunker and that they knew about Sir Dennis and the Fire Lord. Despite the revelation that he was a Watcher, Owen still didn't entirely trust the Professor. All he knew at the moment was that Owen had been to the Realm. He had to think fast. Everyone was waiting for him to continue.

"There's an old church in the woods there." He waited a moment for the Professor's reaction, but his expression gave nothing away. "And underneath, there's a sort of bunker – corridors and rooms and stuff – a library and I think a lab."

"A lab?" This interested the Professor.

"I haven't seen it," he admitted, "but we heard people talking about it. That's why I think Nana's there." He had gone too far to stop now. "We were hiding, and we heard this woman saying how the old lady must know where they are." He glanced across at his friends. "And how Sir Dennis would be back soon, and it would be out of their hands."

"Dennis!" The Professor practically spat out the word. "It would be, wouldn't it?"

Aggie nodded slowly. "He wouldn't hurt her though."

"You think not?" Professor Vishnami sounded distinctly unconvinced. "I don't think there is anything he would stop at these days."

"Why do you think they were talking about Nana?" Aggie changed the subject, but not before Owen noticed the warning look she gave the Professor.

"Well... that white room, it sounds like somewhere down in the bunker. Everything was painted white and there were strip lights and...," he hesitated as he tried to work at how best to put it, "I think the *they* that they were talking about, is us." He looked to his friends for support.

"Go on." Professor Vishnami prompted him.

He had to tell him something, but he certainly wasn't about to bring up the subject of the Sath.

"Sir Dennis has this company, Megaco," he began.

"Yes, yes." The Professor nodded impatiently. "We know all about Megaco."

"You do?" Owen was astonished.

"No." Aggie frowned at the Professor. "We don't know *all* about Megaco. We do know it is Dennis' tool." She chose the word carefully.

"Have you heard of someone called The Baron?" He tried to make it sound as casual as possible.

"The Baron?" Vishnami frowned. "Baron who?"

"Just 'The Baron.'" Owen had no idea if he was Baron anything.

Aggie and the Professor both shook their heads, looking puzzled.

"What about the Fire Lord?"

That got a reaction.

"What do you know of the Fire Lord?" Professor Vishnami leant forward, his yellow eyes narrowing.

"I think he's Sir Dennis' friend." Owen hesitated. "No, not friend..." Friendship wasn't the right word to describe how Sir Dennis had grovelled when he saw them talking on the terrace of Bale Castle. "Sir Dennis calls him 'My Lord.'"

Time seemed to stop, as the Professor's eyes bored into him, the drone of chainsaws and engines outside hanging suspended in the air.

Finally, Vishnami broke the silence. "Are you absolutely certain about this?" His voice cut the air like a blade of icy steel.

"Ye-es." Owen said in a small voice, feeling anything but certain at that moment. Had it been a mistake to mention the Fire Lord and to give away the fact that he knew there was a link with Megaco?

Aggie looked aghast but spoke more gently. "'Fire Lord'..." she frowned as she chose her words carefully, "is it perhaps a sort of title, like Bishop, or something like that?"

He shook his head. "No. Sir Dennis didn't call him the Fire Lord." He was sure he remembered it correctly. "He called him 'My Lord'. 'The Baron' was what he called himself."

"So what makes you think this was the Fire Lord?" Professor Vishnami interposed sharply.

Owen tried to recall the scene he had witnessed that night on the terrace of Bale Castle. "He didn't have a shadow," he said slowly, "and... I didn't know when I saw him what he was, but I've seen other ones – Baarashes they're called."

Professor Vishnami nodded impatiently. He obviously knew what a Baarash was.

"And I don't think Sir Dennis would have been like that with just an ordinary Baarash." It wasn't terribly convincing, but he didn't want to go into detail about the conversation he had overheard that night about the Sath and the key. He tried not to meet Professor Vishnami's piercing eyes.

There was another long silence.

"How do you know about the Fire Lord?" Professor Vishnami changed the tack of his questioning.

"How do you know about him?" Owen retorted, sounding braver than he felt.

"Yes." Raya joined in. "Owen's not going to tell you anything else until you tell us what you know!" She gave the Professor her fiercest glare.

"And who might you be?" The Professor looked at Raya as though he had only just noticed she was in the room.

"I'm Owen's *friend!*" Raya laid heavy emphasis on the last word.

"So are we," Aggie sighed. "Look, Owen, you really must trust us. We all want the same thing."

But he couldn't silence the little warning voice in his head. He did trust Aggie, but there was something about the way Professor Vishnami was looking at him, that reminded him uncannily of the Baarash on Mount Meru.

When no one spoke, Aggie continued. "We know that Dennis is involved with Elemental magic, and that Megaco is a front for... other things. We've known this for a long time."

Owen noticed that she avoided the Fire Lord question.

"Why do you think Dennis is looking for *you?*" she asked softly.

"Don't answer," Raya broke in, but he shook his head.

"It's OK." He had worked out a story that was loosely connected to the truth. "I think he knows we've been to the Realm – to Dayah at least." He shot a warning glance at Raya, who had opened her mouth to speak. "There was an eye watching the Dayah Gateway, and I think it saw me... us... use the key." He paused, expecting questions, but when there were none, continued, "And I think that's why. I think they want to get hold of my key, so they can open the Gateways and go through." It was probably not wholly untrue.

Aggie frowned. "So he knows about the key." She hesitated a moment. "There is something you probably should know." she trailed off and looked uncertainly across at the Professor.

He shrugged. "I don't see any point in not telling him. Nana ought to have said something when they first came back."

"I think she would rather tell him herself." Aggie sounded like she regretted having spoken before.

"Tell me what?" Owen wasn't going to let it go. "Nana's not here, is she, to tell me whatever it is. If it's got to do with Megaco, you've got to tell me."

Aggie sighed. "It may or may not be relevant to why Nana has disappeared." She paused. "Has your mother ever talked to you about your family – your father's family?"

"Not really. I never asked about it." It was half true. His mother had told him everyone was dead, and once he realised his father wasn't coming back, he had tried his hardest not to think about him, let alone any possible family. His father had been his hero: the man who could make fire dance between his fingers, who could call down lightning. When he had first disappeared, Owen had been sure he was on a great adventure and would be back soon. But as the weeks turned to months his certainty had begun to crumble and with it everything he had believed about his father.

"She never mentioned his brother?" Aggie asked tentatively.

"No." He felt suddenly apprehensive. What was it Nana had said when he questioned her about the photos he had found in the attic? That the brother was dead to her or something like that and she had refused to answer any more questions. "I know he had a twin though. I've seen photos."

Aggie glanced at Professor Vishnami before continuing. "Yes. They were twins, but so unlike each other you'd never have guessed if you'd met them. Ned was a lovely boy, a bit too trusting, not the brightest. His brother though..." She shook her head. "Totally different. Always too clever for his own good. Very talented with Earth magic." She frowned. "If things had been different, if Alfred and Rose hadn't died in that crash... Anyway, it was Ned Alfred chose as his heir, to be the Key-Bearer, despite the fact that his brother was by some way the stronger magician. Ned never told him, I'm sure of it, but I think he sensed that Ned was special. He just tried harder, always wanting to outdo Ned, and as they got older the difference in their abilities was more and more obvious." She sighed. "Ned took his responsibility as Key-Bearer very seriously – perhaps a bit too seriously. He thought it meant he must have a special role, a great task to fulfil." She gave Owen a searching look. "And he became rather er... idealistic."

"I think the phrase you were looking for is self-important," Professor Vishnami said. "He believed that he alone could *save the world* and was constantly signing up to one cause or another."

"He wanted to use magic for good." Aggie glared at the Professor. "To heal and to help people. But the more Ned went in one direction, the more his brother went in the other. He was drawn to the darker side, dazzled by the possibilities, the glamour and what it could do for him."

"This brother," Owen asked, thinking of the dark-haired boy he had seen in the boat pictures. "What was his name?"

"That was always the joke," Aggie spoke softly. "They were mirrors of each other, opposites. Ned and Den, Den and Ned." She paused a moment. "His name is Dennis."

Chapter 4

Dennis. Suddenly Owen understood why he had recognized the dark twin in the photos. It was the same person whose face had stared out at him from his computer screen in countless Megaco photos.

"He's... my uncle." He tried out the words. It didn't feel real. The Realm, Elemental magic, the Sath, all felt more real than the idea that Sir Dennis Fairfax-Bale was his uncle.

"So Piers is your cousin!" Raya added unhelpfully.

Aggie nodded. "He wasn't always how he is today. When they were younger, they were inseparable – best friends."

Owen understood this. Tamus and Dar had been best friends too once. They had taken a vow of eternal brotherhood.

"And if it hadn't been for the key," Aggie continued, "if Den hadn't felt that Ned was being favoured in some way, maybe none of it would have happened." She paused. "I suppose he was about twenty, twenty-one, when it really changed. They were living in the Mill with Nana, and Den was spending every minute studying magic. Your father," she smiled, "was more interested in girls and sailing, and of course his latest 'cause'. Anyway, at some point, Den fell in with some strange friends, a secret society, he called it, and secret it may have been, but he couldn't resist boasting to Ned about it, making all sorts of claims about the power and influence of the people involved. Suddenly he wasn't interested in what we had to teach him. He was particularly rude to Nana, I remember, saying Wood magic was just for feather-brained simpletons, and childish." She sighed. "It wasn't him speaking, not really. He was totally under their spell and just lapped up everything they told him. Anyway, one day he comes home from one of their meetings, almost bursting with self-importance, and announces that an extremely important, well-connected person, who of course he can't name, is backing him to set up what would become Megaco. I have to admit that in a way we were quite relieved," she glanced at Professor Vishnami, "because he moved away, went to London, then to America for a while. We thought it was better for Ned to be apart from him."

"We weren't wrong about that," Professor Vishnami said bitterly.

"He was gone a few years without much contact really, other than the odd letter and card at Christmas – that sort of thing. But eventually he came back," Aggie continued. "We knew he was doing well. His letters had told us that, but we hadn't known how well. Megaco kept things quiet in those days. You heard about the different companies they owned, but not much about who was behind them." She shook her head. "It all changed when he came back. Ned had got married by then, and Helena had recently had a baby – you," she added, "but they were still living in the Mill with Nana. Ned was... a bit lost." She looked to the Professor for agreement, but he just pulled a rather disapproving face. "He had started to get very interested in Fire energy."

Owen jumped guiltily at the words.

"And he had decided to study volcanology," Aggie continued, "but he was worried that he couldn't support a wife and child. Anyway, along comes Den, rich and successful, married to that awful woman Bunty Fairfax. Dreadful creature," Aggie snorted, "but her family had a title." She paused. "Den had changed. I hardly recognized him. And he didn't want anything to do with any of us. He even changed his name, first to Fairfax and then, when he bought Bale Castle, he added the Bale bit, to sound posh I suppose, but I think he didn't want anyone knowing his background either. It was only Ned he wanted to see. We wouldn't have known what he was doing if Ned hadn't told Nana and he only told her later...afterwards."

"If Ned had told us what he was up to at the time, we could have helped." Professor Vishnami gave Owen a very hard look as he spoke. "If he had *trusted* us, we might have prevented what happened later."

"He was sworn to secrecy." Aggie came to Ned's defence. "Oathbound," she added with a wry expression. "He had joined them, you see. Not for the power and glory." The words made Owen jump. "But because Den tricked him, told him that the group used magic under the cover of science, to improve the World. All those things Ned had dreamed of were possible through this secret society. They would control the Elements, no more natural disasters, no more illnesses, no poverty, no suffering, no more *hand of God*." She watched Owen carefully as she spoke. "He told Ned that they were like gods controlling their own destiny, and to make it even more appealing, he offered Ned a job in Megaco."

"WHAT?!" He couldn't believe what he was hearing. "He didn't take it?!"

But Aggie nodded. "Yes. You see..." she hesitated. "Bunty had recently had a baby too – Piers, and Ned could see only too well what Den could provide for his family, and he wanted the best for you and your Mum too. And I'm sure he believed Den to start with. Den told him they wanted people with magical talent. Maybe he really did want to help Ned," she said pensively.

"Huh!" Professor Vishnami wasn't having that. "Far more likely he wanted to lord it over his brother, prove once and for all that *he* was the special one. Ned would have had to start at the bottom – that's how they work these *secret societies*," he said contemptuously. "And Den, he would have been surrounded by toadies, hanging on his every word. You may be right, Aggie, about why Ned joined, but *I* can't help thinking that he believed that with the key," again he gave Owen a searching look, "he would soar through the ranks, thought it was the way for him to *save the world* as you so aptly put it."

"Whatever the reasons, he joined," Aggie continued. "We didn't know about it then, not even Nana. He wasn't working for Megaco itself, you see. It was some other company, Magma-something, and we had no idea it was part of Megaco. Not even the Professor knew," she added pointedly. "Anyway, everything was fine for a while – a couple of years or so. Ned seemed really happy. He was earning his own money, saving up for a home for you all. We knew by then that he was working with Den, but as long as he was happy, we thought it was probably all right. And anyway, Den was hardly ever around. We didn't think Ned actually had much to do with him."

"But then things changed. Something was worrying Ned, something he wouldn't even talk to your mother about. He told Nana a bit afterwards, said it was all lies, and Megaco was just after money and power, and that they were doing bad stuff. But he never said exactly what." She frowned. "Then one day I got a call from your mother, saying Ned had had a fight with Den. She wasn't there, fortunately. But Nana was. It wasn't..." she hesitated, "an ordinary fight. They fought with magic."

Owen could hardly believe what he was hearing.

"Nana was horrified. She was sure Den would win. He was so much stronger. But Ned used Fire magic. I still don't understand how he was able to do it, where he learnt that sort of stuff." She shook her head. "It's a very rare talent and not one that is generally taught much – for good reason," she added.

Taught... Owen had so many questions that he didn't know where to begin.

"But Fire magic it was," she continued, "and according to Nana, he nearly killed Den. We had to act quickly." She glanced across at Professor Vishnami. "Ned knew too much about Megaco and this secret society. There was no way they were just going to let things be. You left the Mill that night, and we made sure there was no trail left for them to follow."

"That's why we kept moving..." He only had hazy memories of the places they had lived before Olafssey. Friends had come and gone, houses merged one into the next.

"Yes," she nodded. "It was only after the accident that you were out of danger – ironically." She shook her head sadly. "We did all we could to protect him, wove protections, shielded you all from any attempts to scry or dreamwalk."

"I don't think it was an accident," Owen cut in. "I think they found him."

There was a long silence.

"Why do you think that?" It was Professor Vishnami who finally spoke.

Owen hesitated a moment. He had told this to no one, not even his friends. "I climbed the volcano last year," he said eventually. "I know it was dangerous, but I just wanted to see the place he'd died. I thought... I don't know... I thought I might find something. And afterwards, I thought maybe I had imagined it all, or was mixing it up with a dream. But I know now that it was real, what I saw." The memory was as vivid as if it had happened that morning. "There were eyes – bright, burning orange eyes, like shards of flame, staring up at me from the heart of the volcano. They... they pulled me in. If it hadn't been for a bird flying past my face, I... I think I'd have fallen into the volcano and died – like my father."

Aggie's mouth fell open in horror. "That's not possible. It would mean that they knew Ned would go to Olafssey, that he wouldn't be able to resist visiting the volcano. But there are countless volcanos erupting every year, all over the world. How did they know he would go to that one?" She stopped. "They must have known where Ned was, that he was near to Olafssey. But how?" She turned to Professor Vishnami. "The Watchers were the only people who knew he was there and there is no way one of us would have betrayed him."

An icy chill ran down Owen's spine. There was indeed no way he could believe Nana or Captain Sigursson would have betrayed his father, nor Aggie. He had never known her be anything other than straightforward, unless she was an extraordinarily good actress! Which left only one person.

"It would also mean that the Fire Lord was waiting for Owen," Professor Vishnami said quietly. "Why else stay there so long after Ned's death? This puts a whole new perspective on things." He got to his feet. "If you are right, and they have Nana – and I fear you are right – then she is in even more danger than we thought. There is no time to delay. Aggie, you must go to Torquay and find Sigursson. I shall go home and work out a plan of action. You," he turned to the four children, "will stay here. Do not go out of the house. Do not answer the door, and keep the curtains closed. Is there anything else you should be telling us before I go?" he added, fixing his gaze upon Owen.

Owen began to shake his head, but then froze. It felt almost as though an ear fish had got inside his brain. He couldn't move a muscle, as something slid into his mind, probing, poking, like little needles stabbing at his thoughts. No! He forced a great rush of Fire energy up into his head. Briefly, for no more than a second, a blinding white light burst into his skull, roaring and blazing as though all the air inside him had suddenly ignited in a fiery inferno. Professor Vishnami staggered back, clutching his head.

"Professor?!" Aggie rushed forward. "What's the matter?"

"It's nothing." Professor Vishnami was white as a sheet. "A migraine attack." He steadied himself with an effort, all the time avoiding Owen's gaze.

"You didn't...?" Aggie trailed off, looking from Owen to the Professor, with an expression of growing alarm.

"No, no. Come on." He headed for the door. "The sooner we get going, the sooner we rescue Nana."

Owen sat rooted to the sofa, his heart pounding in his ears as he watched Vishnami hurry Aggie out of the room.

"We'll be back soon," Aggie called over her shoulder. "Don't worry. Just stay here and you'll be safe."

For a few moments after the front door banged shut, no one moved. Then Finn jumped to his feet.

"They've gone," he said, with some relief, as he let the curtain drop.

"What are we going to do?" Raya turned to Owen for an answer. "We can't just sit here."

He agreed wholeheartedly, but just now he could barely string two words together, let alone think what to do. If the revelations about Sir Dennis hadn't been enough to send his mind into a spin, the Fire energy had left what he could only describe as an 'after burn' in his brain. He felt totally frazzled.

"Owen," Arin was giving him a funny look. "Just now, when he looked like he'd been hit by lightning, what happened?"

Owen took a few deep breaths before he spoke. "It was like Baarash on Mount Meru. He was trying to get into my head."

"What?" Raya was appalled. "He didn't..."

"No." He gave his head a final shake to clear it. "I stopped him." He didn't go into detail. The fact that he had used Fire energy might not go down all that well with his friends.

"I knew there was something funny about him the moment I saw him," Raya exclaimed.

"Do you think it was him betrayed your father?" Finn had another look out between the curtains.

Owen nodded. "It can't be anyone else."

"But why?" Arin wasn't convinced. "Why would he want to help the Fire Lord? It doesn't make sense. If he is a traitor, surely he would have told them about your key. And you said before that they were looking for it, so they can't know you've got it."

He frowned. Arin was right. The Fire Lord and Sir Dennis *had* talked about searching for the key. "I don't know why he hasn't told them," he admitted, "but he's up to something. Why was he trying to read my mind? And I don't believe that stuff about making a plan. I think he wants Aggie out of the way so that he can go and tell them we're here."

Finn agreed. "We can't risk it. Staying here we're like sleeping doolobs, just waiting to be eaten."

Owen nodded. Whatever a doolob was, he understood Finn's meaning. "There's a track across the fields at the bottom of the garden. If we go out that way, we should be able to get away without anyone seeing us." He led the way to Aggie's back door. "I know a good place we can hide."

Before reaching the open fields, the little track passed by the back gates of several other houses, Professor Vishnami's being one of them, and despite the thick, high hedge between the path and the garden, Owen still ducked low and ran. The other houses were probably empty, he guessed, but it wasn't until they had safely cleared the village and crossed the first field of sheep, that he slowed down. Crouching behind a hawthorn hedge, he took stock of where they were.

"We need to head that way." He pointed towards the familiar landmark of Gog's Hump, rising up in the distance beyond the rolling fields and woods. "I've got a camp in the woods. No one knows about it, not even Nana. We'll be safe there for a bit." He quickly pushed away the thorny question of what they could do longer term, with it no longer safe to stay in the Mill and nowhere else to go.

"That sounds good." Finn brightened up at the mention of the woods. "I'll cast a circle round it to make sure that the Professor doesn't do any of that dreamwalking stuff again."

Getting to the camp proved rather harder than Owen had expected. The path across the fields was fine, but once they reached the edge of the woods, there might as well have been no path. Fallen branches and uprooted trees had transformed the once familiar woods, and not only was there no clear path, but with half the landmarks gone, Owen had only his sense of direction to rely on. But finally, just as he was about to admit defeat and confess to being lost, a giant oak tree came into view.

"Druids' Oak!" He let out a sigh of relief at the familiar sight. "It's not far from here." He set off again with a renewed confidence.

His camp, fortunately, had survived the worst of the earthquake. A few small branches had come down on to the rhododendron, but apart from some of his twig-lattice ceiling having been shaken loose, the space under the roots was clear and his platform in the spreading oak tree above looked to be intact.

"Not bad." Finn was inspecting the camp critically. "This roof isn't great, but..."

"It wasn't like that," Owen jumped in defensively. "It's the earthquake that's done that. It's survived better than some of those houses in the village anyway."

Finn however, was already rooting around amongst the trees beyond looking for a birch stick he could use to cast his circle. Owen and the twins watched in silence, as he carefully moved clockwise round the oak tree and the rhododendron, tracing a wide circle in the earth, as he intoned the words of protection.

"It's just like we do in Bryah," Arin said, once Finn was finished. "Only of course we do it in the sea." He stopped. "I suppose it does work here in your world, Owen?"

"Yes. I'm sure it does. Other stuff works doesn't it?" he began, but then another thought occurred to him. "You know what *is* a bit weird – Professor Vishnami said he couldn't get into my dreams when I was inside a protective circle. But the circles haven't been Air magic, have they?"

"I don't see what difference that makes," Raya replied. "You used Air magic in Bryah when you tricked those Sutekhim off their boat, and it worked."

"Yes, and you used Earth magic in Dayah to open that iron door," Finn said.

"Mmm." He couldn't deny it, but at the back of his mind was a niggling little voice telling him there was more to this than met the eye. "I'm not about to fall asleep anyway, so he shouldn't be able to go poking round in my head." He made a mental note though always to cast circles before settling down for the night from now on, wherever he was.

There was just enough room under the rhododendron roots for all four of them to get safely concealed. For a moment Owen considered whether someone should go up on the platform as a lookout, but based on the state of the paths in the wood, he decided it was pretty unlikely anyone would be walking past.

"What's the plan?" Raya turned to him expectantly. Back in Assyah, Owen had got increasingly fed up with his friends always expecting him to have an answer, but here, in his world, he accepted the responsibility for deciding what to do.

"I think," he began slowly, "we have to rescue Nana. They said," he hesitated a brief second before saying the name, "Dennis would be back soon – a couple of days – and that was yesterday."

He waited a moment for the full impact of this to sink in before continuing. "That means we have to find her tonight, because they didn't say when tomorrow, did they? So it could be tomorrow morning..." he trailed off.

"But if you're right about the Professor," Arin said, "then they'll know that we know where Nana is and..."

"They'll be waiting for us," Raya finished his sentence. "We'll be walking into a trap."

"You can't go." Finn broke the silence that followed Raya's statement. "It's you they really want Owen, isn't it? You can't risk it. What if they caught you?"

"*We* could go though," Arin said, before Owen had a chance to reply. "We couldn't tell them where the Sath were, could we, if we got caught? And we don't have the key."

"No way." Owen shook his head adamantly.

"Arin's right." Raya said. "What if they did catch you and there was a Fire Spirit like that one on Mount Meru, or worse?"

He knew what she was saying. It was one thing breaking the hypnotic hold of a Baarash, who hadn't known who they were or that they had anything to hide, but imprisoned in that bunker, under the gaze of the Fire Lord himself...? Despite his new-found Fire magic ability, he doubted he could withstand that sort of interrogation.

"You might as well just give them the Sath," Raya said.

"And the key," Finn added.

But their arguments were to no avail. He knew that his friends were right, but he wasn't going to sit there and do nothing, while they risked their lives.

"It doesn't make any difference anyway," he said finally. "If they got you, that would just mean I had you *and* Nana to rescue."

The sun was already high in the sky and the day was passing far too quickly. If things had been different, he would have tried to find Captain Sigursson, asked for his help. But if the Captain was home, Aggie would have found him by now anyway. He glanced at his friends, hoping the rising sense of fear he felt wasn't written on his face. He felt overwhelmed by what he was facing. It was one thing being a hero in the Realm, but quite another in his world. Somehow anything seemed possible in the Spirit Realm. Here though... it just didn't work like that. People like Sir Dennis always ended up winning.

Ten minutes later, no one had come up with any good ideas. Owen didn't hold out much hope of being able to open the iron door that gave access to the castle grounds. Not only was there no keyhole to work with, to guide him into the mechanism, but when he, Finn and Arin had been waiting there for Raya to let them through before, he had noticed a familiar, faint humming sound, which suggested electricity. It would explain how people got in from the outside, if it opened like a garage door, with an electronic key, and he had no idea what would happen if his Earth magic met electrical wiring. It had to be the front gate, he decided, like the first time he had been into Bale Castle. A smile spread across his face as the realization hit him. It was that simple. Straight through the front gate.

"It worked last time," he concluded, after explaining his idea to his friends.

"And I've got plenty of fern spores here." Finn tapped the pouch hanging round his neck. "It should be easy."

But the confused faces of Arin and Raya told him that it wasn't going to be as easy as he and Finn thought.

"I've never heard of a camouflage spell." Raya looked to Arin for confirmation.

Her brother shook his head. "It's Wood magic, isn't it?" He looked doubtfully at the fern spores that Finn had pulled out. "It won't work for us. We can't do Wood magic."

A gaping hole opened up in Owen's plan.

"Could we make them camouflaged too?" he asked Finn, without any real hope of a positive answer.

"I don't see how." The Sylvan boy frowned. "You have to 'become' a part of the Wood energy, sort of merge with whichever tree you're working with."

Owen nodded. That was exactly how it had felt – as though the boundary between him and the oak tree he had leant against, had blurred and then gone. But he couldn't see how he could extend it to merge with Raya and Arin too.

"Finn and I will go." There had been some sense in what they had said earlier, about him not going.

"No, look," he continued, as both Arin and Raya opened their mouths to protest. "We don't need four of us. We'll just make more noise and be more likely to be seen. And *if* anything went wrong, at least we wouldn't all be caught."

"I think we should stay together." Raya wasn't giving in that easily. "Anyway, I know my way around there better than the rest of you." She made it sound as though she had had a full guided tour on her brief visit to Piers' party.

But another idea had just occurred to Owen. "No. It gives us a backup this way. You and Arin wait here in the den and give us until sunrise. That should be long enough." He paused. He could only think of bad reasons why they might not be back by sunrise. "If we're not back, go and find Captain Sigursson. He'll help, but you have to get him on his own and tell him not to trust the Professor."

He outlined how to get to the Captain's house, regretting, not for the first time, the fact that he had not put a pen and paper in his rucksack. "You'll know him when you see him. He looks like a Delfan." There was no better way to describe him! "I'm sure we will be back in time though. It gives us ages."

Chapter 5

Owen decided to leave his rucksack containing the little book with Arin and Raya. Since discovering its importance, he had kept it close, but taking it into Bale Castle was an unnecessary risk.

"You should probably leave the key too," Arin suggested.

He reached up to the key which hung round his neck. He didn't like the idea of leaving it. It felt like a part of him now. He wondered how his father had felt leaving it behind in Nana's care when he fled after the fight.

"I think I should keep it with me," he said finally. "What if we got down into the bunker and got trapped and the only way out was the Gateway?"

As he spoke, an image flashed briefly into his mind of him falling through a Gateway, running away from something or someone. Strange... It hadn't been like a Tamus memory. The Key-Bearer memories were just that – memories, familiar, things he recognized, and afterwards they stayed in his head like videos burnt on to his brain that he could access again. This had been more like a TV screen turning on for a second behind his eyes, sharp and bright, and then gone – no after-image.

Arin didn't look entirely convinced by his reasoning but made no attempt to argue. "I suppose they can't use it without you anyway," he conceded.

"No..." He trailed off. Was that right? The book had certainly said that only the Key-Bearer could read it, so only the Key-Bearer could find the riddles which would lead to the Sath. But as far as he could remember, it hadn't explicitly said that only the Key-Bearer could use the key.

He was keen to get going now that they had a plan. Waiting

only gave his enemies longer to set a trap, and since they were going through the main gates with a camouflage spell, there was no advantage waiting until nightfall.

"See you later," he called back to Raya and Arin as he clambered out through the hole between the rhododendron roots, trying to sound as confident as he could. But despite the risks that might lie ahead, he was glad he was going. Staying behind in the den waiting, not knowing what was happening would have been far worse.

He and Finn made their way through the woods and across the fields that lay between the camp and Bale Castle gates in silence, ears and eyes alert for any signs of danger. Once, he heard a car pass along the road below them, but they were well hidden from view and soon the sound of the engine had faded into the distance, leaving only the reassuringly normal woodland chorus.

However, as they drew nearer to the castle grounds, a potential problem suddenly struck him. He had just been thinking how nice it was in his world not to hear the constant background hum of electricity and car engines. But what if the earthquake damage meant Bale Castle itself had been evacuated? What if there was no one going to be there until Sir Dennis came back tomorrow? No people meant no cars, and no cars meant the gates would stay firmly shut.

His heart fell further as the gates came into view. Whatever other damage the earthquake had caused, it hadn't touched the walls or gates around the Castle. They stood firmly shut, an impenetrable metal grill, like bared teeth, warning intruders to stay out. Finn crouched low beside him, hidden from the road by the hawthorn hedgerow.

"I can hear that nasty buzzing noise again," Finn whispered, as he peered over the hedge. A moment later there was a high-pitched mechanical whine and the surveillance cameras, mounted on the walls beside the gate, swivelled round. Just in the nick of time, he pulled Finn down out of sight, as the cameras panned towards the exact spot where they were hiding. At least that meant that the electricity in Bale Castle was working. There must be a generator, he realized, and that surely meant it was more likely that there would be people there – gardeners, cleaners, Bob, the man who looked after the horses – people who at some point would leave work to go home and drive out of the gates.

They settled down to wait.

"We need to be quick," he said. "The moment we know a car is going through, we have to do the cloaking spell." He remembered what Finn had called it back in Dayah. "We won't have long. The gates are only open a few moments." He reached up and double checked that the fern spores that Finn had given him were still safely tucked away in his pouch.

For the first few minutes, he was poised to move at a moment's notice, like a cat waiting to pounce on its prey. But he couldn't keep up that level of alertness. The day which had started off sunny and bright, now threatened thunder. Dark, ominous clouds were building, rolling in from the moors, and it was growing ever more humid. He batted away what felt like about the hundredth fly to land on the back of his neck.

"They bite!" Finn too was being plagued by the tiny flies. "I wish I'd brought some penny royal and lemon grass water with me." He swatted one on his arm, leaving a squashed, bloody mark. "Ow!" He hurriedly rubbed off the remains of the fly with a leaf. "It's burnt me!" He pointed indignantly at his arm. "What sort of flies are these?"

"That's weird." He frowned as he peered at the patch of skin on Finn's arm. A blister was rapidly bubbling up, as though he had been burnt by acid. "I've never heard of flies that do that." He scratched his hand where one had bitten him, and felt a familiar hot, prickling sensation – Fire energy.

"Urgh!" He shuddered, as another one landed on his head. For a moment he was filled with the urge to jump to his feet and run, to try to escape the biting, tickling, itching, to find some icy cold water and submerge his whole body in it.

"Whatever you do don't squash one!" Finn said through gritted teeth, rubbing his burnt arm.

"They must be Fire things – like those horrible weaselly animals in there." Owen glanced towards the gates as he spoke, trying as hard as he could to ignore the sensation of thousands of tiny little legs crawling over his skin. But the harder he tried to ignore the itching, the worse it became. He forced his attention back to listening out for a car, but a few seconds later, he was flapping furiously again at the cloud of flies buzzing round his head.

The afternoon seemed to stretch on forever, and though the flies dissipated as the clouds cleared, it felt to Owen as though the sun was moving extraordinarily slowly through the sky. But just as he was beginning to think that he had made a mistake and they would have to find another way in, Finn went rigid beside him. "Car!" He turned his head to one side, like a bird, listening intently. Owen could hear nothing at first, but a few moments later, he too could make out the hum of an approaching engine. He quickly pulled out his fern spores.

"I call upon the guardians of woodland and wild places, you who protect the balance within nature. Hear me, Spirits of the forest, grant to me your assistance and cast around me the aura of camouflage, that I may walk your ways hidden from unfriendly eyes." He closed his fist tight around the fern spores, and pressed his cheek against the broad oak tree, which had served him so well the first time he had tried the spell here. Beside him he could hear Finn chanting similar words.

"Ready?" He glanced across at the apparently still visible Finn and sincerely hoped he had done the spell right. But there was no time to make sure. The car had arrived outside the iron gates. He peered cautiously over the hedge. Despite the camouflage spell, he wasn't taking any unnecessary risks. He let out a small sigh of relief. It wasn't a car he recognized, and most importantly not the one he had feared it might be – shiny and black, like a cockroach, the car with the number plate 'B1'.

A moment later, with a metallic clang, the gates began to swing to open. With a quick nod to Finn, he was off, running beside the hedge, out on to the road, through the wide-open gates and into the cover of the trees that bordered the driveway.

"Finn?" he whispered loudly. He could see no sign of his friend.

"I'm here!"

He jumped as Finn appeared beside him.

"Could you see me?" He hoped his spell had worked as well as Finn's.

Finn nodded. "I was following you so I made sure I could see you. You disappeared for a moment when you got into these woods," he said, frowning at the regimented ranks of Supertrees, "but then you made so much noise that it was obvious where you were."

Since the camouflage spells seemed to be working, Owen decided to stay on the drive for as long as possible. Even though the clouds had cleared and the sun was high in the sky, few rays managed to penetrate the dense canopy of the woods. They would have to go deep in amongst the trees eventually, to get to the chapel, but for now the sunlit strip of tarmac felt like a sanctuary from the menacing gloom of the woods.

Now that the car had gone, a foreboding, heavy silence hung in the air. He had noticed it before – a stifling, oppressive stillness that seemed to suffocate the normal chorus of birdsong and the chitter and hum of invisible insects and small animals. He couldn't even hear birds beyond the outer wall, as though a soundproof barrier stood between him and the living world outside.

He focused his attention back on the driveway in front of him, on the perfectly smooth, pristine surface. When he had first brought the Wood Sath back, it had been so effective at attracting Wood Spirits that he had been afraid that Bale Castle would be overrun by nature, but clearly someone had been busy. Not one stray blade of grass broke through the monotonous grey of the ribbon of tarmac, and as the Castle itself came into view, he could see that the weeds which had bravely invaded the artificial rose garden, had all vanished. Sir Dennis was clearly back in control of his domain.

They turned off the main driveway on to a smaller path which ran along the back of the stable block. When the plan had been discussed earlier, Raya had been confident that this was the right one to take.

"On the way to the party, I saw a path leading off in the right direction," she said, "just before you get to that weird grass that isn't grass. I would have taken it, only that stupid Ed saw me first."

Owen heard a horse whinny in the stables as they passed. He wondered what had happened to Tango. It all felt a very long time ago that he had hidden in the back of the little pony's stall, after rescuing the fox. That Owen seemed like another person, someone much, much younger.

The path continued on across the astroturf lawn. He glanced back at the glittering walls of the Castle. If the camouflage spells had worn off, they were in full view of anyone who happened to be looking out of one of the back windows. For once, he was glad to get back under the cover of the trees.

"The spell is still working, isn't it?" he asked Finn, as they set off into the woods.

"I don't think so," Finn replied, a frown crossing his face. "It was to start with, but..." he paused, "there isn't enough Wood energy here. It doesn't last that long anyway and without anything 'Woody'..." he trailed off.

Owen remembered his words when they were down in the bunker the previous day. He had told him then that a camouflage spell wouldn't work there. How had he forgotten that? He had envisaged them going down under the chapel invisible, finding Nana, giving her some fern spores to work her own spell, and all escaping together, still invisible. But there was no going back now. They were almost at the chapel and there was no time to come up with a new plan.

They walked on in silence. Now he knew the camouflage spell had worn off, the woods felt far more menacing. He jumped at the slightest sound, a twig cracking beneath Finn's foot, the distant rumble of a plane engine, a rustle in the leaves overhead. He was sure they were being watched, sure that the black scaly Fire creatures were lurking just behind the trees, their blood-red eyes following his every move.

He knew they were close to the chapel before it came into sight, as the damp, putrid smell of decay began to break through the antiseptic sterility of the Supertrees. Ahead of them stood the blackened yew tree stump. He glanced at Finn. Io, the yew tree, was his root tree, his 'family tree', as he had called it. But Finn wasn't looking at the yew tree. He was staring blankly ahead, his head tilted slightly to one side.

"I can hear something." He held one hand up to silence Owen. "Voices. People. Coming this way."

Owen's heart leapt into his mouth. They must have been seen. "In here!" He ran through the churchyard gate and ducked down behind a thick clump of brambles, nearly tripping over a broken gravestone in his haste.

For a few moments he could hear nothing but his own breathing, but then he too recognized the sound of voices. Beside him Finn began to mutter under his breath.

"What are you doing?" he asked in a hoarse whisper.

"Shh!" Finn hissed at him and continued mumbling. "No." He finally shook his head. "It's not enough." He released his hand from the bramble he had been gripping, and Owen understood. Of all the places he had seen in Bale Castle grounds, the graveyard was, ironically, the one with the most life, the only one that had been left to nature. Finn had tried one last attempt at a camouflage spell, using the bramble thicket, but to no avail.

The people were now just beyond the gate, and it sounded as though there were at least three or four of them. Owen held his breath, half expecting to hear someone say, "Search the graveyard," but instead there was a burst of laughter, followed by a rapid string of words in a language he didn't recognize, as the people walked straight past their hiding place. Very carefully he peered through the bramble leaves. Four men were heading for the iron ring and the doorway. He let his breath out. It didn't look like they were searching for him and Finn after all, just on their way to the bunker. But his relief was tempered by the realization that they couldn't risk going down to find Nana now.

"We'll have to wait until they come back out," he whispered. And that might be a long wait, he thought grimly.

The sun was already sliding lower in the sky and the one thing he been absolutely set against – a night-time rescue attempt, was looking ever more likely, especially when he heard a second group approaching, and then a third. Something was clearly going on down in the bunker, something that he desperately hoped had nothing to do with Nana.

They had no option now but to stay put. Without a camouflage spell, venturing back out on to the path through the woods was far too risky. But the longer they waited, the more chance there was of Professor Vishnami talking to his enemies, and a trap being laid for him.

Yet another group of people was arriving, a larger one this time. He heard a female voice with a heavy foreign accent – the same woman he had heard previously in the bunker, he thought.

"Careful!" A male voice barked the warning. Owen was sure he knew this voice too, but he couldn't place it. He didn't think it was the man who had been with the foreign woman before. Feeling more confident now that three groups had passed the bramble thicket without spotting them, he parted the thorny branches a fraction to get a better look. He could make out six or seven people gathered

46

by the gate, waiting for something. But whatever it was they were all looking at, Owen's attention was fixed at on only one thing: a man standing slightly to one side of the main group, a man with unnaturally smooth, tautly stretched skin and flat, dead eyes, who looked strangely isolated without the shadow that followed his companions. A Baarash. And not just any Baarash. Owen was sure it was the same one he had seen with Darius at the fair, and later in the garden of the Mill. He didn't dare move a muscle. He had no reason to believe Baarashes could hear or see better than normal people, but after seeing the way the Fire Spirit dispatched Ayin Dragontooth on Mount Meru, he wasn't taking any risks.

But then he saw what it was the group were all staring at. Moving slowly through the gate and along the path was a white-cloaked, hooded figure, from whose waist stretched a long, slender leash that shimmered in the evening sunlight. He leant cautiously forward to get a better look, but at that moment the figure turned towards him. He let out a gasp of surprise. The face that was revealed under the white silk hood would have been beautiful, but for one horribly familiar feature – an impossibly long nose, which was now sniffing intently in his direction. An Aelva!

She tugged at her leash as her nose twitched more and more rapidly. She had smelt them! Though he knew that it would make no difference, he pulled Finn down flat to the ground and closed his eyes, as he had done when he was a child, believing that somehow, if he couldn't see them, they wouldn't be able to see him.

"She's smelt something," a male voice said. "Look!"

"Hold her. I'll go and have a look," the voice he thought he had recognised spoke.

The commanding tone left no room for argument. Owen opened his eyes. That was it. He looked across at Finn, resignation written across his face. It was over. He could hear footsteps approaching the bramble bush, then saw legs walking round, stopping a metre in front of him. He looked up, trying to muster the last of his courage to meet the eyes of his captor.

Chapter 6

No! He froze, wide eyed with shock, unable to comprehend the face that looked down at him, a face that like the voice, he recognised – Darius! A moment later, without so much as a blink, Darius turned away from him.

"It's a fox," he called back to his companions, his voice heavy with disdain. "This is the problem with these creatures. They're not reliable until they have been *properly* trained." He laid heavy emphasis on the word.

'*Stay here!*'

Owen nearly jumped out of his skin as the words rang out inside his head.

"Take her down." Darius nodded towards the bunker, then cast a swift warning glance back at Owen, before following the Aelva down through the open door.

For several moments after the door had closed, neither Owen nor Finn dared move. Then slowly Finn edged forward and rose up on to his knees.

"They've gone," he whispered. "Let's go!"

But Owen shook his head. He didn't understand what was happening, why Darius had been with his enemies or why he hadn't said anything about them being there, but one thing he did know was that Darius had probably just saved his life. What's more, he had definitely heard those two words, '*stay here*,' ring out loud and clear in his head.

"No." He shook his head. "It's too dangerous." He spoke in a hoarse whisper.

"But he knows we're here," Finn replied, confused. "We have to…" He stopped mid-sentence at the sound of yet more people approaching the churchyard gate.

This time the footsteps hurried past without stopping, making straight for the door to the bunker. "We can't just stay here," Finn continued once he heard the door clang shut. "We'll never get Nana out tonight. Not with all those people down there." He hesitated a moment. "That was the man from your house, wasn't it? The one we saw in the garden."

Owen didn't reply immediately. A part of him knew Finn was right. They should make a run for it, get as far from the graveyard as possible. But another part wanted desperately to trust Darius, to do exactly as he had been told and stay put.

"I think we should just wait until we're sure no one else is coming, and we can get out without being seen." He didn't want to tell Finn about Darius' voice in his head. "He's not going to tell anyone we're here," he continued. He couldn't explain to Finn how he knew this, why he suddenly felt so certain that Darius wasn't about to betray them.

Finn frowned. "I don't know how you can be so sure about that. He was with a Fire Spirit in your garden, wasn't he?"

"I just... know," he replied.

It wasn't exactly a convincing argument, but the arrival at the gate of another visitor to the bunker at least reinforced the danger of leaving straight away. They waited in silence, expecting more people to turn up, but after about five minutes, Finn was getting impatient.

"How long are we going to wait? We should go and find that captain friend of yours, the Delfan, before it's too late."

It was hard to disagree. Now that their plan of rescuing Nana had been wrecked, it was probably the best option. But Darius had told him quite clearly to wait where he was, and the more time that went by, the more certain he was that Darius hadn't revealed their presence to anyone else.

"Come on!" Finn didn't understand his friend's reluctance to move. "Let's go." But just as he was speaking, the door to the bunker gave a heavy click and swung open.

Owen could hear footsteps approaching along the path, and for a moment his hopes were raised. Maybe the people had just met up in the bunker and were now heading off somewhere else – the Castle itself perhaps. Maybe they would still get their chance to rescue

Nana. But then instead of continuing along past their hiding place, the footsteps stopped. The walker had turned off the path and was approaching the bramble thicket.

"What on Earth are you doing here?" It was Darius, his voice taut and angry. "Come on! Quickly! Follow me. Quickly," he repeated the command when Owen didn't react. "Now."

Owen scrambled to his feet, followed hurriedly by Finn. His head was a whirl of questions, but now clearly wasn't the time to ask them.

Darius cast a swift glance back at the door to the bunker, then took hold of his arm and pulled him across on to the path towards the gate. Owen stumbled and almost fell, but Darius yanked him back up again, with surprising strength, as though he was just a small child. Only when they were clear of the graveyard and under cover of the wood, did Darius release his grip.

"I'll explain everything later." He was breathing fast, and even in the shadow of the trees, Owen could see the warning in his dark eyes. "You're a fool to come here. You could have ruined everything."

"I don't understand..." Owen began.

"Not now." Darius shook his head. "We need to get out of here and fast." He tilted his head to one side just like Finn had done earlier, and for a moment his eyes glazed over. "Come on. Follow me." He turned away and set off deeper into the wood.

Owen didn't need telling a third time. Whatever Darius' explanation for being there was, he was right that he had been a fool. If anyone else had followed the Aelva to his hiding place, he dreaded to think what might be happening to him now. He hurried after him. To his surprise, instead of leading them to the iron gate, Darius was taking a path he hadn't seen before, one which wound round to the opposite side of Bale Castle from the stable block. A couple of times Darius stopped, listening intently for a few moments before continuing along the track. Finally the path opened on to a wide gravel car park, sheltered from view by high walls on three sides. Owen recognized Darius' car parked close by.

"In!" Darius swung open a door.

Finn hesitated, looking at it warily.

"It won't eat you," Darius huffed impatiently. "It's not a dragon!"

"It's OK." Owen got in first and a great wave of relief swept over him. It *was* going to be OK. Darius was rescuing them. They would soon be safe. He should have trusted him all along. Finn followed him in rather reluctantly, wrinkling his nose at the expensive leather smell inside the car.

"Right." Darius turned back to them from the driving seat. "The windows are tinted so no one can see you there. But just to be sure, when we get near the gates, get down on the floor until we're through."

Finn jumped as Darius started up the engine and looked even more unhappy than before but bit his lip and said nothing. The dark woods rolled past the window as they drove along the driveway towards the gates in silence. Owen felt safe cocooned inside the car, as though somehow the metal chassis could keep out any danger, but he still ducked down behind the front seats when the gates came into sight, and let out a sigh of relief as the car pulled away on to the road outside.

"OK. You can get up now." Darius too sounded relieved.

As Owen sat back up on the seat, he caught sight of Darius' eyes in the rear-view mirror, watching him with a very peculiar expression. Darius swiftly looked away, focusing back on the road.

"Where are your friends?"

"They're waiting for us in the woods," Owen replied immediately, realizing a second too late that he hadn't mentioned Raya and Arin to Darius before. "How do you...?"

"Listen." Darius cut him short. "None of you are safe. I've told you I'll explain it all, but for now you've got to trust me. Tell me where to go and I'll get them to safety too. OK?"

"OK." Owen tried to push away the little voice of doubt which was whispering in his head. After all why would Darius have rescued him and Finn if he didn't want to help them?

"Good." Darius spoke gently. "Now where do I go?"

Five minutes later, Owen was leading him through the woods towards his camp. Darius had parked the car just off the road at what Owen judged to the nearest point to the den. Finn hadn't spoken since getting into the car, and Owen could tell he wasn't happy with what was happening. He glanced across at his friend, but Finn was very deliberately keeping his head down.

As they approached the camp, he could see no sign of Arin and Raya. No one appeared to be up on the lookout platform and there was utter silence from the rhododendron bush.

"Raya, Arin, it's me. It's OK. You can come out." He pushed through the leaves that hid the entrance and peered into the dark space between the roots. It was empty. "They're not there." He crawled back out into the open, puzzled. "They were meant to wait until sunrise before going to get help if we didn't make it back," he explained. "I don't understand why they're not there."

"Did anyone see you come here?" Darius asked quietly. "Could you have been followed?"

Owen shook his head. "No..." But was he certain? What if it hadn't been a person following them? He tried to remember if he might have felt the hot pricking of Fire energy at any point, or anything else unusual. "I don't think so."

A moment later however his worries were allayed.

"Here." Raya's voice rang out from the opposite side of the clearing. "We're up here."

He turned to see her peering down at them from high in the branches of another oak tree.

"What's *he* doing with you?" She looked accusingly at Darius.

"It's OK," he hastily reassured her. "He's a friend. He rescued us."

"Where's Nana?" Raya asked as she and Arin clambered down from their perch.

"We couldn't get her," he began, but Darius interrupted.

"You can talk when we're back in the car. There'll be plenty of time later, but right now we need to get away from here. And fast," he added.

Raya gave him one of her best glares but said no more as they made their way back to the waiting car.

"Why weren't you in the den?" Owen asked, as soon as Darius started up the engine.

"We were to start with," Arin replied, "but after a bit we thought we should move, because if you got caught," he glanced at Darius, "they might make you tell them where we were. So we hid close by so we could make sure it was safe before we came down."

Owen guessed the '*we*' who had thought of this was Arin.

"That was a good idea," Finn said, frowning at Darius' back as he spoke.

They lapsed into silence as the car sped along the narrow country lanes. Owen wanted to tell Raya and Arin what had happened in the graveyard but wasn't happy talking in front of Darius until he knew exactly what he had been up to down in the bunker. Suddenly, the car swerved sharply, throwing him against the door and narrowly missing a white deer which had run into the road.

"A roebuck!" Finn let out a low whistle and gave him a warning look. He was obviously meant to understand the significance of the deer, but he couldn't recall any mention of roebucks in Nana's lessons.

The roads were thankfully empty. The last time Owen had been in Darius' car, on the ill-fated trip to the Dolphinarium, holidaymakers had slowed traffic to a standstill in some places. At least there was one positive thing to come out of the earthquake!

They turned off the main road on to a smaller one which he was surprised not to recognize. He thought he had ridden his bike along all the roads round here and couldn't understand how he had managed to miss this one. But as the road rounded one last corner and emerged from the woods, he had an even bigger surprise. Ahead, rising up from the surrounding fields was a peculiar, unnatural-looking hill, and soaring skywards from its peak, a tall, white-painted lighthouse.

Owen was flabbergasted. The fact that there was a lighthouse so far inland wasn't such a shock. Professor Vishnami had told him about how the sea once came in further, and the Gateway to Bryah, the rock arch, stood today in the middle of a field, miles from the shoreline. But how could he possibly not have seen this before? He was sure it wasn't marked on any maps.

The road wound up the hill in sinuous curves, like a giant snake, and he was reminded suddenly of the web-worm that had taken them from Bryah to the Earth Temple. He hastily pushed the thought away. This was just an ordinary road winding up a hill.

"I never knew this was here," he said.

"No," Darius replied. "I don't suppose you did." He looked amused by something. "This is where I live when I'm here in Devon."

Owen was surprised. He had thought Darius stayed on his boat. He wasn't sure why he had made that assumption, but someone must have given him the idea – his mother perhaps. "Has my mother been here?" he asked.

"No." Darius hesitated a moment before replying. "She hasn't.

There are things we keep private, aren't there?"

Owen couldn't really argue with that. He craned his neck to get a better view as they drew closer. From across the fields he had noticed something rather peculiar. The lamp house had looked strangely small, sitting in the middle of a wide, flat circle of roof, whilst to one side stood what appeared to be two tall, grey stones, pointing skywards. But with the lighthouse now towering directly above them, he could no longer see the top.

"There has been a lighthouse on this site for a very long time," Darius continued after a moment. "And before that, there was a tower – some sort of temple, I believe."

Owen fixed his eyes on the road ahead, trying not to let any emotion show on his face. "Oh, really?"

"Yes." Darius replied. "Really." He smiled slightly. "Those stones you saw on the roof, they were a part of the original ancient structure." He paused a moment. "Something to do with the Air Element, so I'm led to believe."

Owen was sure Darius must be able to hear his heart pounding.

"Why is there a lighthouse *here?*" Raya broke in suddenly. "There's no sea, is there?"

Darius looked up into the rear-view mirror. "No." His eyes scanned across the passengers on his back seat as though he had only just noticed them. "Not now. There was once. All these fields, woods, they all used to be under water. This hill was an island, not far from the shore. You could sail out here in a little boat easily enough back then." His eyes met Owen's as he spoke and a look almost like regret crossed his face. But then a moment later his gaze was back on the road ahead, leaving Owen wondering if he had imagined it.

He slowed the car as it rounded one last curve and pulled up just in front of the lighthouse. A flight of stone steps led up to a yellow-painted door. "Don't worry." Darius smiled encouragingly at Finn, Arin and Raya as they climbed out of the car. "You're safe here. This place is... protected, hidden. No one can find you here. *No one.*" He laid extra emphasis on the word. Finn still didn't look convinced, but he followed the others up the steps and through the door.

A spiral staircase wound up through the tower ahead of them, like a continuation of the serpentine road. Owen was slightly surprised as

Darius led them up past several firmly closed doors. The steps were of bare, light grey stone and the walls painted a stark white, rather like those of the bunker, not the sort of opulent luxury he would have expected in Darius' home. But when Darius finally opened a door and led them into a large, hexagonal room, his original expectations were realized.

It looked like something out of a film, not the sort of place where ordinary people lived. The walls were hung with peculiar paintings of shapes and colours, which he guessed were probably very expensive – even though he had no idea what they were meant to be, while the chairs and sofa were all made of white leather so immaculately clean that he was afraid to sit down.

A vase of tall white flowers got a frown from Finn. "Not real," he whispered as they walked past.

He could see no sign of a TV amongst the carefully positioned sculptures that decorated the room. It felt more like being in a museum or art gallery than a house.

Darius beckoned him over to the sofa. "Sit down." He smiled at Owen's disconcerted expression. "It's all a bit too white, isn't it? The truth is, I haven't been here much. I got a designer to do it all for me and ended up with this. I should get your mother in when she's back to help me make it more homely."

That got Owen's attention. "Do you know when she's coming back?"

Darius shook his head. "No. I haven't heard anything."

Owen was suddenly on guard again. Did Darius know about MARS, the Megaco Antarctic Research Station that his mother had been heading for in her last letter?

"Would anyone like something to drink?" Darius asked, before he had a chance to pursue the subject of his mother.

Silence greeted the question.

"Well, I'm going to have something." Darius headed for the door. "I'll bring you glasses in case."

The moment he had disappeared out of the room, Raya turned accusingly to Owen.

"What's going on? Who is he?"

"Darius. My mother's friend. You know... the one with the boat," he replied.

"Oh! Him!" Raya's attitude changed in an instant, as she remembered the pictures Owen had shown them of Darius' new boat.

"So what happened?" Arin asked.

Owen glanced quickly at the door. "We nearly got caught." He outlined as fast as he could what had happened at Bale Castle.

Darius was taking a very long time getting the drinks, and he had got as far as the escape back through the woods before the door swung back open.

"Here you go." Darius put down a tray with five glasses and a jug of an orangey liquid that looked suspiciously like Smah. Owen took a tentative sip. It tasted like Smah too.

"Right." Darius set his glass back down. "Now I don't know what you were doing in that graveyard, but I'm guessing that it wasn't just chance that you were there."

Owen glanced at Finn. He knew his friend didn't trust Darius, but then he hadn't wanted to trust Beith either. Anyway, he had to tell Darius something.

"What were you doing there?" Finn cut in abruptly before he had a chance to speak.

Darius hesitated a moment before replying. "I'm not really sure how much I should tell you... whether I can trust you to keep this in confidence."

"Trust us?!" Finn exclaimed. "We're not the ones..."

"You can trust us." Owen frowned at Finn. "I'll tell you why we were there, but not until I know why *you* were there. I didn't realize you knew the Fairfax-Bales."

Darius leant back in his chair, giving Owen an appraising look. "I know Dennis." He paused, "I've known him for a long time. His company, Megaco – have you heard of it?"

Owen nodded.

"We've been watching it for several years now." Again he hesitated, as he chose his words carefully. "It's not what it appears to be in certain respects. It's a front essentially. Do you understand?"

"Yes. I think so," he replied slowly. "We know about Megaco, the Supertrees and stuff. And all the disasters."

Darius nodded encouragingly. "Right. So I don't need to explain to you how dangerous Megaco is." He didn't ask how Owen knew about Megaco in the first place.

"No. We know it is." Owen was feeling more confident. "When you said 'we,' who did you mean?"

"I said 'we,' did I?" Darius smiled again. "Well, let's just say we are a group of concerned people, people who have the greater interest of this World at heart. It's taken us a long time to infiltrate the inner circle of Dennis' organization – or rather it's taken *me* a long time." He laid heavy emphasis on the word.

"You mean like a spy!" It all suddenly made sense. That was why Darius had been with the Baarash at the fair.

"Like a spy," Darius agreed. "They would have jumped at the opportunity of bringing in someone like me anyway, but I had to make sure it was the inner circle, the initiated, as they call themselves, not just as a business associate. I have had to befriend some very unpleasant characters to get there, like that strange man you saw me with at the fair."

Owen gave a start. It was as though Darius had just read his thoughts!

"So you can see why I was so alarmed when I saw you there, Owen. You risked blowing years of work out of the water if they had found you first. You were unbelievably lucky that it was me," he continued.

He *had* been unbelievably lucky, Owen realized, and not just in escaping in one piece from Bale Castle. "This group of people you belong to..." he began.

"I'll tell you more about us later," Darius stopped him. "What I would like to know now is exactly why you were hiding behind a bramble bush in that graveyard."

"Nana." Owen had been so absorbed in Darius' revelations that he had almost forgotten his purpose in going to Bale Castle to start with. "I think they've got Nana there. We went to try to rescue her." He expected Darius to ask why he thought this and was ready to tell him all about the Realm and the key, but Darius said nothing. "We've got to get her out or..." He trailed off. Or what? "We heard someone – one of them – talking about it and they said Sir Dennis would be back soon and then it'll be too late." That wasn't quite what they had heard, but he needed Darius to understand how urgent it was.

Darius' eyes locked on to his and just for the briefest of instants, held him with an unnerving intensity, just like the Zadi in Bryah. But then a moment later Darius blinked, breaking his gaze.

"OK," he said, his voice soft, reassuring. "Here's what I'm going to do – what *we're* going to do." He paused a moment. "We need to talk more. There's a lot I think I should tell you and a lot you have to tell me. But right now, if you're correct, Nana is in danger. I should go back anyway before anyone notices that I'm missing, and if she's there I *will* find her." He got to his feet. "And I'll get her out. Don't worry. But in the meantime, you stay put. No one will find you here. There's food in the kitchen, beds made up upstairs. It's going to be OK. Everything is going to work out just fine."

Chapter 7

"Are you really sure we can trust him?" Arin asked the moment he heard the front door shut.

"Yes," Owen nodded. Darius' story had all made sense to him and what's more when he had been explaining about the mysterious group he was part of, the words *'Priests of the Elements'* had popped into his head so vividly that it was as though Darius had shouted the phrase inside his ears. What was also clear, was that it had been a message intended only for him, not for his friends. That must have been why Darius hadn't wanted to pursue the conversation then, he guessed.

"There's something... not right." Finn was frowning, still unconvinced.

"It's just because you don't know the whole story yet." He realized he wasn't going to be able to convince Finn without revealing too much. "Just trust me. He's on our side." He felt a shiver of excitement run down his spine. The Priests of the Elements, the Wardens! He had been right, back in the bunker library, when he had come to what had seemed an almost impossible conclusion about the phrase he had overheard – *'Old fossils'*. He had guessed then that this was referring to the Priests of the Elements. And now he had found them...almost.

They decided to explore the lighthouse while they waited for Darius to return. Owen was particularly keen to investigate the strange stone columns on the roof. It was too much of a coincidence, the fact that the lighthouse had been built on the site of an old temple, like the church on top of the old Wood Temple. The Air Gateway had to be here somewhere, and the most logical place to look was as high up as possible. He wondered if Darius knew about the Gateways. He must know about the Spirit Realm at least.

By the time he had reached the top of the spiral staircase, he had made a decision. When Darius got back, he would tell him everything. If he had trusted him from the outset, he could have had the help of the Wardens all along. They would know what to do with the Sath, could even help him find the last two.

At the top of the stairs stood a wooden door, of a similar design to the one that led to the Earth Temple, only carved from a much lighter wood.

"Ailim," Finn declared as he touched the door approvingly. "Pine."

Pine! Owen remembered Nana saying pine was an 'Airy' tree. This looked promising. He half expected to find it locked, but when he lifted the latch, the door swung open easily. Ahead, at the centre of the flat roof, stood the lamp, a huge diamond-paned lantern, encased in an octagonal glass structure. From where he was standing, it looked to Owen at first as though the lantern was hanging suspended in mid-air, but as he stepped out on to the roof, he realized that it was sitting on top of a glass cube.

He had noted the low ramparts which circled most of the tower with some relief, thinking that they might provide some shelter from the wind. But he had worried needlessly. Although the branches of the trees far below were swaying in the wind, the air up on the roof was utterly still, as though the lighthouse stood in the eye of a storm.

"Mmm. Lavender." Finn was sniffing the air. "That's good."

"Is it?" Raya asked, puzzled.

"It helps when you're travelling, which is what we're doing, isn't it? And it's an Airy plant," he added.

Owen reached up for his pouch and pulled out the key. Warm. The light violet strip in the shaft gleamed in the sunlight, standing out from the red, green, blue and yellow. Violet for Air.

He walked across to take a better look at the two stones, which stood on the opposite side of the roof from the doorway. From the ground they had looked a solid, uniform grey, but he could now see that they were streaked with fine veins of violet amethyst quartz. The ramparts which ran round most of the roof stopped once they reached the stones, leaving a very precarious edge. He wondered if it was deliberate or if the walls had been damaged in the earthquake.

He stepped forward, reaching out to touch one of the stones, but then staggered back as something small and hard hit him square in the centre of his forehead.

60

"Ow! What was...? Whoa!" He ducked as a bee shot towards him like a dart, missing him by only a few millimetres. He looked round alarmed, half expecting to see a swarm approaching, but there were no more.

His friends meanwhile were staring at him as though he had gone mad. "What are you doing?" Raya exclaimed.

"That bee..." Owen began, then stopped. What bee? Only a second earlier he had seen it buzzing in front of the stones. Now it had vanished. "Didn't you see it?" He turned to his friends. "It dive-bombed me." He could still feel a sharp pain on his forehead.

"That doesn't sound like a bee to me." Finn shook his head. "It wouldn't just attack you for no reason. There isn't a hive here or anything is there? And anyway what's a bee doing all the way up here. Too high for flowers."

But Owen was sure it had been a bee – a bee which had just mysteriously vanished, as the fox had done in the church and Brock, the little badger in the Earth Temple.

Very carefully he took one step towards the stones and reached out into the space between them. Slowly he extended his arm, then with a gasp of surprise pulled it swiftly back.

"That's really weird! It's like..." he struggled to find the right words, "like a fan or jet engine... sort of." That didn't help his friends. He tried again. "When I reached out my hand just now, it was all normal until I got to in between the stones and then there was suddenly a wind whirling round, so fast that it felt like it was going to suck me in." He stopped. "Look, I'll show you." He bent down and picked up a feather from the ground, held it in his fingertips and stretched out his arm. The moment it touched the swirling air, he let it go. For a few seconds it spun round as though it had been sucked into a whirlwind, and then shot out on the far side and floated down out of sight over the precipitous edge of the tower.

"Do you think that would have happened to you if you'd gone any further just now?" Raya sounded more curious than worried.

"People might be too heavy," Arin said, "though there are quite small waterspouts that can do that to a whole boat in Bryah!" He gave Raya a stern look as he said this.

"I wouldn't want to risk it!" Owen was very grateful to the little bee. He gazed back at the stones. The fact that the bee had vanished between them suggested that the Gateway was indeed there, but if he couldn't step through without being hurled over the edge, finding the keyhole was going to prove difficult. The key itself was giving him no clue. It was warm, but no more than that. It didn't seem to get any warmer at any particular point.

His friends said nothing as they watched him run his hand slowly along the amethyst veins. This was something they couldn't help him with. He took a few steps back and looked up at the tops of the stones. They weren't actually perpendicular, he noticed, but leant in at an angle, so that had they been longer they would have met high overhead and formed a triangle shape.

'Centrum, in Centri Trigono.' The words floated up to the surface of his memory – or rather *someone's* memory. He frowned. This wasn't a Tamus memory, he was sure. It was one of the other Key-Bearers, and a language he didn't recognize. 'Centrum in Centri Trigono.' He stared at the gap between the stones. Trigono sounded a bit like triangle and centrum and centri – like centre. Then suddenly it *was* Tamus' memory in his head, and a lesson about the still point at the centre of a wheel, a lesson which had given him a headache trying to understand. Air magic had always given him headaches. It was Dar's strongest point and his weakest. He just wasn't clever enough.

He focused back on the stones. Most of the memories made no sense to him. He couldn't see what a triangle had to do with a wheel. But the still point at the centre of a wheel, the axis round which it spun – that did make sense. He took a few steps back to get a better view of the stones.

"If these stones met at the top so they made a triangle shape," he began, then stopped. He was trying to imagine a wheel inside the triangle, but was that right? Wasn't the triangle meant to be inside the circle? He could feel a headache beginning.

"If there was a circle round that triangle, where would the centre be?"

Finn and Raya looked bewildered by the question, but not Arin.

"Up above your head," he squinted slightly as he tried to work out the exact point, "about... two arms' length I reckon."

"I need something to stand on then."

"The ladder," Raya replied a moment later. "Just inside the door."

Owen hadn't noticed a ladder before, but sure enough a small stepladder stood propped against the wall. A lucky coincidence, he thought as he carried it across to the stones. He set it down, making sure it was steady, then climbed up carefully. With the precipitous edge just a few feet away and the whirling winds even closer, he wasn't taking any risks.

"OK, tell me when you think I'm near the centre." He pulled the key out of his pouch, and holding it firmly so it didn't get sucked in, reached out into the space between the stones.

"Down a bit." Arin stepped back to get a better view. "And a bit to the right."

"Here?" He held his hand motionless.

"Yes... that's pretty close," Arin nodded.

Slowly he moved the key forward, a fraction at a time. Then suddenly it touched the wind. His arm was pulled violently forwards, and he nearly toppled off the ladder as he yanked it hastily back.

"I think it's a tiny bit further up actually," Arin said apologetically.

Owen bit his tongue as he tried again. He moved the key even more slowly, but this time when he reached the point where before he had hit the wind, nothing happened. He edged it in another millimetre and another, and then 'click'. The keyhole! Gently he turned the key. It was as smooth as if it had just been oiled. A moment later, a now familiar black hole began to open. The Gateway. Raya already had one foot on the ladder, about to follow him, but he pulled the key back out. The Gateway stood open for a few moments, then vanished.

"Not yet," he said as he climbed back down the ladder.

There was a peculiar shimmering, glassy quality to the air where the Gateway had been, with the light round the edges slightly distorted as though seen through a prism. It wasn't unlike the air on the Plain of Shells in Assyah, he thought.

"I want to wait till Darius gets back so we know Nana's safe," he explained. "And I want to tell him. I want him to come with us."

Late that evening as they sat in the lighthouse kitchen, finishing a rather Spartan meal of bread and cheese, Finn made one more attempt to change his mind.

"I still think you're making a mistake," he said through a mouthful of bread. "When I first saw him, he was sneaking around your house, and I remember you saying you didn't like him. And I don't think

Nana likes him either," he added.

"I was just being stupid," Owen retorted. "I didn't know then that..." he hesitated, "that he was only friends with that Fire Spirit so that they would trust him."

"It's a bit of a coincidence though, him being your mother's boyfriend, isn't it?" Arin too was unconvinced.

The thought had occurred to Owen, but he could see no other explanation. "I'll ask him if you want. But what other reason could there be? He couldn't have known I was, you know, the Key-Bearer," he felt a bit self-conscious calling himself that in front of his friends, "because he was friends with my mother before Nana even gave me the key."

"Dennis could have told him to watch you," Arin suggested.

Owen shook his head. "No. Why would he care what I was doing? Anyway, if he'd wanted to get to know me, he could have just come and introduced himself, couldn't he? '*Hello, I'm your uncle!*'"

And that was that. He knew there were a lot of unanswered questions but was sure Darius would be able to explain everything. It just felt like such an enormous relief to know that there was an adult on his side – a powerful one, one who could help him, guide him – a Priest of the Elements.

They waited late into the night for Darius to return, but finally not even Raya could keep her eyes open.

"We'll hear them if they come in, won't we?" she said with a yawn. "He probably just hasn't had the chance to get away yet."

Owen hoped she was right. He had expected Darius to be back hours ago, thought he would just walk into the bunker, find Nana and leave. Since 'hearing' the words *Priests of the Elements* he had begun thinking of Darius in almost super-human terms, a mighty wizard who could easily thwart Sir Dennis' people. But maybe he was wrong. Maybe someone had seen him with them, and he too had been captured. Whatever the answer, trying to stay awake and getting more and more worried, wasn't going to help.

They had found the bedrooms earlier – four half-moon shaped rooms, each one as immaculate as an expensive hotel room. Darius' own room was on the floor below. Owen had felt rather embarrassed as they had explored the vast bathroom with its sunken bath, and Raya had commented on the size of the enormous bed.

"It doesn't really look like he lives here, does it?" she said, as she opened a wardrobe door to reveal several shelves of identical white T-shirts. "I mean, how can anyone be this tidy?"

"He'll have a cleaner." Owen couldn't imagine Darius hoovering. "You know, someone from one of the villages who works for him." But as he spoke, he realized how unlikely this was. The existence of the lighthouse wouldn't stay a secret for long on that basis.

"Probably a Fire Spirit," Finn muttered under his breath.

Owen had lain awake for what had felt like a very long time. His head was still spinning from all the revelations of the day. The story of the Watchers hadn't come as a great shock. He had already begun to put two and two together in Bryah when Raya had spoken of the Arivala Isles. He had recognized the word, remembered Captain Sigursson talking of Arivala. It hadn't been a great leap to connect Nana to Dayah and then Aggie to Assyah, and from there to assume that their presence might have something to do with him. Dennis though... He still couldn't get his head around the idea of him being his uncle, Piers and Iona his cousins! What's more, he had learnt more about his father in those few minutes with Aggie and Professor Vishnami than in all the years with his mother on Olafssey. And finally Darius. It felt as though his world had been turned upside down. No one was who he had thought they were, nothing what it appeared to be.

"But it's not true Tam!" His brother was laughing at him again. "Why do you always just believe what they tell you?"

"I don't *just* believe..." he began.

"Yes, you do." Dar sat down on a flat rock overlooking the pool and opened his bag. "Here." He threw an apple across. "You don't need them. I *know*. Why don't you believe me?" He paused a moment. "If I tell you something..." He hesitated a moment before continuing. "Two nights ago I went dreamwalking."

Tamus stared at his brother in disbelief. "No. I don't believe you." He stopped. If anyone was going to do it, it would be Dar.

"It was... like nothing you could ever imagine." Dar ignored his brother's comment, his eyes bright with excitement now. "I saw things... wonderful things."

"Then you're stupid," Tamus retorted. "There are Dreamspinners there who'll trick you off the path if you're not properly trained. And then you're lost. Some people have gone there and never come back!"

"Huh!" Dar snorted with contempt. "That may be true if you're weak. But me, I know what I'm doing. In fact," he paused for dramatic effect, "I might have done a bit more than just *walking*."

"What are you talking about?" he demanded, alarmed by his brother's words.

"Never mind." Dar had clearly changed his mind about whatever it was he had been about to say. "All I'm saying is, if you're strong enough, you can control what happens. You can learn more there than in a lifetime sitting in a stupid class repeating poems and being a slave to those Wardens."

"I'm not their slave." He was angry now. "You don't know what you're talking about. I may not have been dreamwalking, but I've been through the Gateway." He knew he shouldn't be talking about it, but Dar's constant taunting made him so angry that now he couldn't stop himself. "I've been to the Spirit Realm, to Dayah, Bryah, Assyah, Yezirah, Azilut – all of them!" he declared. "And if you think you've seen incredible things…!"

For a moment Dar said nothing. Then he shook his head. "I don't believe you. They'd never let a novice like you go there."

"Hah! That shows what you know then," he retorted. It might be wrong to tell Dar, but it felt good, really good, for once to be the one with the upper hand.

"Prove it." Dar took a step towards him. "Go on."

"What?" He hadn't expected that.

"Prove it!" Dar's eyes locked on to his, the challenge thrown down.

Chapter 8

"Wake up! They're still not back."

Owen woke with a start to find Finn poking his arm. He struggled to get his head together. Who wasn't back? And where was he? Then the events of the previous day came flooding back. Beside the bed a clock said half past nine.

"He should be back by now," Raya said the moment he stepped into the kitchen. "Even if he couldn't get out last night. It's nearly midday!"

That was an exaggeration, but even so Owen was struggling to think of a good reason why Darius should be so late.

"I suppose at least it means Owen's right," Finn conceded. "I don't see why he'd have waited if he was going to tell them about us."

It was little consolation though, if Darius too had been caught...

"It's too early," he replied. He wasn't willing to give up yet. "And I don't believe they've got him."

However, as the morning passed, his fears grew. But just as he was about to admit that they should probably try to find Captain Sigursson, he heard the sound of a car pulling up outside. He jumped to his feet and ran to the window, relief flooding over him. But the car which he could see below, parked in front of the lighthouse steps, was not one he recognized. The two people who stepped out of it however, were a different matter. It was the woman and one of the men who had been in the group with Darius and the Aelva in the churchyard. For a moment, he hesitated. They could be Darius' friends. But Darius hadn't said anything about anyone else infiltrating Sir Dennis' secret society with him, nor had he mentioned the possibility of someone else coming to the lighthouse in his place.

"It's not him." He turned away from the window, his eyes darting rapidly round the room. "We need to hide..." He stopped as he heard the clunk of the front door shutting below them.

But there was nowhere to hide, no convenient large cupboard or pile of boxes lying around. And with the couple making their way up the spiral staircase towards them, there was only one way to go – up.

He signalled to his friends to follow, moving as fast as he dared without making too much noise, and stopping only to dash into the bedroom to grab his rucksack. The door to the roof swung open silently and he hurried out, closing it softly once everyone was through.

"Can we lock it?" Arin spoke in a hoarse whisper.

Owen couldn't see how. He had noticed before that the door hadn't been locked. It didn't really need to be after all. No one was going to break in from the roof.

"They might not come up here," Raya said. "If they're just looking for Darius... maybe..." She trailed off as down below another door banged shut, this time higher up. They were definitely moving up the stairs.

The Gateway. He reached for his key. They could go through, wait, and then come back when the coast was clear. He hurried over to get the stepladder, and quickly positioned it in front of the pillars. It looked a very long way down to the ground below, over the precipitous edge of the roof, and briefly the unpleasant thought flashed through his head that the exit from this Gateway might also be high up. But they had little choice now. It was the Gateway or be caught.

"Here?" He held the key out to about where he remembered the keyhole had been.

Finn took a few steps back. "Just a bit to the left and down."

Owen carefully lined the key up. No matter how much of a hurry they were in, it wasn't going to help if he got it wrong and got sucked into the swirling vortex of air and thrown out over the edge! Click. He heard the familiar sound of the key successfully finding its target then slid it in as quickly as he dared and turned. The Gateway entrance opened up before him. For a moment he hesitated. Even though he knew this was the Gateway, knew that he would step through into a tunnel, a part of his mind was telling him that beyond that dark hole lay open air and a long drop down.

"Go on. We'll be right behind you." Arin was already two steps up the ladder and Owen realized it was going to be even worse for him with his fear of heights. He took a deep breath and jumped forward off the ladder top into the dark hole.

For a split second he thought he had made a terrible mistake, as he dropped like a stone into the gaping darkness, but then he began to spin, hurtling down the familiar spiralling tunnel as though on a helter-skelter. He caught the briefest glimpse of a sparkling, turquoise sea beneath a rainbow of spray and foam – the wake of a seahorse, he realized, just as the window vanished behind him. He smelt the rich, woody tang of Dayah a second before he shot past a magnificent russet stag standing proud in a sun-dappled forest glade. And then he was out, tumbling headlong into open air.

The scream came from his mouth before his thoughts had caught up, before he had time to understand consciously that he was at least a hundred feet up in the air and plummeting towards the hard earth far below. But then he stopped. Abruptly, as though someone had just pressed a pause button, his descent halted, leaving him suspended some fifty feet off the ground. He gasped, winded and shocked, tried to move and failed. He could have been back in Odora's web, immobilized utterly, only this time the threads that held him hanging were invisible. A moment later he heard a scream from above, then Raya appeared in front of him. He tried to speak to her, but though he could open his mouth, though he knew he was speaking, no sound came out. A second and third yell rang out above him – Finn and Arin. He could just make out Arin to the far left of his field of vision but couldn't turn his head even an inch to see him better. Finn was nowhere to be seen.

"Finn!" He called out his name, but in vain. A deafening silence enveloped him. In front of him Raya was mouthing something, trying to tell him something, but he had no idea what. Only when her eyes stayed fixed in a downward stare, did he force his own to look down. Immediately, a dizzying wave of nauseous vertigo swept over him. He shut his eyes quickly. As much as he wanted to be released from the invisible bonds that were holding him, the alternative looked far worse. Not only did the ground look a very, very long way down, but as far as he could see from his brief glimpse, the field below was carpeted in jagged crystals of amethyst, all pointing up towards him. He took a deep breath and cautiously opened just one eye, trying as hard as he could to convince himself it was all fine, just another Gateway. But the memory of the rock arch in Bryah was still uncomfortably fresh. If it hadn't been for the dolphin, his guide, even though he passed the ear fish test, he would have drowned. And if he was right, he couldn't see how a bee was going to help him here!

Far below the amethyst glinted menacingly, like a sea of razor-sharp blades waiting to cut to shreds anyone who fell on to them. His mind was racing now, trying frantically to remember this place. Yezirah, the Professor had called it. Tamus had been here, hadn't he? Surely he had? What had he done? But before he had a chance to remember what Tamus had done, he became aware of a peculiar rushing, whirring noise behind him, growing louder and louder as though a whirlwind was bearing down on him. And then it was on him, blasting straight into him, through his skin, in through every pore, filling him with air, like an inflating balloon. He could feel countless tiny fizzy bubbles popping inside his head, tiny stars exploding, more and more. Then just as he thought his body couldn't possibly hold any more air without bursting, he deflated; It was the only way to describe the whooshing sensation as the air rushed back out of him and then sucked him down, feet first, and dropped him impossibly gently on to a lawn of soft, springy grass – a lawn which had suddenly opened up in the middle of the field of amethyst.

A moment later his friends landed beside him. Finn let out a low whistle of relief. "I thought I'd done something awful and got stuck in the middle of the Gateway. I couldn't see any of you when I stopped falling."

"You were looking the wrong way. You were behind Owen, but I could only see the back of your head." Raya laughed, her eyes shining with excitement. "That was brilliant!"

It wasn't how Owen would have described it, but now they were all safely down, he had to admit the 'balloon' test was less unpleasant than the salt or the ear fish! And if he had only been able to recall Tamus' memory in time, had known he wouldn't crash to earth on the field of amethyst, he might actually have rather enjoyed the sensation of 'flying'. There was only one problem. His original plan had been to come through the Gateway, wait in Yezirah for a couple of hours or so, perhaps explore a little, but then return back to the lighthouse to make sure Nana was all right and to tell Darius everything, before setting off again with him at his side. But now as he looked back up to the sweeping vault of cornflower-blue sky, streaked with ribbons of feathery cloud, the Gateway entrance looked no more than a tiny black dot.

"How do we get back?" The same thought had struck Arin.

Owen frowned. Tamus must know. But try as he might, he couldn't reach his Tamus memories. They were there, he was sure, like a word on the tip of his tongue, but as always, the harder he tried to remember, the further away the memories seemed to get.

"I'll work it out," he said finally, rather lamely.

"So... What? Are we just going to sit here while you do?" Raya clearly had other ideas. "It seems a bit of a waste of time. We could go and have a bit of a look round. I mean, it doesn't exactly look dangerous, does it?"

Owen brought his attention back down from the Gateway above. There was indeed nothing obviously dangerous-looking about the blue-green grasslands which stretched as far as the eye could see in all directions. But neither was there anything terribly inviting; no distant mountains to aim for, not even a solitary tree to break up the monotony. The land seemed to stretch out unbounded, melting into the sky on the hazy horizon. They could be walking for ever out there, lost, in a grassy version of the Endless Ocean in Bryah. There was also the small problem of the field of amethyst. Although they were sitting comfortably in a circle of grass, as smooth and even as if it had just been mown, they were still surrounded by an unbroken ring of dagger-sharp amethyst a good ten metres wide.

"Raya's right." Finn got to his feet. "Because unless you reckon you can work it out pretty soon, we're going to be in trouble." He pulled a flask out of his bag and tipped it upside down to illustrate his point. "I haven't got anything to drink or to eat, and I bet none of you have either."

The silence that greeted his statement confirmed it. Owen slowly walked round the edge of the grass circle, examining the amethyst, looking for any spot where it looked in any way different, but without success. He knelt back down and reached out a very tentative finger. As he had feared it was sharp as a shard of broken glass.

"Any ideas?" He started to stand back up, but at that moment, a bee appeared from nowhere, buzzing loudly, and to Owen's ears, angrily, and headed straight for his eye. He flapped wildly at it, his immediate instinct to protect himself, staggered backwards, tripped and fell straight on to the spikes of amethyst.

"Owen!" Someone shouted. Someone else screamed, and for a moment he was too dazed to think straight, but as he looked up towards the horrified, wide-eyed faces staring down at him, he realized something very peculiar had happened. He had landed hard on his back and was winded, but apart from that, as far as he could tell, he was uninjured. There was no pain and no blood. Cautiously he moved his hand and touched one of the amethyst spikes. It yielded instantly as though made of the softest goose down. He pressed his whole hand down and it came to rest, flat and unharmed.

"They're like feathers!" he exclaimed.

"But just now," Finn looked bewildered, "when you touched one..." He trailed off.

"I know. It was sharp. But these aren't." Owen picked himself up. "Come on." He beckoned to his friends. "It's OK."

Finn took one step forward and tentatively reached out his foot. "Ow!" He pulled it straight back. "They *are* sharp. We can't walk across that!"

Arin bent down and touched one, a frown on his face. "Maybe it's just the closest ones that are sharp."

Owen moved slowly to the edge of the amethysts and placed his foot carefully on the spot Arin had just touched. "No. Still soft."

"You must have done something to make them soft for you," Finn said.

Owen shook his head. "I didn't do anything. I just fell over."

"So if..." Raya began, then stopped. She hesitated a brief moment, and then ran at the carpet of amethyst, leaping into the air just before the edge and landing as deftly as a cat, just beyond Owen.

"Easy!" She turned back laughing, to face Finn and Arin.

"How did you do that?" Finn was flabbergasted.

"I just jumped." Raya sounded very pleased with herself. "It's like catching an arpage. If you touch it in the sea, it stings you, but as long as it's out of water, it can't hurt you," she explained, seeing Finn and Owen's bewildered expressions.

"Yes!" Owen exclaimed. "Like Antaios, the giant. He loses all his strength if he doesn't touch the Earth. I read a story about him. He's not real," he added, "but..." He trailed off. How did he know he wasn't real? The once clear division between real and unreal was now decidedly hazy.

"Come on!" Raya held her hand out towards Finn and Arin. "Jump."

"You'd better be right!" Finn said, still sounding rather doubtful, as he took a few steps back and then with a yell, hurled himself forward on to the amethyst. A moment later Arin followed, rather less dramatically.

Owen had hoped to see the bee again, hoped for some guidance as to which way to go, but she had vanished. There was nothing to provide any clue. Every direction looked identical. Despite his suspicions, he wished he had asked Professor Vishnami more about Yezirah! But he had to make a decision, and given that all the options looked the same at the moment, he might as well just pick one blindly.

"Why don't you divine which way to go?" Finn suggested. "You might know, really, mightn't you? I mean, if Tamus has been here, he would know, so you know too," he added.

Owen didn't understand.

"Look." Finn rummaged in his bag, pulled out an odd assortment of pieces of bark, stones, twigs and what looked like roots, and proceeded to lay out four of them. "North, south, east and west. Right?"

Owen nodded, still not clear how this would help.

"Now, come down here." Finn indicated the ground next to the four objects. "Close your eyes and try and remember one of your Tamus memories – the clearest one you can think of."

Owen did as he was told.

"Keep doing that but hold out your left hand straight in front of you," he continued. "When you've got that memory clear in your head – really, really clear, ask yourself which way to go. And when you've asked the question, move your hand around in front of you until you feel it get hot."

Owen tried to recall his Tamus memories. There had been a lot of hillside and sheep ones, but they had merged together, and it was hard to distinguish a specific one. The fishing with Dar dream? The burning temple? He shuddered, pushing that one out of his mind as quickly as he could. Morph making? Another memory he wanted to forget. No, it had to be last night's dream. Sitting by the rock beside their favourite pool as Dar told him he had been dreamwalking. The memory was so vivid that for a moment, as it filled his whole consciousness, he forgot all about asking the question about which way to go.

Finn's voice echoed hollowly in his head. "Which way should we go?"

Owen was confused for a few seconds at the strange voice.

"Owen! Tamus! Move your hand." Finn spoke again very deliberately, stressing each word.

Slowly he began to circle his hand – a hand which seemed strangely disconnected from his body... His eyes flew open. "It's hot!" There was no doubt about it. It was as though he had just moved his hand over a flame.

"See!" Finn was beaming with delight. "I knew you would know which way to go!"

Owen looked down at the twig directly beneath his hand, the twig that indicated east.

An hour or so later, he was beginning to wonder if he had made a mistake. Nothing appeared to have changed. The vast, open plains still stretched as far as the eye could see. The only break in the monotony was the occasional sudden gust of wind sweeping past.

"Strange wind," Arin had commented, the first time it happened. It was indeed strange, Owen thought – a warm, moist air, a bit like standing over the steam from a kettle, and not the bracing chill he would have expected out on the plain.

"Maybe it's a dragon, like Draco," Raya suggested unhelpfully, just at the same moment that the identical thought occurred to Owen.

"Well, if it is, it's got a very funny way of breathing!" Finn retorted. "Even dragons must need to breathe more often than that!"

Owen glanced back in the direction they had come from. For quite a while he had been able to see the light reflecting back off the amethyst shards, but now he could see nothing but the hazy green-blue of grass. The Gateway had vanished.

He stopped. "I think we should try to mark our route so that we can find our way back."

Arin nodded in agreement. "Yes. It's not like we've got a compass or anything. Just heading back west isn't going to be enough to find that Gateway again."

However, it was one thing deciding to mark their route, quite another working out how. The only stones they could find were tiny pebbles and to build a cairn from these, that was big enough to see from a distance, was an impossible task.

"Maybe we should just go back now and let Owen work out how to get up to the Gateway," Arin said gloomily. "We could probably still find it, but if we go much further..." He left the statement hanging.

But in the end, it was the bee that decided it. Just as Owen was beginning to think Arin was right, it buzzed past his face, tracing a figure of eight shape in the air, before darting ahead in a straight line, heading due east as fast as if it had been shot from a bow. He let out a huge sigh of relief. He was sure now that he was right. The bee *was* his guide, and it was indicating unequivocally where they should go – onwards to the east and whatever lay beyond the hazy horizon.

Chapter 9

As they walked on across the vast, sweeping grassland, it began to dawn on Owen that all was not quite as it had at first appeared. He had thought the plain was flat, a constant level stretching to the horizon. But now he realized he was wrong. Where before the ribbons of cloud had drifted past high overhead, they were now like tendrils of mist reaching ever closer to the ground. Either the sky was slowly coming down towards them or the land was rising in an imperceptibly slow gradient. His spirits rose. Going up felt as though they were getting closer to some sort of destination, whereas the endless flat monotony that he had thought they were walking through before, had begun to fill him with a sense of hopelessness and despondency.

"Mieuw."

He nearly jumped out of his skin at the sound. High overhead a tiny dark shape hovered for a moment, then dived, slicing through the air like an arrow shot from a bow. A hawk!

His friends had all stopped and were gazing up at the bird wheeling through the wispy cloud.

"So *something* lives here!" Finn sounded enormously relieved. "I was beginning to think it might just be grass forever and nothing else."

"I think they normally live in trees." Owen tried to remember what he knew about hawks, and it didn't amount to much! "There are always hawks over the fields near the woods where my den is. I'm sure they have nests in the trees." When no one volunteered any more information, he continued. "So maybe this means there are woods somewhere near here." A second hawk emerged out of the mist, swooping high above the first, as he spoke.

They set off again with renewed enthusiasm. Owen's

disappointment that Darius wasn't with them was receding the further they got from the Gateway, his spirits rising with the land. He drew in a big breath of air and nearly fell over as his head spun wildly. He tried again, this time more slowly, letting the air spread into every part of his body. And then he was off, speeding across the plain with vast, elongated steps, fast as a cheetah. 'Far-striding' – that was what it was called! The memory came flooding back to him as he raced on towards the horizon.

"Owen! What are you doing?!" Raya's voice carried across the open space as clearly as if she had been shouting over water. He stopped reluctantly and looked back. His friends were already small, distant figures. It looked as though he had cleared almost half a kilometre in a matter of seconds, and he wasn't even out of breath!

He sat down to wait for them to catch up, struggling to contain his impatience. This was a brilliant discovery! He wondered if it was just the air in Yezirah or if he would be able to repeat it back in his world. No one could possibly catch him. He could break every running world record there was, win the Olympics! But even as he thought it, a part of him realized it could never be so. There were rules, things you didn't do, things you didn't speak of. Dar had thought these were stupid. He remembered clearly how dismissive his brother had been. *"Who are they to tell me what I can and can't do?"* he would say. It was the same old argument – the Priests of the Elements and their *'right'* to make the rules. *"Tam, you're such a sheep sometimes! If someone's good at singing, they sing; if they're good at swimming, they swim. I'm good at magic – it's my talent and I'm going to use it!"*

Finn was the first to reach him, his expression a mixture of bemusement and annoyance.

"What was that?" he exclaimed. "I thought you'd turned into one of those morph things!" The comparison to the unbound morphs racing past them on the Plain of Shells wasn't one Owen liked very much.

"It's called Far-striding," he replied rather defensively. "There's nothing wrong with it. It's just er... Air magic."

"So we can't do it." Raya sounded disappointed.

"Well," he hesitated, "maybe..." He wasn't really sure. Was it Air magic or was it something special about the air here in Yezirah that could affect anyone. But a quick experiment answered his question.

Try as they might, none of his friends could even sense anything different about the air, let alone consciously direct it into their bodies. He somewhat regretfully decided not to try Far-striding again for a while. Since the others were limited to normal walking pace, there was little to be gained from charging on ahead on his own. It could mean running into trouble. He thought of what Beith had said back in Dayah about running into traps if you went too fast. And something else too, something about missing important things, how if they had raced through Dayah, they would never have met Oolugh, and if they had never met Oolugh, he would never have been given the Pearl. He had really been very lucky so far, he realized. Now, with three Sath found and only two to go, it wasn't the time for cutting corners.

Despite having not yet found anything to eat or drink, Owen was feeling more optimistic as the day went on. The land was rising at a noticeably steeper gradient and the higher they climbed, the closer the clouds were to the ground. Frequently now they were walking through bands of cloudy mist, so dense that he could barely see a yard in front of him, only to emerge back into bright sunshine a moment later. Though there was still no sign of anything ahead but more grassland, the fact that so much was blanketed in mist gave him hope that there was something different ahead, which was at present hidden in the cloud.

They had been walking for a good half-hour in mist so thick that Owen felt as though he was pushing his way through a warm, damp mesh of cobwebs, and he was just beginning to wonder whether it would ever end, when suddenly he emerged into sunlight so bright that for a few seconds he was dazzled. Above him, the sky was an extraordinary vivid, azure-blue, a shade so intense that even in Dayah he had never seen a colour like it. He stood rooted to the spot, staring up at the sky, transfixed, all else momentarily forgotten.

"It's like looking down into a bottomless ocean." Arin was the first to speak, his voice hushed, as though he was in a church.

Owen knew what he meant. There was a depth to the sky – that was the only way he could describe it – that he had never seen before. In his world it felt more like a roof stretched high above over the Earth; a thin, rather two-dimensional film of sky. Ahead of them the horizon looked very close.

"We've nearly reached the top," he exclaimed with relief, dragging his attention back down to earth.

He hurried up the last stretch, eager to see what lay beyond, struggling to resist the urge to try Far-striding again.

"It's not just more grass, is it? If it is..." Raya began as she came up behind him. She stopped mid-sentence and let out a gasp. It wasn't more grass. For a moment Owen had thought it was the sea, or a vast lake, stretching endlessly to the horizon, but then he recognised the hazy silhouettes of trees, rising from the mist as though they were floating above the Earth. Further away still, just at the limit of his vision, he could see something that looked like a tiny island.

"Can you see what that is?" He pointed towards it, hoping that Raya's sharp vision could see more.

She shielded her eyes with her hand as she peered into the distance. "A hill... and colours – red and yellow." She paused, "I can't see what they are though." She squinted, trying to get a clearer view. "No, it's too far away."

"Well it's not grass," Finn said, "and those are definitely trees. And where there are trees there's probably food."

Finn was wrong about the food. The trees which they could see turned out to be pines and aspens. They did however prove unexpectedly useful. There had been a unanimous decision that they should make for the hill which lay directly to the east. Easy in principle, but in practice, once they had descended the grassy slope and were below the mist, it was almost impossible to tell which way they were going. It was only when they stumbled upon one of the trees by accident, that Finn had an idea. He had been disappointed at first by the lack of anything very edible. "It was hard to see from back there what they were," he explained defensively. "I couldn't even see really what shape they were when only one bit poked out above all this mist." He stopped, his face lighting up. "I know!" And with that, he scampered straight up the tree like a monkey, vanishing briefly into the mist. "That way!" He announced as he descended, pointing off to the left. "I could see the hill from up there. We've come over too far to the south."

So taking a rather zigzag route across the mist-shrouded plain, they approached the hill. By the time they reached their third tree, they were close enough for Finn to make out more detail.

"It looks like a sort of village. And it's not just red and yellow. There's orange and blue and purple and every colour," he called down.

"What do you mean 'a sort of village'?" Owen asked.

"I'll go and look," Raya said. "Just help me get on to that first branch."

She climbed up after Finn easily enough and a few moments later her voice floated down.

"It *is* a village. But it's like the market at Eridu. It's tents. All those colours, they're tents and streamers I think." She jumped back down from the lowest branch, landing deftly on the springy grass. "There's lots more birds as well up there. Huge ones like albatrosses."

"They're the biggest birds I've ever seen," Finn joined them back on the ground. "Bigger than anything in Dayah."

But Owen was more interested in the tents. "You couldn't see any people?"

"Too far away." Raya shook her head. "But there must be. Birds don't live in tents, do they?"

Before very long she was proved right. Although the hill was still obscured by thick mist at ground level, the unmistakeable sound of whinnying horses indicated that they were getting closer to something more than birds' nests, and a few minutes later Owen heard human voices shouting – children's voices.

One more tree climb was enough to confirm how close they now were. Finn hurried back down through the branches, eager to share what he had seen.

"We're nearly there! It looks as if something's happening, like a festival or that thing, er... the Evocation, in Arktos. I can see streamers and kites and people rushing round, running everywhere. And so many colours! Like a... a rainbow." He was struggling to find the words. "You'll see what I mean."

Finn was right. Only a few minutes later the hazy forms of horses emerged from the mist ahead of them. Finn, Arin and Raya stopped in their tracks, eyeing the horses suspiciously, but Owen walked slowly forward, hand outstretched. He liked horses. Some of his earliest memories were of the small, sturdy horses that roamed free on Olafssey, horses that had been remarkably unafraid of a boy offering carrots.

These horses however, bore very little resemblance to his childhood friends. They were more like the elegant thoroughbreds he had seen the day he had hidden in Tango's stall in Bale Castle. Poised, graceful horses, with long, flowing, silky manes and tails, they stood regarding him with a detached curiosity. Slowly he approached the closest one, a chestnut mare with soft, doe-brown eyes, but just as he got close enough to touch her, she threw back her head, flared her nostrils and shied away from him.

"It's OK," he began, but it was too late, she was already cantering off into the mist.

"They're not dangerous then?" Arin came forward rather tentatively.

"No," Owen hesitated. "I don't think so anyway. They could kick you I suppose, if you went up behind them, but they're not going to eat us or anything like that." He hoped he was right and that these were 'normal' horses. "You've seen horses before. Ator was riding one." His friends hadn't seemed bothered by the chunky, placid natured cob that the big Boryad had ridden alongside their donkey cart in Assyah.

"Yes, but that was a tame one," Arin said. "These are wild."

However, just as he spoke, he was proved wrong, as a figure emerged from the mist, riding towards them, a figure wrapped in a pale-yellow cloak and seated upon a white horse. There had been no thundering of hooves to warn them of his approach and he seemed simply to have materialized out of thin air.

For a moment the thought passed through Owen's head, that maybe he was a ghost, but as the horse pulled up before them, it let out a snort of breath, something no ghost horse was likely to do.

"Who are you?" The man's voice was clear and sharp, but more curious than threatening.

"I'm Owen and this is Finn, Raya and Arin," Owen replied, pointing to each of his friends in turn. He was getting tired of having to think up some story for who he was and had already decided this time to say as little as possible. If other Aevyans were anything like Professor Vishnami, they would probably see through any subterfuge pretty quickly anyway.

Not surprisingly the rider wasn't satisfied with this answer. He leant forward on his horse, peering intently at them from pale violet, yellow-specked eyes. "What is your purpose here?" His voice still didn't sound menacing, but there was a definite note of challenge.

"We're er... wayfarers," Finn said rather tentatively. The man's pale face creased into a frown.

"Wayfarers?" It clearly wasn't an acceptable answer. "Where have you come from and where are you going?" The rider tried again, speaking very slowly and deliberately as though they were very young children or a bit simple.

"We're Seekers of the Truth!" Owen blurted out suddenly. That was the right phrase, wasn't it? That was what the young Air novices had rather grandly called themselves, a phrase Dar had found particularly amusing. The rider apparently agreed, throwing his head back and roaring with laughter.

"Ah! I see. That's what you are is it?" He shook his head. "Well, you're not going to find it out here! Go back to your flock. The Towers are no place to be now. It's war you'll find there soon enough, not the Truth." And with that he wheeled his horse round and galloped off into the mist on silent hooves.

For a moment no one spoke. It wasn't what any of them had expected; capture or a welcome, but not for the rider to vanish as suddenly as he had appeared. The Towers... Bells of recognition were ringing loudly in Owen's head, but try as he might, he couldn't quite retrieve the memory.

"What was he talking about?" Raya turned accusingly to Owen. "And what was all that Seekers of the Truth stuff? Was that Tamus talking again?"

"No," he replied indignantly. "It was me! It's never Tamus talking." He didn't like the suggestion, even though the first time it had happened, when he and Finn had summoned the Eddra in Dayah, it had felt exactly like someone else talking through his mouth! "It was one of his memories though," he admitted.

Despite the rider's warnings about war, they continued on towards the encouraging sounds of laughter and shouting. It didn't sound to Owen much like a place preparing for battle and anyway the term 'towers' seemed so inappropriate to the collection of tents that Finn and Raya had described, that he was sure this couldn't be the place the rider had been referring to. High above, hidden from view beyond the veil of mist, he could hear the high, plaintive cries of hawks, interspersed from time to time with another, stranger noise – a low- pitched whirring and whistle, a bit like the sound made by a bicycle wheel spinning freely.

As they climbed ever higher heading up away from the plain, Owen had the increasingly uncomfortable feeling that they were being watched. He glanced round nervously. It all felt a bit too much like the Eddleshi incident for his liking and though he could see no yellow-green eyes glinting out from the mist, he was sure it was more than simply horses out there. Before long however, the mist began to thin out and his fears were forgotten as the initially blurry sea of colours ahead of them sharpened into the unmistakeable shapes of triangular tepee-like tents.

Owen couldn't stop himself smiling. There was something contagiously cheerful about the brightly coloured tents, each one topped with flamboyant feathers, poking out at jaunty angles. He could see too the streamers Raya had mentioned, fluttering in the wind atop long poles, a rainbow of colours which shimmered in the sunlight as though made of gossamer-thin satin.

A figure suddenly appeared, running out from between the closest tents, racing across the grass towards them, followed moments later by several more. Owen stopped in his tracks, the warning about soldiers preparing for battle ringing in his ears. There were at least ten of them, running full pelt down the slope, shouting and whooping in a definitely war-like manner. But then Raya burst into laughter.

"They're children, little kids!" And in an instant the tension evaporated. It wasn't a hoard of Aevyan soldiers tearing down the hill to attack them, but a laughing, excited bunch of young children.

Chapter 10

"Seekers of the Truth!" The first child to reach them stopped just in front of Owen and dramatically drew a very realistic looking sword from his belt. "This is the Truth!" He sliced the sword theatrically down through the air, in a gesture which would have been alarming if he hadn't been only about nine years old.

"No! This is." A dark-haired girl of about the same age stepped in front of him holding her own sword high above her head, her pale-yellow eyes glinting with mischief.

"What are you talking about?" Raya didn't like being teased, let alone by little children. "And stop waving those around like that. It's dangerous."

She sounded so pompous that Finn could barely stop himself laughing out loud. "You'd better do what she says," he spluttered. "Or she'll get angry and er... turn you into slugs."

For a moment there was a silence as the children turned and stared as one at Raya, then the girl who had spoken, laughed. "No she won't." She turned her head to one side regarding them quizzically. "Why are you wearing those horrible clothes?" The other children had all gathered in closer now and were watching the conversation keenly, heads turning in unison from their friend to the strangers and back again, reminding Owen uncannily of a flock of starlings. He could see nothing 'horrible' about the clothes he was wearing. In fact it was one of his favourite puffin T-shirts, but it was true to say that they did look rather dowdy next to the rainbow garb of the Aevyan children, and what's more it wasn't simply the clothes that were brightly coloured. Arms, legs and even their hands were painted with vivid swirling patterns like the wings of butterflies.

"How did you know we're Seekers of the Truth?" He changed

the subject. It was better to be the ones questioning than being questioned. It was also a good opportunity to learn as much as they could before they encountered any more adults, because whatever else they might be, he was sure the children weren't Baarash spies! The Fire Spirit who had caught them in Mount Meru had been incredulous at the idea of him and his friends being entrusted with such a role, so children as young as the bright-eyed little Aevyans were hardly likely to have been recruited. It felt rather good to be the older, wiser ones for once. It soon became clear, however, that he might have underestimated the children.

"Hive Mind. There's a Bee Strain in our colony. That's why we're so much stronger than other Butterfly Tribes." This time it was the boy who had reached them first who spoke.

"Er... right..." Owen was floundering.

"You don't know what 'Hive Mind' is, do you?" The boy looked surprised.

"Not exactly, no," he admitted.

"Well..." the boy began, but before he had a chance to get any further, all the other children had joined in with their own explanations.

"Whoa! Stop!" Owen held his hands up. "Stop!" It was like being surrounded by a swarm of gnats. He could hear nothing but an incomprehensible babble of words all jumbled up, one on top of another. "Just one of you," he shouted.

Instantly all the voices fell silent and twenty something eyes widened with alarm.

"One of you," Owen repeated more gently. He hadn't meant to scare them.

Finally the girl with the pale-yellow eyes spoke. "You know how with bees, what one knows, they all know." She paused.

"Ye...es." Owen didn't know this, but it sounded familiar. Nyxa had said something similar about Undines.

"Well, because we have a Bee Strain, we have 'Hive Mind' a bit, see?"

Owen really didn't like confessing ignorance to someone who couldn't have been more than nine, but he didn't see. "What do you mean *a bit*?"

The girl frowned as she tried to find a way to explain it. "We don't all know what we're all thinking, but we can sometimes. It's different thinking."

Arin was nodding. "Like Raya and me. Selenian twins."

"Huh?" Finn was totally confused by the whole conversation.

"I'll explain another time." Arin turned back to the Aevyan girl. "So that man we saw before, on the horse, he told you about us in this different thinking, this Hive Mind."

"Yes!" The girl beamed at Arin, delighted to find that at least one of them wasn't a numbskull.

"And you're all part of this Butterfly Tribe?" Owen brought the subject back on to securer ground.

"Of course we are!" The first boy broke in with a laugh. "Come on!" He beckoned to them to follow then set off running back up the slope towards the tents. An instant later the rest of the children were hot on his heels.

"Hang on!" Owen called after them. He had wanted to ask more questions before venturing into the camp, but his words went unheard. He looked at his friends. "We might as well go with them." After all, a Butterfly Tribe didn't really sound too dangerous, despite the fact that the children carried swords.

By the time they reached the first of the tents, Owen was out of breath. He had started off running in an attempt to catch up with the children, fully expecting to be significantly faster than them, but the gradient of the slope was deceptive and in no time he was puffing and panting like an old man, his chest heaving.

Finn too was gasping for breath. "Something wrong." He bent forward, hands on knees to recover and was struggling to speak in between sucking huge gulps of air into his lungs. "This air."

Owen nodded in agreement, momentarily unable to talk. "I think it's because we must be really high up," he gasped eventually. He had heard of thin air high in the mountains and though they hadn't climbed up very far, perhaps the whole plain was high up to start with.

The children had vanished into the camp just ahead, but he could still hear their laughter and high excited voices. They passed between a violet and yellow striped tent and one artfully decorated in every conceivable shade of blue, just as a small child raced past carrying what looked like a kite in his arms.

86

"Where are the adults?" Raya said, as yet another child peeped out at them from behind the tent opposite, before running off laughing. "And why is everyone rushing round like zigga fish?"

Owen had never heard of zigga fish, but he understood what she meant. The children were dashing to and fro between the tents, apparently frantically busy going somewhere extremely important, as fast as possible.

"What's going on?" he called out to a boy he thought he recognized as one of the group who had met them on the hillside, waving his arms for him to slow down.

"Huh?" The boy stopped in his tracks and gave him the rather peculiar head-tilted-to-side 'starling' look.

"Where are you all going in such a hurry?" He tried again.

The boy stared at him for a moment, blank incomprehension written across his face, but before he had a chance to reply, a man emerged from inside one of the tents.

"Shoo! Shoo!" He flapped his hands at the boy as though swatting a fly, then turned to face Owen and his friends. For a few seconds no one spoke as he looked them up and down.

"Seekers of the Truth, eh?" The man finally spoke, a look of amusement flitting across his face.

"Ye... es." Owen answered hesitantly. He couldn't see what the man found so funny about the phrase, nor for that matter the rider they had met earlier. He was sure that was the correct term, the title taken by Air novices. "And er...we're looking for the Guardian." He couldn't see what harm saying it would do. The Fire Lord knew about his key and knew about the Sath, but that seemed to be as far as it went. There had been no indication in Dayah, Bryah or Assyah that his enemies knew of even the existence of his book, let alone the role of the Guardians in reading it.

However, the man's response took him totally by surprise.

"Well, obviously!" He shook his head with some bemusement. "What are they teaching you back in Paralda? That the Butterfly Tribe have no brains or something?"

Owen was utterly lost by the conversation, but luckily the man continued. "It seems a very strange and illogical thing to send novices out to the Rainbow Guild at this time. Very peculiar indeed." He frowned. "Unless of course..." He looked more closely at them and for a moment Owen had the awful thought that he might be about to say, *"You are Owen Shepherd, the Thief we are all looking for"*, or something similar. But instead he laughed. "Hah! Yes, that's it isn't it? You've run away, looking for glory! Well, you're fools," he tutted, suddenly serious again. "All you'll find at the Towers is bloodshed. Go home. The battlefield is no place for children."

"Battlefield?" It was Arin who spoke, alarm evident in his voice. "What do you mean, battlefield?"

The man looked so taken aback by the question that Owen feared Arin had made a bad mistake revealing their ignorance, but then his eyes widened in apparent understanding.

"Oh! Of course. I forget not every Tribe has Hive Mind. You don't have Bee Strain, do you?"

Owen was able to shake his head quite definitively on this. "No. Not at all."

"Right." The man hesitated. "Look, I'm really too busy to explain it all, what's going on with the Guild and the Palace, and to be honest, I don't care that much. We're going to the Chrysalis Fields, war or no war." He gestured back towards the tent from which he had just come. "Grandma Saiki can tell you what you need to know." And with that he turned away, disappearing between the tents opposite.

Owen glanced round at his friends. The word Grandma had triggered an unfortunate memory for him – that of Gramps, the Solochi who had tricked him in Bryah. But Finn had no such qualms and pushing the light fabric door flap aside, ducked down and entered the tent.

It was surprisingly cool inside and surprisingly light. Owen had assumed from a distance that the tents were made from canvas, but now he was inside, he could see that he was wrong. The light streamed through the walls as though they were made of chiffon, bathing the contents of the tent in an extraordinary pale yellow and blue light. He blinked, feeling momentarily disorientated.

"So it's the Guardians you're looking for?"

Owen nearly jumped out of his skin as a high thin voice broke the silence, a voice that reminded him of the wind whistling past his window on a cold winter's night on Olafssey.

"Come on in and sit yourselves down." The owner of the voice moved as she spoke, raising herself very slowly from the hammock-like structure in which she had been lying, so that she was sitting facing them. Owen couldn't stop himself staring. He had never seen anyone who looked so old – even Nana looked young by comparison! Yet despite this, she was beautiful. The painted swirls on the limbs of the Butterfly children were pale and watery imitations of the deep, rich colours which covered the frail old lady's skin. They had a peculiar depth to them, as though the dyes permeated right through into her bones. She raised her hand to beckon to them again, her yellow-specked, violet eyes watching their every move unblinking. "There's sugar water in the bowl over there if you're thirsty." She nodded towards a wide, shallow bowl, raised up on three legs.

"Thank you." Owen hadn't realized how thirsty he was until she mentioned it. Once he had drunk his fill of the surprisingly refreshing sweetened water, he sat down on the rush matting that covered the ground. "Everyone seems to be in such a hurry," he said.

The old lady smiled ruefully. "Always in a hurry, Butterfly Tribe. In a hurry to be born, then in a hurry to die." She turned her head to one side just like the little boy had done before and gave him a quizzical look. "I thought it was usually the brightest that they sent to the Towers."

"Just because we don't know about Butterfly Tribes doesn't mean we're not bright," Raya retorted indignantly.

But Owen interrupted her. "We weren't sent. We ran away." It seemed sensible to go along with the story that had just been suggested to them.

Grandma Saiki nodded. "Hmm..."

He wasn't sure whether she believed them or not.

"Not a very wise thing to do." The old lady shook her head as she spoke and he noticed for the first time that her long hair, which had appeared white before, now reflected the pale blues and yellows of the tent walls, as though transparent. "No, not at all." She gave Owen and his friends a long, appraising look.

Owen bit back the questions that were on his lips. One thing he had learnt from talking to Nana was that it was generally better to let her carry on speaking, than to ask a string of questions. All sorts of unexpected revelations came out that way.

"Even out here on the Plains we've heard of the war. There have been many voices in the wind." She paused. "You're not from Paralda, are you?"

"No," Owen admitted. "We never actually said we were."

Grandma Saiki nodded slowly. "It was a hasty assumption that I made. Forgive me."

"It's fine," Owen said quickly. "Please... er... we do need to find the Guardians."

The old lady sighed. "Foolish. You are all the same, no matter whether Butterfly or Bird, or whatever tribe you are, you youngsters want to fight. What quarrel do you have with the palace of Paralda that you wish to throw your young life into this battle?"

"We don't. We... we just... we're looking for something." Owen ended lamely.

"Yes. You are looking for the Sword of Truth. You have already told us that. But if the Prince is right and the Guardians have found it, they are not going to hand it over to you, are they? And the Prince will attack the Towers any day now. Nothing is going to stop him. The Singing Head has been telling of the finding of the Sword each morning for nearly three months now."

Owen sincerely hoped at least one of his friends could understand what on earth she was talking about, but the flummoxed expressions on their faces weren't promising.

"Is that why everyone is rushing around?" Arin came to his rescue, bringing the conversation back on to securer ground. "Because you're getting ready to move, to escape this battle?"

"Oh no," Saiki exclaimed. "We don't need to escape it. It's not our battle this time – thankfully! Life contains enough sorrow without needing to take on that of another. We lost too many young ones only last year. A quarrel with another Butterfly Tribe about the correct colour for a baby's first dream-wings." She pulled a long face. "It has still not been resolved. But now we are on our way back to the Chrysalis Fields. We need to replace all those we lost last year. We leave tomorrow."

"Tomorrow?" Owen had just begun to formulate a plan in his head, which involved spending at least a couple more days in this bright, dynamic camp. He was sure he could learn a lot more from the chatty Butterfly children and more importantly, it felt as unlikely a place as he had ever been for a Fire Spirit to take up residence. There was something so sharply alive in the curious bright eyes of all the people he had met so far, that seemed utterly at odds with the dull, flat deadness of a Baarash gaze. But if they were leaving tomorrow...

"You can travel with us if you wish." Saiki had read his thoughts correctly. "But only to the edge of the Great Plain. Beyond that limit you may not come. The Chrysalis Fields are for the Butterfly Tribe alone. No one else may ever venture there."

"Thank you." He hesitated, unsure how to phrase his next question. "Which way are you going?"

Instantly the old lady's eyes darkened, and he felt a sharp pain, as though someone had just stuck a needle into his temple.

"Ow! Stop!" He clapped his hands to his eyes, breaking the contact with her. "Please! I wasn't trying to find out where the Chrysalis Fields were," he exclaimed hastily. "I just... I still need to find the Guardians, even if it is dangerous."

Grandma Saiki relaxed. "You are determined to go there? No matter what?"

He nodded, still not trusting to make eye contact again and making a mental note to be very careful in future when talking to Aevyans. "It's important for us," he added quickly, hoping she wasn't going to question him further about why it was important.

"Then it's east you'll be going. Not with us. We travel in a different direction." She paused. "You will need to take care though and travel fast. The Winds are stirring." She frowned, as though considering whether to say more. However, Finn's stomach chose this moment to rumble hungrily. The old lady's face broke into a smile. "You must stay with us tonight. We have plenty of food, enough to share. If you leave early enough tomorrow and make good speed, you should reach the foothills with time to spare."

Owen too suddenly felt a pang of hunger. Breakfast in the Lighthouse seemed a very long time ago. It was clear that the old lady had said all she was going to say on the subject of the Guardians and the Towers, and although he was tempted to ask her more, he didn't want to risk her enquiring further about their supposed quest for the Sword of Truth. He had already learnt enough to know that the Towers was the place he had to head for, which was more than he had known in Dayah, Bryah or Assyah, and he had a good idea of what it was he might be searching for. Even finding the Gateway had been easy this time. It was all going remarkably well really.

Chapter 11

Owen had hoped to learn more about Yezirah and Aevyans from some of the children rushing hither and thither about the camp, but they seemed to be too busy to talk to him. Busy doing what, wasn't really clear. Young and old alike, everyone was in a hurry.

The tents were pitched apparently randomly on the slope, and it took Owen and his friends longer than he had expected to weave their way up to the summit of the little hill. He stopped when they reached the last tent, suddenly apprehensive about stepping out from the cover of the closely packed tents on to the open hilltop ahead. But Finn had no such reservations.

"They'll all know who we are, won't they?" he reasoned as he led the way out into a riot of colour and noise that reminded Owen rather of the village fete that summer back in Devon.

Brightly coloured streamers fluttered from long painted poles like a wide ring of sentinels standing guard around the flattened summit of the hill. Finn had been right about the kites as well when he had described the camp from his treetop vantage point.

"It looks like a game." Finn nodded towards the centre of the field, where a crowd stood gazing upwards at a flock of gaudily decorated kites which were swooping and diving with extraordinary skill and speed... impossible skill and speed... No kite could fly like that! What's more Owen couldn't see any strings attached and if there had been they would have become hopelessly entangled with one another in seconds. But as they drew nearer to the crowd, he spotted a boy not much older than himself, moving his hands as though controlling a kite. He watched, fascinated, as the boy wove his hands through the air apparently tugging invisible cords.

"No!" The boy let out a wail as one of the kites plummeted to the ground. "Why didn't you defend me Loki?" he called across the field as he went to retrieve his fallen kite. Whatever Loki had to say in response, however, was drowned in a great cheer as another kite crashed to the ground.

"One all!" Owen jumped as a voice boomed out over the cheering, from just behind him. "It always happens like that," the man who had shouted out the score sighed in exasperation. "One team scores, they let their guard down, and then the other equalizes straight away! I don't know how many times they've been told to stay focused after scoring, but it makes no difference. They always do the same thing!" He shook his head in mock despair and turned back to the game.

No one seemed to be paying any special attention to the four drably dressed children, but Owen suspected Finn was probably right, and everyone knew who they were already. Grandma Saiki may well have passed on everything they had told her via the Hive Mind. It was a rather disconcerting thought and put paid to any ideas he had had about choosing children to question on the basis that they were less likely to be Baarash spies. He ducked quickly as a gleaming gold and purple kite swept low over his head and the crowd let out a roar of approval.

"It would be hard to keep a secret with this Hive Mind business," Finn said, scanning the crowd ahead. "I mean... if someone was hiding something..." he trailed off.

Owen hadn't thought of that side of things. How could you be a spy if everyone knew what you were thinking?

But Arin shook his head. "Not necessarily. If it's like me and Raya, Selenian twins, you don't know everything the other one's thinking."

Raya let out an exclamation of mock horror. "No way! Urgh! I wouldn't want to see all the weird things in Arin's head!"

"So what bits do you know?" Owen had meant to ask this question a long time ago. Both Raya and Arin had mentioned being Selenian twins, but neither had ever given a very satisfactory explanation of what this really meant.

"I told you before," Raya began. "It's a different..." She stopped mid-sentence, staring wide-eyed with surprise over Owen's shoulder. He spun round, fearing for an instant that it was a Baarash that she had seen. But instead he saw a tall, skinny man with feathers braided into his hair, striding very deliberately towards him, and talking in an animated fashion to thin air. Owen automatically took a couple of steps back. He had seen someone just like this only a few months earlier outside Exeter Station, talking to himself, gesticulating wildly at an invisible creation of his mind.

"No, no, no!" The man exclaimed. "It cannot be done." He seemed thoroughly annoyed about something.

"They hold the nectar." Owen jumped in surprise as a soft, feminine voice suddenly came out of the man's mouth, a voice which sounded very weary and long-suffering. "If the Chrysalis Fields are not fed and watered…" the female voice continued.

"But you don't understand!" the male voice interrupted impatiently.

Owen recoiled further as the man passed by him. His friends however, looked intrigued.

"An Angekok," Raya whispered under her breath. Arin nodded in agreement.

"A what?" Finn had never heard the word.

"Like an oracle," Raya began.

"He is a 'Cracked Brain,'" a voice broke in.

Owen turned to see the young girl who had spoken to them outside the camp watching them, her head held at the odd, bird-like angle that he was becoming accustomed to.

"He channels the ancestral voices through the split inside his head."

"Oh! Like a shaman," Finn exclaimed.

"What?" Owen was confused. His friends all seemed to understand what the girl was talking about, but to him the man had just looked crazy.

"The Knowledge of the Butterfly Tribe – like Hive Mind, but with the ancestors' Hive Mind. See?"

Somewhere in his memory a little bell was ringing – something Nana had taught him, or tried to teach him, about Io, the Yew Tree. Finn would know.

"All the wisdom of the Ancestors," she continued. "It's all in his head."

Owen watched the gangly man wander off between the tents, still deep in conversation with himself. "So you mean that other voice, that was the Ancestors?"

The girl nodded, pleased to see that her explanation had apparently been understood. "And does she, they... talk to him all the time," Owen was beginning to feel distinctly uncomfortable about this, "even if he doesn't want them to?"

"Why wouldn't he want them to?" The young girl peered curiously at him.

"I don't know... er... if he was just having a normal talk with someone, say."

The girl shook her head. "He doesn't have normal talks. He's a Cracked Brain."

That was clearly meant to suffice as an answer and judging by their nods, Finn, Arin and Raya appeared to think she had explained the situation perfectly adequately. But Owen wasn't happy with it. The moment the girl had mentioned channelling voices, the disconcerting memory of the Eddra grove had flashed into his head, and the strange voice that had spoken through his mouth. It had happened again with Hathor in the Temple of the Navel. Perhaps more alarming still was the increasingly frequent intrusion of memories that didn't belong to him, into his consciousness. How long before Tamus started speaking regularly out of his mouth without him having any control over it?

"When do you eat round here?" Finn broke in rather unsubtly, and the subject of the Cracked Brain man came to a close, but for the rest of the evening Owen kept a wary eye out for him. It might all seem quite normal to his friends, but they weren't the ones with a bunch of other people's memories knocking around inside their head!

Food turned out to be better than Owen had expected. They had been invited to eat by the young girl whose name they discovered was also Saiki.

"She's my grandmother," she explained, when he commented on the fact. "The first-born girls are always Saiki in my family." She set down a bowl of what looked like soup, in front of him. "Pollen broth," she said as she sat down on the ground beside him. "I helped gather the pollen and Rui, my brother, he did the condensing."

Owen took a wary sip. "It's good!" he exclaimed in surprise. It reminded him of something he might have eaten in Dayah, rich and nutty and slightly sweet, as though honey had been added. He drank down his bowl hungrily and found himself feeling as full as if he had eaten a whole three-course meal. Even Arin and Raya enjoyed it, despite the lack of extra salt!

It was already getting dark by the time everyone had finished eating and Owen was relieved when Saiki and several other children started to string up hammocks between the poles of the tent nearest to them. The long day had suddenly caught up with him and he could barely keep his eyes open.

"You can sleep in here with us," an older boy declared, noticing his yawn. "Only you'll have to sleep on the floor. We haven't got any spare hammocks."

Owen didn't really care where he slept at that moment. The pile of brightly coloured canvas that the boy was pointing to looked as comfortable as a soft feather bed to him and he fell fast asleep almost the instant he closed his eyes.

"We are one. Forever." He repeated the words solemnly as he drew the blade across his brother's forearm.

"Deeper." Dar sounded annoyed. "That's barely a scratch. I did yours properly!"

Owen glanced down at his own left arm, at the blood running freely from a deep gash. Strangely he could feel nothing but a heavy throbbing sensation. He clenched his fist tighter round the knife hilt and holding Dar's wrist with his left hand, pulled the long thin silvery blade sharply across the pale flesh.

His brother winced in pain. "One forever!" he gasped as he grabbed hold of Owen's hand, pressing their forearms together. "My blood, your blood."

"My blood, your blood." Owen repeated.

"My destiny, your destiny."

"Forever."

And then it all changed. Owen became aware of Dar again beside him, but it was a different Dar, an older Dar who was laughing at him, as he always did. "I told you I could control them." There was a mocking tone in his brother's voice and Owen instantly knew what he was talking about. Dreamwalking. Dar had been dreamwalking again. "They're just Dream Spirits – our servants!" He gave Owen his most superior look. "And they are trapped there, in the Dream-Lands. They need us to get out."

But he knew it wasn't that simple, knew too that there were other things walking the paths of the Dream-Lands. "Dar, please don't go there." Last time Dar had spoken of dreamwalking he had got angry with his brother, fed up with the constant teasing about him being a sheep and doing whatever the Wardens told him. Last time he had bragged about visiting the Spirit Realm and Dar had called his bluff. This time he would take a different tack and under no circumstance would he lose his temper. "I mean it. It really is dangerous. Look," he hesitated, "why don't you let me talk to the Ruach?" Not that he was keen on the idea of approaching the High Priest of the Air Element, but if that was what it took. "He must know about you already. Everyone does. And you're *so* good at Air magic, I reckon you'd be able to skip loads of the novice stuff and..."

"Huh!" Dar snorted in contempt. "You still don't understand, Tam. I don't want to be one of them." He laid heavy emphasis on every word. "And he wouldn't want me anyway, because he'd know that...well, I might not be stronger than him yet, but I soon will be." Coming from anyone else it would have sounded a ridiculous claim, but Dar was different. Tamus felt an involuntary shiver of premonition suddenly run down his spine.

"I'll tell you what though." Dar's tone of voice was deceptively casual. "I'll make a deal. I promise I'll stop dreamwalking and even go and talk to your Ruach, if you can convince me that what they can offer is better than what I can find myself, on my own."

Tamus frowned. "What do you mean?"

"Take me through the Gateway. Show me the Spirit Realm. Then I'll believe you."

It was still dark when Owen woke up. Something knobbly was poking into his back through the spare tent canvas he was lying on. He rolled over on to his other side as quietly as he could, not wanting to wake his friends. The dreams were both still vivid in his mind. He rubbed his left arm unconsciously where Dar had drawn the blade across. He had dreamt before about a bonding ritual with his brother, hadn't he? Or had he? He struggled to remember and vaguely recalled something about one of the Wardens telling him that he and Dar had a shared destiny. He gazed up at the apex of the tent where the faintest sliver of moonlight cut through the darkness below. He missed his brother...

he, Owen, missed him, despite the fact that they had never met.

He forced himself to focus on the second dream – reluctantly. Tamus was a fool to let Dar get to him like that. Owen knew this with one part of his mind, but with another he understood exactly how Tamus felt – the frustration of yet another day tending sheep, the growing seeds of doubt as his brother's magical abilities raced on far ahead of his own. What if Dar was right? What if he had been chosen by the Wardens rather than his brother, simply because they had thought him more obedient and sheep-like, more easily fooled?

He heard someone stir in one of the hammocks close by and his attention came back to the present. The Butterfly Tribe were planning to pack and leave as soon as everyone was up, and since Owen and his friends weren't travelling with them, there was little point hanging around while the packing was going on. He knew the direction they had to head in, back down into the mist on the other side of the hill, and at least today he knew what he was making for – the Towers and their Guardians; knew too that the vast plain ahead wasn't the endless expanse he had feared the previous day.

They shared a very brief breakfast with Saiki and her friends. Once they had woken, the Butterfly children were all keen to get going as quickly as possible and a few mouthfuls of some flat cakes that tasted of honey were all that they bothered with before they set to dismantling the tent.

"You should go," Saiki said as she unstrung her hammock. "The Winds are stirring up in the caves." Owen remembered the old lady, Saiki's grandmother, saying the same thing.

"What winds?" he began, but she had already turned away, distracted by a younger boy tugging at one of the tent poles ineffectively.

"Not like that!" She hurried over to help him.

"We might just as well go." Arin glanced round at the chaos unfolding.

He nodded. He wasn't quite sure what he had been waiting for. Maybe he had been hoping someone would come with them, that there was an Aevyan version of Finn, Raya or Arin, who wanted to travel with them, but it looked as though, like in Assyah, they would have to find their way through Yezirah unaccompanied. Not that it would have been easy travelling with one of the Butterfly Tribe, he thought, as they set off down the hill away from the rapidly disappearing camp. Only Saiki had said goodbye when they left and had soundly mildly annoyed at the interruption to her packing. The enthusiasm of the children the previous day had fizzled out as quickly as the flame of a match doused in water, once they had known that Owen and his friends were about to disappear from their lives and he had the distinct suspicion that even if they had found a companion, the moment something apparently more interesting had come along, they would have been abandoned like broken toys.

The cries and laughter of the camp and the whinnies of excited horses gradually grew fainter, until all he could hear were their soft footsteps on the coarse turf and the occasional distant rumble of what he hoped was merely thunder.

"Reminds me of Draco," Finn remarked after a while.

"No." Arin shook his head. "Someone would have told us if there was a dragon out there, wouldn't they?"

Owen hoped he was right. Now they were back down under the mist cover, it was impossible to see more than a few yards in front of your nose. Anything could be lurking out there. He tried to focus on listening with his inner ears and watching with his inner eyes as Beith had taught him but could sense nothing. High above, the plaintive cry of a lone bird echoed forlornly across the plain and he shivered. The sound always reminded him of Olafssey and the volcano. But then suddenly he felt something different. He stopped, tense and wary as an all too familiar hot, prickling sensation crawled across his skin. Fire energy.

"What's wrong?" Raya stopped too. "What is it?"

'Caw, caw'.

It was another bird, invisible above the mist. But he had an ominous suspicion that he knew exactly what the bird was.

"An ixephat," he began, then stopped. "A sort of ixephat," he corrected himself. He was willing to bet that it wasn't one of the dark, golden birds with feathers liked speckled sand, that had lured Beith into Odora's web, but something closer to the black, scaly creatures of Bale Castle, something just like the black bird he had seen flying high above the sea in Bryah.

"Like we saw before." Raya remembered it.

He nodded, relaxing a little now that the Fiery feeling had passed.

"It's a Fire creature," he explained to Finn and Arin, "a bad one." It sounded rather a feeble explanation of what he had sensed, but it *was* bad. The golden ixephat in Dayah had been under the spell of Odora and her poppy juice but hadn't been a minion of the Fire Lord. For the first time it occurred to him that perhaps not all Fire creatures were bad.

He kept his guard up as they continued on across the mist swathed plain. Occasionally another bird passed by, soaring high overhead, but nothing that sent hot prickles crawling across his back. The rumbling thunder noises, however, were getting steadily closer and more frequent.

"It does sound like Draco." Finn wasn't letting it go. "Like something breathing heavily."

Or like wind. The warning words of both the young and old Saikis rang loud in Owen's ears, but just as he was about to mention this, he found himself walking into bright, dazzling sunlight. The mist had dissipated peculiarly quickly. He glanced back behind him and could see what looked like an opaque wall of cloud. Only a few straggly tendrils remained, stretching long, frail fingers out across the vivid blue sky.

Finn let out an exclamation of relief. "Now we can see where we're going!"

"Huh." Raya sounded less than impressed. "More and more grass is all I can see. I think I preferred the mist. At least then there might have been something interesting coming up."

Owen gazed out over the plain ahead. It did indeed look unpromising. But Grandma Saiki had been quite clear that this was the direction in which they should head in order to reach the Towers, so that was what they would do. Anyway, Raya wasn't totally correct. There was more than grass out there. At first, he had thought he was imagining the tiny sparks of light flashing past the periphery of his vision, thought he must still be dazzled by the brightness of the sunlight after the mist. But when one flashed up right in front of his nose, he realized they were real.

Finn too had just reached the same conclusion. "Did you see that?" he exclaimed. "That flash of light just then – like a tiny Eddradi!"

"They're like fireflies... sort of." Arin was squinting, trying to get a better look at one. *Fire* flies! Owen's heart skipped a beat but a moment later he realised that there was nothing Fiery about these little bursts of light. He closed his eyes, trying to sense their energy, took a deep breath and waited.

'*Pop.*'

He gasped as one of the tiny sparks flared up for a split second, close by.

'*Pop. Pop.*' Two more.

They sounded like bubbles in a fizzy drink, felt like tiny stars exploding – just like he had felt, hanging in the air just after passing through the Gateway. Only this time he was standing on firm ground, this time he was able to enjoy the intoxicating sensation of light and space and clarity.

"Owen."

He jumped in shock as a voice rang out in his head.

"Owen. Listen to me."

He staggered back, his hands clasped to his ears. "No! Go away." His head was spinning as panic gripped hold of him.

"Owen!"

It was Professor Vishnami's voice.

Chapter 12

"What is it?" Finn grabbed hold of Owen's arm to steady him.

"Nooooo!" Owen tried frantically to find the Fire energy that he had tapped into last time, tried to find the source of the blazing rod of light that had blasted the Professor from his head before. But just as he thought he had it, just as he felt the spark ignite, it fizzled out. The Professor, however, seemed to have gone too. Cautiously he opened his eyes and removed his hands from his ears – not that they had really been doing any good. The voice had come from inside his head, not outside.

"It was him," he said, his voice small and shaky.

"Him? You mean... the Fire Lord?!" Raya's eyes widened in alarm.

"No... no." He managed to steady his voice. "The Professor – Professor Vishnami. He was trying to get into my head again."

"But... but... how?" Finn was confused. "I thought you had to be asleep."

"I don't know." Owen hesitated. That wasn't totally true. "I maybe let my guard down." The dream about Dar and dreamwalking flashed into his mind and he reached automatically for his rowan charm. "It's like he's been waiting, watching me until he saw a chance." Until he saw him drift off into Airy Realms where he could get to him.

"A chance?" Finn shook his head. "You can't let him do this. There must be some sort of Air charm that can protect you, like 'Luis'."

"It's OK. I won't let him in my head again. I don't need a 'Luis'. It's not enchantment." He released his grip on the rowan charm as he spoke. "It's OK," he said again. "I know what happened." And he did... sort of. At least, he knew not to go floating off into that bright Airy space again in a hurry.

For the next hour or so he concentrated as hard as he could on the ground in front of him and putting one foot in front of the other. The strange winds that had disturbed their journey the previous day were becoming more and more frequent and Grandma Saiki's words of warning were ringing in his ears.

"These winds are definitely not normal." Raya echoed his thoughts as a hot blast of air tore past them, whirling and dancing like a dervish across the grass.

Ahead of them the vast grassy plain stretched apparently endlessly. Owen screwed up his eyes as he tried to get a clearer view of the distant horizon. It looked slightly different, slightly hazier. He hoped it wasn't more mist rolling in towards them. But as he squinted into the light, he noticed something else, something flashing and spinning like the colours in a kaleidoscope, whirling across the plain to his left. He turned towards it, focusing his eyes normally again, and in an instant it vanished.

"What is it?" Arin came up alongside him. "What's wrong?"

"I saw something." He frowned as he scanned the now seemingly empty plain. "Like a waterspout, only without water. A sort of rainbow-coloured whirlwind thing."

"Where?" Raya scanned the plain. "I can't see anything."

"No... I can't see it now either." He stopped as a thought occurred to him. "Hang on." He turned to face the east and tried glancing out of the corner of his eye. Nothing. But then he carefully focused on the farthest point he could imagine, way out beyond the horizon, and everything else blurred, just like he had done in the church at the beginning of his quest, when he had found the first Gateway in the Noah's Ark painting. And suddenly there they were, dazzling vortices of air spinning past with wild abandon. They weren't close enough to be a danger yet, but he had no idea for how much longer they would be safe. It was one thing ducking out of the way of a galloping Morph on the Plain of Shells, but quite another avoiding a tornado. He blinked and again the image vanished.

"Grandma Saiki was right," he said. "We have to get off this plain as fast as we can." He explained what he had seen. "They're quite a long way away at the moment, the big ones, but they look like they're directly ahead of us."

He didn't need to say any more. The smaller winds were whirling past close by almost continuously now and growing steadily stronger, and though the others might not be able to 'see' the big rainbow twisters, they could feel the blasts of their smaller cousins. Had he been alone, Owen would have turned to 'Far Striding' with no hesitation, despite the possible risk of a Professor Vishnami intrusion, but this was not an option for Finn, Raya and Arin. All they could do was walk as fast as they could, stopping every now and then for him to check on the progress of the winds.

"It's fine. They're not heading straight for us," he reassured his friends. What he wasn't telling them was how much closer the towering tornadoes were. Each time he looked now, they were markedly nearer. "Perhaps we should run for a bit." He tried to make the suggestion sound far more relaxed than he felt.

So they ran for a while. But eventually they had to stop. It was Owen who ran out of steam first, much to his shame. "Got... to... stop!" he gasped as he collapsed to his knees. It didn't seem to have made any difference anyway. The horizon still looked just as far away and just as unpromising. But just at that moment a wind tore past them, roaring like a jet engine and knocking Arin's legs from under him.

"Ooph!" He landed hard on his bottom. Finn and Raya staggered backwards but somehow kept their balance. Owen tried to get his eye in, to focus on that distant point which brought the winds into his field of vision, and for an instant he had it, an instant in which he caught sight of a huge, roaring vortex heading straight for them. He looked frantically for somewhere that could at least offer the hope of some shelter, but there was nothing. It would hit them in less than a minute at the rate it was travelling. Time perhaps to run, but the whirlwinds didn't trace a straight path. He had watched the distant ones veering wildly from left to right, following no discernibly logical route. Should they run to the left or to the right or stay put and just hope it swung off on a curve that missed them? He was rooted to the spot by panic, totally incapable of deciding one way or the other. He could hear it clearly now, rumbling, booming like thunder rolling round the plain before them.

"What...?" Finn began but stopped mid-sentence as he saw Owen's expression.

"We can't just stand here!" Raya had realized what was happening. "We..." But her words were drowned out beneath the roaring, howling wind. It was too late to do anything but fling themselves to the ground where they stood.

Owen clapped his hands over his ears in a vain attempt to block out the deafening thunderous roar, as his whole body tensed with fear, waiting for the full blast of the wind to hit. Waiting. And still waiting. Slowly, cautiously, he let his breath out and opened his eyes. He could still hear the rumbling boom of the twister, but it was behind him, to the left.

"It's missed us!" Finn gasped, wide-eyed with incredulity. "How... how did it miss us!?"

Owen had no answer. The tornado had been almost directly upon them when he had thrown himself to the ground.

"Luck!" Raya was already back on her feet. "We're lucky!" She laughed in relief. "Don't you see, Owen? You're luck-charmed!"

"Huh!" Finn snorted. "I knew a lucky person once. He was always lucky until the day he wasn't! He got caught by Eddleshi and *didn't* escape." His last words were directed at Owen. "You might be happy risking your luck out here, but I'm not. The quicker we get out..."

Finn never finished his sentence. A low thundering rumble shook the earth beneath their feet, a sound which Owen instantly feared was another whirlwind hurtling towards them. He spun round ready to run. But it was no whirlwind this time. It was a herd of horses in full gallop, charging across the plain in a cloud of dust. For a few moments he feared the worst, but at the very last instant the horses wheeled to the left, as one.

"Whoa!" A man's voice rang out, bellowing above the pounding hooves. "Whoa!"

As the dust cloud settled a grey cloaked figure rode out towards them. At first Owen wondered if it was one of Butterfly Tribe come to find them, but as the rider drew closer, he sensed something different from the sharp brightness of the Butterflies.

"What fool's errand are you on to be out here on foot?" The rider exclaimed. "Today of all days!"

"Er..." Owen stammered. "We... er..."

"Come on!" The man shook his head impatiently. "I really haven't got time to waste picking up waifs and strays, but you're dead if you stay out here much longer. The Winds are raging. Any time now the fighting will begin. Quickly now." He gestured towards the herd of horses.

It was clear what he meant, but the only horses Owen had ever ridden before were sturdy little Dartmoor ponies, and not only did they bear very little similarity to the wild-eyed beasts pawing impatiently at the ground and snorting through foam-specked, flaring nostrils, but they had also had saddles and reins.

"I can't..." he began in a very small voice, but the rider snorted with impatience.

"Of course you can." He swung himself down from his horse. "It's your choice though. Come with me and live or stay out here and die."

Put like that it wasn't really a choice! It was Raya in the end who made the first move. "Let's do it! It can't be any worse than those aurox can it?" she said eyeing the closest horse.

She hesitated, uncertain what to do next, but the grey-cloaked man swung her deftly up on to the horse's back.

Owen expected the horse to shy away or rear up, but instead it remained still, as though transformed by the presence of a rider from a wild beast into a placid cart horse, and it was with slightly more confidence that he accepted the still nameless man's assistance to mount the relatively calm-looking grey waiting beside Raya's horse.

He looked down warily. The ground seemed an awfully long way away. Not as far as from atop Clover, the aurox, but he had been safely ensconced in a saddle then, with a firm, solid pommel in front of him. He took hold of his horse's mane, trying to get as firm a grip as possible, but still felt horribly unstable. It was all very well getting on the horse, but he felt a grim certainty that the moment it began to move he would be tumbling straight off on to the hard earth below.

Beside him Finn looked just as unhappy. "I don't think I..." he began, but whatever it was Finn didn't think was never revealed as at that moment the grey-cloaked rider swung himself up on to his own horse, gave a loud whooping cry, and they were off. As one, the horses began to run. There was no gentle easing in, no chance for Owen to accustom himself to the sensation of riding; the horses were racing as though a pack of wolves was on their heels. But strangely he didn't fall off. It was like flying with Beith or skimming through the ocean with the dolphins, and though he was clinging on tight to the mane in front of him, it hardly seemed necessary, so smooth was the ride. He could hear a pounding of hooves beneath him, but it felt as though the horse was galloping on air. On and on they rode, the grassy plain tearing past in a green-blue haze. It occurred briefly to him that were he to fall off at this speed, he would be seriously hurt, but he knew it wasn't going to happen. He turned his head to see where his friends were.

"Hey!" he called across to Finn, but his words were snatched from his mouth by the wind howling past.

It was impossible to see clearly ahead. Every time he raised his head to try to focus on the distant horizon, his eyes were blurred by streams of tears, and despite his confidence in not falling off, he didn't dare let go of the mane even with one hand to wipe them away or shield his face from the wind.

He had lost track of how long they had been galloping across the plain. Ten minutes, an hour... he had no idea. All he was aware of was the constant blur of green racing past beneath him, and the pounding of hooves. Finally the horses began to slow and as they slowed, the velvet smooth ride came to an abrupt and unwelcome end. Instead of feeling as if he was gliding effortlessly across the plain on wings, Owen became a sack of potatoes, bumping up and down on his horse's back with no control over his movement whatsoever.

"Whoa! Whoa!" He called out desperately, clinging to handfuls of mane in an attempt to save himself. "Ooph." Not for the first time since his quest had begun, he hit the ground with a resounding thud.

As he picked himself up, he became aware for the first time that the landscape had changed. Instead of the flat monotony of the plain, the land around him rose and fell in gently rolling hills. He frowned, bewildered by the transformation. It hadn't felt as though anything had altered during the ride and he had had no sense whatsoever of having gone uphill. Yet that was what had evidently happened. Behind him, far below, lay the plain, vanishing into a misty haze on the horizon, whilst ahead soared the vertiginous peaks of snow-capped mountains. He couldn't understand how they hadn't been visible earlier. They must have travelled an incredibly long distance on the horses for it to be possible.

His confusion was cut short by the return of the grey-cloaked rider.

"Are you alright?" He jumped down from his horse and hurried over to them. "I should have warned you. If you've never ridden Aolian horses before, you wouldn't know." He sounded rather sheepish. "Easiest horses in all Yezirah to ride fast, but the hardest to ride slowly," he explained.

Fortunately, apart from a few bruises, no one was hurt, and Owen wasn't convinced that it would have helped if they had been warned. There was absolutely nothing he could have done to stay on the back of his horse. In the distance he heard the familiar rumbling roar of a whirlwind. He squinted in the direction the sound was coming from and caught a brief glimpse of a flashing kaleidoscope of colours spiralling skywards before it whirled out of view behind the swell of a hill.

"It doesn't look like we're going to be going any further today." The rider sighed as he eyed the four children. "The horses can't gallop flat out forever, especially not on this ground." He scanned the hummocky hillside as he spoke. "Anyway, now we're off the plain we can find some cover for the night. Those trees over there, they'll do just fine." He nodded towards a copse of poplars, clustered in a dip.

"But those Winds aren't just down on the plain. I saw one over there, just behind that hill," Owen said. He couldn't see how the copse would be able to protect them if a full-blown tornado swept through in the night.

"Oh, don't worry. Those are Whispering Trees." The man seemed to think that was sufficient explanation.

Once they were safely under the trembling canopy of poplar leaves, the rider introduced himself.

"Enlali." He held out his hand in greeting and pushed back his grey hood. "I didn't mean to be quite so short with you earlier, but what in the Sword's name were you thinking of, walking around out there with the Winds stirring like this?"

He was younger than Owen had expected. The grey cloak had given him the impression that the person underneath must be grey too, but the fair-haired, yellow-eyed man facing him couldn't have been more than a few years older than Owen himself.

Raya was the first to break the silence that followed Enlali's question. "I'm Raya and this is Arin, my brother, and Finn and Owen. We didn't deliberately try to get killed," she added. "We just sort of got blown off course."

For a moment Enlali's eyes opened wide with surprise at the phrase, but then he burst out laughing. "Very good! That's very funny. I'll have to remember that one."

Raya frowned, seeing nothing at all 'funny' in the expression. "You were out there too!" she retorted.

"With horses!" Enlali exclaimed. "It's rather different." He looked at them seriously once more. "What are you doing though? Where were you going before you got *'blown off course'?'*

Owen was suddenly wary, even though Enlali had given him no reason to distrust him.

"We were with the Butterfly Tribe," he said, carefully choosing his words.

"You're not Butterfly Tribe," Enlali stated.

"No. We're not. I didn't say we were." He hesitated. Why was he so reluctant to tell Enlali where they were going? He could think of no good reason not tell him. After all he had probably just saved their lives. What harm could it do? "We're going to the Towers to see the Guardians."

The moment the words left his lips he knew he had made a mistake. A look of suspicion flashed across Enlali's face and his eyes narrowed, before he gave a very forced snort of laughter. "Oh, are you? You want to become magicians, is that it?"

"We're seeking the Sword of Truth actually," Raya chimed in, repeating the words of the Butterfly children. Owen's heart sank like a stone as she spoke.

"And what do you know about that?" Enlali asked, staring intently at her.

"Er... we... er..." Raya was floundering.

"We heard it might be there." Owen tried to sound as casual as he could.

"You heard it might be there?" Enlali repeated his words incredulously. "So you thought what exactly? That you would rescue it for the Prince... or something else?"

Owen was now way out of his depth and as Enlali stepped towards him, his cloak swung open slightly to reveal a sheathed sword.

"I don't know," he stammered. "We... we just wanted an adventure."

For a few seconds Enlali didn't reply, then he burst out laughing.

"An adventure! Well you'll certainly get that. Come on." He shook his head in amusement, reminding Owen for some inexplicable reason, of Darius. "We had better get on and make camp here. Until these Winds have blown themselves out, none of us is going anywhere."

Any hope Owen had had for a comfortable night's sleep, rapidly dissolved when the Aevyan called his horses into the shelter of the trees with a high-pitched whistle.

"I can't leave them out there in the open," he said, noticing Arin eyeing suspiciously a particularly high-spirited looking horse. He gave another high whistle and the horses gathered closer still. "Don't worry. They won't step on you or anything while you are asleep." He seemed to find their unease around the horses amusing.

There was no sign of any sort of supplies or baggage, except a very small pack on Enlali's own horse – no tent, not even a hammock like the Butterfly Tribe had slept in.

"Not much to eat I'm afraid," Enlali apologized as he pulled the remains of a loaf of bread and a couple of lemons out of his pack. "I had hoped to be able to ride on further today, up beyond the Caves of the Winds."

"The Caves of the Winds?" Owen still felt uneasy about Enlali, but his curiosity got the better of him.

"Yes, we're very close to them now. Just over the next rise and you should be able to see the cliff itself – where the Wind Masters live," he added, seeing Owen's blank expression.

"Oh... er... right." He nodded, trying hard to look knowledgeable.

Enlali took a long drink from his flask, then handed it on to Finn before continuing. "That should help you sleep. It's going to be quite a night, I fear. With those big Winds fighting down on the Plain, the Wind Masters are sure to be out hunting. It's always the best time for them to capture another Wind for their bag – when they're so preoccupied with fighting one another. And from what I've seen, there are some impressive Winds intending to give battle tonight."

Whatever was in the flask, it was certainly strong. Owen spluttered and nearly choked as the yellow liquid slid down his throat, burning like a fire inside him. Even Arin and Raya, used as they were to Smah, were coughing and gasping. Only Finn seemed to be unaffected.

"Mmm. Not bad," he said appraisingly. "A bit like a hazel and lavender cordial."

Enlali took back his flask and drained the remainder.

"I would rather not have had to stop this side of the cliff," he sighed.

"You said that we'd be all right here because of the Whispering Trees." A worried look crossed Arin's face as he spoke.

"Yes, yes... we should be. It's just..." Enlali hesitated a moment. "Well, if all the Wind Masters ride out tonight, there'll be very little to protect the Wind Bags and there are always mischievous Spirits around looking for trouble, or mischievous people wanting a chance to ride a tame Wind." He frowned. "Stupid! And the likelihood is they open the wrong bag and let out an Ill-Wind, and then..." He pulled a grim face. "I would just rather have been the other side tonight, that's all."

With that he got to his feet. "I'd better check all the horses are safely in. There's one or two always want to do the opposite of what I tell them!"

Once he was out of sight, Finn jumped up. "This will have to do." He picked up a poplar branch, looking very dissatisfied, and began to trace a wide circle in the earth, walking slowly backwards in a clockwise direction and softly incanting words which were now familiar to Owen. Raya and Arin watched silently until he had finished.

"It might not work here, Wood magic," Arin said grimly. "I know what you said before Owen, but that was in your World. This is the Air Realm."

"It'll work," Owen reassured him. "This may be the Air Realm, but if it was only Air, well... these trees wouldn't be here to start with, or the ground, or... any of this." He gestured around him. "It's all sort of mixed together, only here it's Air that... er... rules... I think," he ended rather lamely.

"Eadha isn't the best wood to cast a circle with," Finn sighed, "but it does help protect you from illnesses I suppose, so if one of those Ill-Wind things comes this way, it might help."

Owen wondered if that was what Enlali had meant by an Ill-Wind. He hadn't wanted to ask any more questions, since clearly they were expected to know about the Winds and he didn't want to face an inquisition from the Aevyan man about this ignorance. Somewhere in the back of his memory, or rather Tamus' memory, was something about Air magic being particularly connected to interrogation and inquiry! In truth though, it wasn't really the mention of the Ill-Winds which had grabbed his attention, so much as the phrase *'ride a tame Wind'*. Could that be what it sounded like? Was it possible? It was something he had dreamt of all his life, something, which despite all his adventures with Elemental magic, he had never really believed possible. Riding a Wind. Flying!

Chapter 13

Long after his friends and Enlali had fallen asleep, Owen lay gazing up through the rustling poplar leaves. He could hear the thundering of the Winds, mingling with the snores and steady breathing of his companions, but felt strangely safe inside the poplar grove. Close by the dark forms of the horses stood like sentinels against the outside world. He understood now why Enlali had referred to the poplars as Whispering Trees. The shivering leaves did indeed sound as though they were whispering secrets to one another. He was reminded of the elm tree he had lain under on his journey to the Temple of the Navel. He felt a shiver run through him, mirroring the leaves above, despite the warmth of the night.

The storm was building down on the Plain below, flashes of distant lightning now joining the rumbling thunder. He caught a glimpse of a whirling vortex of light beyond the copse, pulsing a rainbow of luminous colours as it spun past, and glanced round at his sleeping companions, wondering whether to wake them. But they had been unable to see the Winds before and he had no reason to think anything had changed.

Carefully he got to his feet. As an afterthought he grabbed his bag. What if Enlali woke while he was gone? With the increasing volume of thundering and roaring from the Plain, this was a distinct possibility and however friendly the Aevyan appeared, Owen still didn't entirely trust him. There was definitely more to his interest in the Sword than met the eye. He tiptoed past Finn's sleeping form and stepped carefully out of the protective circle. It shouldn't be a problem, he thought to himself, since he had no intention of falling asleep. All he wanted to do was go to the edge of the copse, where he could get a better view of the Plain and the battling Winds.

One of the horses gave a gentle whinny as he crept past, but otherwise all was calm within the safety of the poplar grove. As he drew closer to the limit of the trees, a thrill of anticipation gripped him. Even without doing the *Magic Eye* trick, he could see brilliant flashes and whirling vortices of light ahead of him. He stopped beside one of the outermost trees, remembering Enlali's words of warning. This was far enough. Any further out on to the hillside and he risked being caught up in the maelstrom of a passing whirlwind.

Slowly he focused out beyond the dark horizon, training his eyes on a point far out in space, and in an instant the panorama before him was transformed. The flashes he had seen before were swept up into a vast kaleidoscopic tableau of dancing, swirling colour and light. No fireworks display came close. Not even the spectacle of the northern Lights illuminating the sky on Olafssey, could compare.

Time passed, but he had no sense of it. He was transfixed, everything else forgotten but the glorious battle of the Winds on the Plain below. But gradually the frenetic dance began to slow, and then suddenly he lost his focus. He blinked briefly, seeing double, and struggled to bring the scene back into view -- but to no avail. His eyes were aching, too tired by the unfamiliar experience. He tried once more, but finally admitted defeat and turned back towards the shelter of the copse. But as he turned, a sheet of lightning lit up the sky, delineating the dark silhouettes of the mountain peaks. By an optical illusion they seemed to loom far closer by night than they had during the daylight. He stopped. A thought had just popped into his head. He glanced around the empty hillside surrounding the copse. All was calm. Down on the Plain below he could still hear the occasional roar of a Wind, but the battle seemed to have largely blown itself out. What harm could just a look do? And with the Winds gone there was surely no real danger out on the hillside. He made up his mind. He would just walk to the crest of the little hill and see what lay on the other side, then come back again.

But though he was trying to convince himself that this was his only intention, as he made his way up the slope away from the copse, his heart was pounding with both fear and excitement. He reached inside his pouch for his rowan charm. Not that he expected to need it, but it always made him feel safer, not least because of the link with Nana. But instead of the knobbly little twig, his fingers found a hard, cold object with a sharp point at one end – the Tooth! His hand froze. He had forgotten it was there. Slowly his fingers closed around it and he drew it out. For a moment he just held it and stared at it, but then he began to roll it between his thumb and fingers. What was it Raki had said about the Tooth? *'Power beyond your wildest dreams'.* And Owen's wildest dream was suddenly within reach…

He hurried on up the hill, his heart now racing. Even Dar had never done this, had he? For all his supposed mastery of Air magic, the most he had been able to achieve as far as Tamus remembered, was simple levitation. And dreamwalking didn't really count. It wasn't the same thing at all.

He ran up the last few metres of the slope, brimming over with anticipation. But when he reached the top, his heart sank like a stone. Enlali had been wrong. There was nothing ahead but more rolling grassy hillside and beyond it what looked like a bare rocky cliff. But then another sheet of lightning flashed across the sky, and he saw them – small dark holes, no more than pockmarks in the face of the cliff at this distance, but he was sure he was right. These were the Caves of the Winds, where the Wind Masters kept their bags!

Ten minutes later he was standing at the foot of the cliff. It had looked from a distance, in the brief glimpses that the lightning had provided him, as though there was no way up the cliff other than climbing, but even that prospect hadn't daunted him with the Tooth in his hand. However, as it happened this wouldn't be necessary. Now that he had reached the rock face, he could see a narrow path zigzagging precipitously up. With no moon to light his way, this wouldn't be easy. But then he had an idea. Rummaging deep in his rucksack, he found what he was looking for – a tiny fibre bag, containing a powdery substance. Taking care not to overdo it, he began to weave Woody energies between his fingers as Finn had taught him, and a moment later a perfect little glow ball sparked to life in his hand. Reluctantly he tucked the Tooth back into his pouch. He needed one hand for the glow ball and couldn't risk the path without one free hand to find handholds if necessary.

It didn't take him long to reach the first cave. He could hear no sound coming from the darkness within but was still cautious as he peered through the entrance. Enlali had expected the Wind Masters all to be away chasing the Wild Winds down on the Plain, but what if he was wrong? What if one of them had stayed behind? Somehow Owen didn't think he would receive a warm welcome. But the cave looked to be empty. He crept in, holding his glow ball in front of him. The yellow-orange light poured into the darkness, revealing a rush mat on the floor towards the back and a small pile of what looked like animal bones to one side. But that was all. He was puzzled. This didn't look right. He had expected something more akin to Moshi's house in Assyah. He turned back out of the cave. Perhaps this one was just not occupied at the moment.

After two more almost identical caves, however, he was beginning to think Enlali had been talking nonsense. Clearly people had visited the caves. Someone had brought in the rush mats and stacked the bones in tidy piles, but as far as he could see, there was no evidence that anyone had been there recently. He paused as he stepped back on to the path. He hadn't gone very far up the cliff yet, but it still looked a long way down to the rocky ground below. Was there any point carrying on up? But as he glanced up the path, the thought of flying came back to him. Even if there was just the slightest chance that Enlali was right, it was worth going on.

The fourth cave looked at first sight disappointingly like the first three. But just as he was turning to leave, he caught sight of something out of the corner of his eye, something so innocuous looking that normally he wouldn't have given it a second glance. Hanging from the rocky wall, half hidden in the shadows, was a brown sack. It could be just that, he told himself, as he stepped slowly towards it, just a plain brown sack, nothing special. But his heart was in his mouth as he reached up and very gently unhooked it from the wall.

It felt empty. For a moment bitter disappointment swept over him, but then he almost laughed out loud. Of course it felt empty! How heavy were Winds going to be?

The sack was tied firmly at the top with a cord. However, it looked easy enough to open. He hesitated. This was all well and good, but what if he was right and there was a Wind trapped inside the bag? Did it wait calmly like Enlali's horses for him to climb on to it? He frowned and reached back into his pouch for the Tooth. He was sure Tamus had known all about the Wind Masters. He sat down on the floor of the cave to think, laying the brown sack down carefully in front of him.

"Wind Masters, Wind Masters." He repeated the words softly to himself out loud, trying to trigger the memory. But it wasn't a memory that came into his head, but a dream. As a young child, amongst his many flying dreams, there had been one odd one in which he hadn't been the one with miraculous flying powers, but simply an observer. It was a dream that had recurred unchanging, time after time, and now as he thought back to it, there was something very familiar about the scene, something he recognized about the hillside overlooking a turquoise sea, and the building that stood just behind him, a building with a doorway painted in four quarters of olive, citrine, russet and black. His heart was pounding. That was what they were called wasn't it, the three colours that he had seen in his dream as greenish, yellowish and reddish? Now he remembered their names. And more importantly he remembered exactly what it was that he had seen, sitting, watching, from the hillside.

Barely able to contain his excitement, he jumped to his feet and picked up the sack. The possibility that he might be wrong, that the sack might be empty, no longer concerned him. All he could think about was riding that Wind, soaring high into the sky. He stopped just inside the cave entrance, giving his Tooth one final roll in his fingers for luck, then stashed it back in his pouch and fastened his rucksack firmly to his back. Taking a deep breath, and with trembling hands, he pulled on first one end of the cord, then the other. And then everything happened so fast that it seemed to him as though one moment he was standing holding the sack and the next he was hurtling out into space, his hands buried in what felt like a warm, wet sponge.

He opened his mouth to scream, but the Wind tore the sound from him. Desperately he clung to whatever it was he was holding, clung to it for all he was worth. A blast of hot, foetid air hit him in the face, and he gagged at the stench. He didn't dare open his eyes, didn't dare let his mind think about what was happening. It took every last ounce of his strength to hang on. But then something buzzed past his ear, and he felt a tickling on his forehead, as though an insect was crawling across it. It didn't occur to him to wonder how an insect could have been up so high, flying so fast that it could overtake a Wind. He raised one hand automatically to swat it away... and fell...

He clawed frantically at the air, but the Wind was gone. He was no longer *'flying,'* but tumbling helplessly through the air, plummeting towards his certain death.

Before he even had time to scream, he hit the ground. For a few moments he lay there, dazed and winded. Was he dead? Surely he was dead, or at least horrifically injured? Tentatively he moved one arm. It seemed to be working. Then his feet. Also working. He opened his eyes, still not convinced that he hadn't been killed. Around him all was dark, but far above the night sky was sprinkled with stars so bright that it looked as though someone was shining an incredibly powerful torch through pinholes in a piece of black velvet. He recognized reassuringly familiar constellations: Libra, the balance, Gemini, and one that he thought was Aquarius, but there were many, many more he didn't know – groups of stars forming shapes that rang distant bells in his memory, but no more.

His arms were stinging as though scratched, and as he put his hand out to push himself up into a sitting position, it met something rough and springy like heather. He sat stiffly up. It was too dark to make out much around him, but as his eyes adjusted to the dim light, he could see that he was right – it was heather. It had broken his fall, cushioned his landing and probably saved his life, although he did wonder now quite how far he had fallen. It had all happened so quickly. But now that the realization that he was alive had sunk in, everything else came flooding back. He wrinkled his nose automatically at the memory of the vile, rotten stench that had blasted him with its full force and took a deep breath of the fresh air now surrounding him – air that smelt of herbs: rosemary, lavender, sage. He sucked it into his lungs, trying to expel any last remnants of the Wind.

A dreadful sense of guilt swept over him. What had he done? Why had he been so stupid? He bashed his fist on his head with anger at himself, tears rolling down his cheeks. Now he was alone. His chest heaved as he cried, not caring that he was meant to be Owen the Bold, the Chosen One. He wasn't. He was Owen Shepherd, and at that moment all he wanted was to wake up and find it had all been a bad dream. But he couldn't wake up, no matter how hard he willed himself to. He rubbed his eyes, sniffing back the last of his tears. It was no good sitting here feeling sorry for himself. He reached into his pouch and this time found Luis, the little rowan twig, the present

Nana had given him for his 12th birthday. It seemed so very long ago now. Everything had been normal then – the Old Mill, undamaged by any earthquake, Nana, mixing up a fruit and herb punch, whilst he and his mother watched 'The Blue Planet' together and shared a pizza. And now? He gripped the rowan charm harder. It wasn't a dream. It was all real. Nana was captured by his enemies and held in Bale Castle, and his mother... He had heard nothing since the arrival of the postcard telling him that she was about to leave for the MARS Station, the *Megaco* Antarctic Research Station. Yet strangely this made him feel better, or at least stopped his self-pity in its tracks. He didn't have the option of giving up, deciding it was all too hard and he would rather do something else. He found the glow ball powder and struck up a light. Heather and more heather. He made his glow ball a little larger, but it didn't help. As far as he could see he was in the middle of a field of heather, a moor perhaps, and that was it – no light in a distant window, no welcoming glow from a campfire.

At least it wasn't cold. He lay back down. There was no point stumbling blindly across a moor at night. He had no idea where he was, how far away from his friends or the Gateway. He suddenly remembered Finn's circle and Professor Vishnami. But what did it matter if he did look out of Owen's eyes tonight? There was nothing to see but heather, and enemy he might be, but he was at least a connection with home, a connection with that long-ago, far-off world of normality.

Owen woke up with his fingers still wrapped round the rowan charm. For a few moments he was confused. The purple moorland that surrounded him made no sense whatsoever. But as he sat up, he flinched with pain. His body felt like one giant bruise. He groaned as the memory of the previous night's adventure returned to him. Never, never would he do such a stupid thing again!

He got stiffly to his feet and took a look around. Vast, foreboding mountains filled the horizon on three sides. Only to the south did the terrain look more promising, with the moorland sloping down towards a wood. That was the path he would take, he decided. After his recent experiences in the Mountains of Assyah, the last thing he wanted to do was risk encountering ogres or dragons alone. He rubbed his shoulder. His arms felt as though they had been pulled out of their sockets during his Wind ride. He had no idea where he was relative to where he had been – where his friends still were probably, he thought bleakly, as he set off. But at least they knew where he would be trying to get to, knew he would be making for the Towers. It was little consolation, however. For all he knew, he could be hundreds of miles away from them now and heading in totally the wrong direction.

But as he continued across the moor, as the sun rose above the mountains in the east and the pale yellow/mauve light of dawn took on a warmer hue, his spirits began to rise. He could hear the soft, reassuring hum of bees busy gathering their first pollen of the day from the welcoming heather. It was like seeing the pod of dolphins following the boat in Bryah, and though logically he knew that it wasn't exactly unusual to find bees where there was heather, it still felt comforting. This wasn't the first time he had been on his own in the Realm after all. When he first set off in Dayah, before he met Finn, he had been alone, and again when he went to Aralu to rescue the Princess. But it wasn't the same. The Owen who had left Varak's Grove had been an excited boy on an adventure, the Owen in Assyah, a hero with the whole of Arktos rooting for him. This Owen was a fool, he thought with a heavy sigh, a fool who had risked everything for the thrill of a ride on a Wind.

He couldn't stay gloomy for long though. A bee buzzed past his nose and then back again – once, twice... He had to duck to one side to avoid it. His bee! Surely it was his bee!? It felt like his bee anyway, he decided. Before long he even found himself humming along with the bees in time with his footsteps as he walked – first of all tunes that he knew, and then new ones, ones he was making up as he went along.

Eventually he reached the edge of the wood. From higher on the heath, he hadn't been able to tell exactly what the trees were and had simply assumed that they would be mainly conifers, but though there were indeed a few pines, the majority of the trees were deciduous – oaks and beeches, clumps of elder, rowans, hazels, even a crab apple and a thicket of what he thought were wild plum trees. He stopped and plucked one of the yellow and red fruits from the tree. It had been a long time since he had eaten a decent meal, and suddenly he felt famished. Tentatively he bit into it and the sweet juices flooded into his mouth. It *was* a plum! He wolfed it down and picked another.

They tasted as good as if they had grown in Dayah!

He was on a path of sorts, a narrow grassy track that wound circuitously between the trees. Whether it was made by men or animals, he couldn't tell, and it did occur to him that it might be like the paths in the Great Forest of Dayah, shifting continually, never staying in the same place for long. The bees were still with him as he walked on through the wood, providing a constant reassuring background hum and this time instead of humming with them, he decided to talk, to tell them his story. Nana had told him that you should do this. *'Talk to the bees,'* she had said. *'Tell them your news.'* He didn't recall her telling him why he should do this, but it wasn't going to do any harm. So talk he did. He started at the beginning, told them about his father and mother, about Olafssey, the puffins and whales, the volcano. He hesitated a moment. He had never told anyone all of this, not even Finn, but it seemed to him that the bees had suddenly fallen silent when he stopped, as though they were waiting for him to continue.

He described the Old Mill, his bedroom, his treehouse, Nana and her concoctions. He even told them about West Ham football club and his favourite bands. On and on he talked. At some point he found himself walking beside a stream and took a long drink; another time he stumbled upon an almond tree with nuts ripe for the picking. Occasionally he found that he had stopped talking, that the words he thought he was saying were inside his head, and then he would simply listen for a while to the bees, to the gentle rustle of the forest trees, the creak of a branch, the crack of a twig, a brilliant arpeggio of bird song, a throaty bark from a hidden animal...

By the time he had reached the end of his story, the sun was slanting low through the canopy of the trees. Evening was falling fast, and he was utterly bewildered by where the day had gone.

"... so here I am," he concluded, "walking through this wood, talking to you. Lost." He paused. "And that's it. That's my story." He trailed off rather lamely. The bees continued to hum. "Er... that's all – the end." He felt suddenly rather foolish. He wasn't sure what he had thought would happen, whether he had thought a Nyxa of the Bees would rise up before him and thank him for his story or something, but the bees just carried on buzzing.

A few moments later however, the bees were forgotten. Just as he was beginning to think he would be spending a night in the forest, the path opened out on to a meadow, below which stretched a wide, dark lake. But it wasn't the lake that had stopped him in his tracks, despite its uncanny resemblance to the lake of the Wood Sath, nor was it the clouds of water lilies that seemed to float ethereally above the water. It was something else, something that lay on the far side of the lake. Seven cloud-capped towers.

Chapter 14

The Towers stood a little way back from the shore, across a dark strip of land – seven vertiginous columns with spire-topped pinnacles wreathed in cloud. In the fading evening light, they gleamed with an unworldly luminescence: red, blue, green, yellow; the closest one a pale violet, the two furthest away dazzling white and jet black. They were breathtakingly beautiful.

He screwed up his eyes, squinting into the distance to get a better look. He couldn't make out their bases. Like the pinnacles, the feet of the towers were shrouded in mist, from which they rose like islands from the sea. If it hadn't been for the strip of land delineating the shoreline of the lake, he would have thought that they stood in the lake itself. But it was too dark now for him to learn any more. He turned back to the wood. The bees had returned to their hives, the birds to their nests, and a silence had fallen over the darkening forest. He felt suddenly like an unwelcome intruder, one who should have been back in his own nest by now, not trespassing in the territory of the nocturnal wood.

He decided to sleep beneath the broad, heavy branches of a willow tree rather than venture round the lake in the dark. 'Strength of Bees', Nana had called it, as she explained some of the qualities of Saille, the Willow. He recalled something about moving forward into the unknown without fear but couldn't remember how it was connected to bees. Nevertheless, it seemed an appropriate place to sleep. This time he did cast his circle, did make sure that Professor Vishnami's searching eye couldn't find him in the night and peer out between the trees to see the lake and the Towers. He pulled a covering of branches and ferns up over him as a rough blanket. Not that it was cold, but even with the thick willow trunk behind him and the circle cast, he didn't feel entirely safe. After all, he had already seen one of the black ixephat birds down on the Plain. What if there were some of those scaly weasel creatures roaming the wood? He shivered and burrowed deeper under his leafy cover.

"It's so easy!" Dar shook his head in mock despair. "Look, if you're scared of the Spirits there, you don't have to take that path. It's up to you. You can just explore a bit."

Tamus frowned but stayed silent. Despite everything, he wanted to hear what Dar had to say. Anyway, before too long surely the Ruach would teach them the first principles of dreamwalking and it would give him a head start on his fellow novices to know at least a bit about it. It would be good to impress the Ruach for once. He was getting a bit fed up with being the worst at Air magic.

"It's like flying," Dar continued. "You choose where it is you want to go to, or who you want to find. As long as you form the intention properly," he said, sounding just like one of Tamus' teachers, "then you won't go wrong. Simple and brilliant," he added. "You can go anywhere. Imagine that! Flying over the forest, over the ocean even. You could go and spy on those other novices, the Wardens themselves... even Endymia..."

Tamus went bright red. "You haven't, Dar! If you have..."

Dar laughed. "No, of course I haven't. I've got better things to do when I'm dreamwalking. But I could!"

Tamus glared at him. Endymia was the most beautiful girl he had ever seen, and the favourite novice of the Water Priestess. The idea of his brother spying on her was appalling.

"And... so could you," Dar added with a grin. "If you wanted to."

Owen woke up with a start. What was all that about? He felt confused and embarrassed. For the first time since he had started to have the Tamus dreams and memories, he felt like an intruder. These weren't his memories. There were plenty of things he, Owen, kept private, and would have been horrified at anyone else knowing. Tamus probably felt the same. He jumped as a fox barked somewhere close by and pulled the leafy branches up over his head. To distract himself from the thought of what else might be out there lurking in the dark woods, he turned his mind to the Towers. First thing in the morning he would set off round the lake. It shouldn't take him too long, a couple of hours maybe, to reach them. And then what? The warnings from Saiki and Enlali rang in his ears. What if he was too late and the Prince and his army had already got there, were already attacking the Towers? He had seen no sign of any battle, but then how much could he see from this distance? Maybe they had the Towers under siege, and he would be walking into the middle of it.

And then he had an idea – an idea which once it had entered his head, he just couldn't cast aside. He would be careful, he thought, really, really careful. And it wasn't like the Wind Bag because it wasn't fun or something he wanted to do for himself. No. This was different. He knew how to do it, he was sure, and it had to be safer than walking into an ambush. Anyway, the first sign of danger he would turn back. His mind was made up.

He closed his eyes and began to breathe slowly, focusing on the air as he had done earlier on the Plain. Only this time he had no worries that Professor Vishnami would turn up inside his head. He was safe inside the circle.

'Pop'. He felt a tiny spark burst inside his head but continued to breath slowly, deeply, letting the bubbles of air fill his whole body. Somewhere close by a solitary owl hooted mournfully but otherwise all was still. He breathed in the dark scent of the nocturnal wood and the night seemed to mingle with the bright bubbles of air inside him. And then suddenly he soared up, up through the rippling leaves of the willow, up towards the great arc of the moonless sky. Below him lay the lake, dark, still, fathomless, and smooth as a mirror. He flew on, leaving the shadows of the forest behind him, his sharp eyes focused in on the silhouettes of the towers ahead. He could see them despite the darkness of the night, as though he was wearing night vision goggles. He was an eagle! He was flying! Flying... He pulled in his wings and dived towards the lake. "Woooo" he let out a whoop of joy as he cut through the air. The towers were forgotten. He just wanted to fly. He pulled out of his dive and swept back up, soaring higher and higher, riding air currents that carried him ever upwards.

And then ahead of him he saw a pale silvery-violet light. He flew towards it, overcome by curiosity. It was round, a perfect circle, a hole in the sky – just like a Gateway Entrance... He approached it slowly. There was a sound emanating from it, like waves breaking rhythmically on the shore. *"It was like nothing you could ever imagine."* Dar's words echoed in his head. *"I saw things... wonderful things... You can learn more there than in a lifetime sitting in a stupid class."* Owen knew in that instant what it was he was looking at – the Gateway to the Dream-Lands. And all Tamus' warnings were forgotten.

He stepped through on to a smooth silvery path, no longer an eagle, no longer flying. *"You must stay focused at all times."* The words of the sharp-nosed Air Priest, the Ruach, rang in his ears. *"Hold firm to your destination."* He could almost feel the pale blue eyes boring into him as he remembered the lesson. *"And under no circumstances must a Dream Walker stray from the path. This is why the Dream-Lands are no place for novices. This is why..."* Owen jumped, his memory cut short by something that shot by just off the periphery of his vision. His glance darted briefly to the side, but he forced his attention back to the path and set off along it. He was meant to have some sort of destination in mind, wasn't he, somewhere he was going? Or was that for before, when he was heading for the Towers? He didn't know. A seed of doubt began to grow inside him. A shadow flickered in the pale, mauve light to the side of the path, then another. He walked a little faster. They were only shadows, weren't they, like on the cave wall in Aralu – not real. He glanced around nervously but they were gone. But then he heard something, an unmistakeable hiss coming from just behind him! He spun round just in time to catch a glimpse of a scaly black creature, scuttling off into the violet mist. Panic gripped him. He could hear laughter now, high pitched giggling like the Eddleshi. He tried to run, his heart pounding with terror, but nothing happened. As though in a dream, his legs ran, but he couldn't move. He remained exactly where he was. Above him, directly overhead, a huge orange eye opened. He tried to scream, but no sound came from his mouth.

And then suddenly he saw it, hanging in the air just a few feet to the side of the path, gleaming with a golden radiance – a sword. *The Sword!* In that instant, everything else vanished. The shadows, the scaly creatures, the eye – all gone. All that remained was Owen, the Sword and a deep silence. He turned slowly to face it, took one step, then another, then, "Argh!" He let out a cry of pain and shock, as from out of nowhere a tiny bee appeared, moving so rapidly that he had no time to duck out of the way, no time to react before it buried its sting straight into the middle of his forehead.

The boy woke up with a yawn and rubbed his eyes. Where was he? He groaned as he stretched. He was aching as though he had been in a fight, and his forehead really hurt. He winced as he reached up a hand to touch the tender skin. What *had* he been doing? He pushed back the covering of branches and ferns and sat up. Nothing looked familiar. A knot of fear twisted in his stomach. Breathe slowly, he told himself. It would all come back soon. Saille! He recognized the willow tree behind him with some relief and wrapping his arms round the trunk, pressed his cheek against the rough, furrowed bark.

"Strength of Bees!" he whispered to the tree. A memory came to him of cutting a wand from a willow tree, the day the catkins turned from silver to gold. He felt a little better. Whatever had happened to him, he hadn't lost all his memory.

He got stiffly to his feet, noticing for the first time his extraordinary clothes. There was no way these were his clothes! He was sure he had never seen anything so peculiar. Maybe on a Boryad perhaps, but... He stopped mid-thought. A Boryad! From Assyah. Images flashed through his head – a stone circle, a temple. He took a deep breath. Was this some sort of trial, a test that he must pass? As he moved, he felt something shift underneath his top. He reached up and found a small cloth pouch hanging round his neck. For a brief moment he thought he might find some answers there, but his hopes were swiftly dashed – a key that meant nothing to him, a strange looking tooth, a red stone and a twig!

Cautiously he stepped out from between the trees on to the edge of a grassy slope. Just below him lay a wide, dark lake. He tensed automatically as he sensed something in the wood behind him- a bright, light energy that fluttered and sparkled in the forest canopy. A Sylph! He relaxed. So he was in Yezirah. Not his favourite Realm. Dayah would have been better, or even Azilut, despite the dangers. His memories were popping into his head as a string of disconnected, apparently random images and words, but at least they were still there!

Then he saw the Towers. Oh no! He groaned. He was right. This was a trial. He remembered the Towers all right, remembered being made to look a fool by his fellow novices for his hopelessness with

127

Air magic, remembered being the idiot who volunteered to study in the Saturn Tower for his first test. He had probably made some stupid mistake to end up lying battered and bruised in a strange wood with his memory in pieces, failed some critical Air test – again. Dar would laugh at him... Dar! The name rang loudly in his head, but try as he might, he couldn't remember who Dar was. He sighed. There was only one thing he could do and there was little point in putting it off any longer. He would have to go to the Towers, the yellow one probably – Mercury – and ask for help to recover his memory.

Just as he was about to set off down the slope, he spotted something lying half-covered by the branches and ferns that he had pushed aside. He bent down to look closer. A bag! His bag, he assumed. Maybe there was something in there that could give him some answers. He tipped the contents out on to the ground: string, a couple of empty tins, a brown cloak, and a small black hide-bound book with no title. He opened it eagerly.

"Welcome reader, enter in," it began. He read on.
"Where only one may tread.
This spell is wrought for one alone,
By one these words are read.

To one alone the Spirits call
From memories long past.
Take up the key, the time is come,
The lots of fate are cast.

So turn this page and find within
A legacy of ages.
The story that will here unfold
The knowledge of the sages."

He turned the pages as instructed but was feeling less hopeful now.
"In the First Age, the Worlds of Man and of Spirit were one." He closed the book with a sigh. It was just a story book. It wasn't going to help him remember who he was.

As he set off on the path round the lake, he tried to recall the name of the Guardian of the Mercury Tower. He could picture him, a dark-haired man with eyes of such a deep yellow that they were almost amber, and a very long, beaky nose. The Exarp! That was it. He didn't have a name as such, just a title. He would surely be able to help him recover his memory.

Although the grassy track seemed vaguely familiar, he had a feeling that last time he had walked round this lake, he hadn't been alone. A sudden wave of fear swept over him. What if he was here alone because he had been cast out? What if this was a punishment for something he had done? He felt an awful stab of guilt. Was that it? But then a bee buzzed passed his face and he relaxed. The bees were his friends. It was always to the bees that he turned when he had an apparently insurmountable problem. When he was little, he had sat up in Grandma's orchard amongst the hives, talking to the bees, telling them all his tales. He began to hum softly to himself as he walked. His voice resonated inside his head, as though there was a bee buzzing round in there, a bee that had coated his memories in a thick, cloudy sort of honey.

It didn't take him long to reach the far shore of the lake. The track was smooth and well-trodden and as he walked, his stiff muscles loosened up and he strode more confidently towards his destination. He had stopped trying to remember things. It only gave him a headache, and anyway, he knew well enough that force was never the best thing to use with elusive Watery things like memories.

Ahead of him, the towers rose like islands out of a sea of mist. He frowned. There was something tugging at his mind, something about that mist... It gleamed with a peculiar, unnatural light, reflecting back at him a pale, watery version of each tower's colour. He continued more slowly along the path away from the lake, across the wide swathe of grass that stood between him and the edge of the mist, and the closer he got, the more certain he was that all was not as it seemed. The mist hung just above ground level, like a shimmering, gauzy blanket, shrouding the land below – assuming it was land below. Maybe it was water. There was something different about the ground where it met the mist. It looked just like a shoreline or... a cliff! He stopped dead in his tracks as he realized what it was he was looking at. Only a few feet from where he stood the land simply vanished, and the mist was no longer a thick blanket lying above the ground, but the surface foam of a foggy ocean of cloud.

He dropped to his hands and knees and crawled towards the edge, feeling suddenly giddy. Very cautiously he peered down into the misty depths, but he could see nothing. He picked up a pebble and dropped it over the edge, listening for any sound of it hitting water or solid ground. Nothing. He sat back on his heels, gazing down at the abyss before him. The answer was in his head somewhere. He had been here before and could even remember going out to pick vegetables for the evening meal from the gardens that surrounded the Towers, gardens that definitely weren't shrouded in mist... Illusion! It had to be illusion. Mist – Air and Water weaving illusion. Air and Water. He let his mind float. You didn't conquer illusion with straight, logical Air thinking alone. Water in the air... He pictured it in his mind, saw the sunlight breaking through clouds, making a rainbow. Yes! He jumped to his feet. That was it. He remembered exactly how it all worked now. Without hesitation he walked forward and stepped straight out over the cliff into the clouds. And in an instant they were gone. For a moment he stood there, suspended in mid-air, a bottomless chasm beneath him, but then like a wave rolling up over the shore, a bridge unfurled beneath his feet, an arch of crystal that shone with all the colours of the rainbow, spanning the abyss that stood between him and the gardens of the Towers.

He felt a rush of recognition and happiness as he walked out across the arch, and despite its narrowness and the bottomless chasm below, he felt no fear. He wouldn't fall, he knew that, knew too that the bridge would only crack and break beneath feet bent on harm towards the Towers. Besides which, his balance was good. It was one of the core magic lessons back home, balance. And for Air magic it had a specific relevance. A disconnected memory flashed into his head of trying to maintain a ridiculous position on one leg for what seemed like hours, holding absolutely still as the teacher described the balance needed for Wind Riding. He frowned. Wind Riding... The words filled him with an utterly inexplicable sense of guilt.

A path led off from the foot of the bridge, winding up through an orchard of apple, pear and quince trees, towards the Towers. They formed a circle at the top of a gentle hill, with the golden white sun

Tower nearest to him and the black Saturn Tower furthest away. From the other side of the chasm it had appeared as though they were much lower, rising up from a flat plain of mist. That was another thing he remembered about the Towers. Nothing was quite what it appeared to be. He glanced suspiciously up at the pale, silvery-violet Moon Tower; that one in particular was a place of illusions and one that he had no intention of visiting this time.

Ahead of him, through the trees, he could see a long wall of honey-coloured stone, beyond which he knew lay the apothecary gardens. He felt more confident now. Surely the Mercury Guardian, the Exarp, would be able to help him. It might be enough just to see a familiar face. That could be the trigger he needed to restore his memory. At the end of the path an intricately patterned metallic gate stood open. It should have been shut, he thought disapprovingly. One thing all his long months of tending sheep had taught him was that gates must always be shut behind you! He could hear the bubbling murmur of water coming from the other side of the high wall – a fountain he recalled. But before he had the chance to see if he was right, a voice rang out behind him.

"Who are you?"

He spun round, nearly jumping out of his skin with surprise. Four boys of about his own age were standing in the path glaring at him as one. His heart sank as he recognized the red belts fastening their white novices' tunics – the red belts that signified the Mars Tower.

"I... er..." he stammered.

"Well?" The biggest one stepped towards him. "Who are you?"

Who was he? He groped desperately in his memory for a moment and then in a flash it came to him. He remembered who he was.

"I'm Tamus."

Chapter 15

"Tamus." The boy who had spoken before repeated the name. "Right. And what are you doing here?"

It wasn't the welcome Tamus had expected, though the aggression of the Mars Tower novices wasn't totally a surprise. He tried to look confident, as though there was nothing strange about his presence there.

"I'm on my way to the Mercury Tower to see the Exarp."

There was a long pause.

"You're not a novice," one of the Mars boys stated bluntly, staring with undisguised contempt at his odd clothes.

"Yes I am," he retorted indignantly. "Just not from here. I've come from the Temple of the Azoth. I'm a Priest of the Elements – at least I will be soon," he added. "Last time I came here I got a better welcome than this!"

A look of incredulity met his statement. "A Priest of the Elements?" the first boy repeated, then turned to his comrades and rolled his eyes. "Definitely the Mercury Tower!"

Tamus didn't understand.

"Come on." The boy beckoned to him. "I'll take you to the Mercury Tower. You tell them that story." One of his friends sniggered and Tamus had a sudden bizarre recollection of a group of boys dressed in similarly odd clothes to him, standing arms crossed in front of them in a field, laughing at him – a field beyond which lay the most peculiar buildings, like nothing he had seen in any of the Spirit Realms, let alone back home.

He followed the red-sashed boy through the gate into the garden beyond. Just how he remembered it, he thought with relief, as they passed between borders of herbs: lavender, sage and fennel. The scent was overpowering. The path led to the source of the watery sound he had heard earlier: a white marble fountain topped with an eagle. But he had no time to stop and admire the intricate carvings that wound up the central pillar.

"This way." The Mars Tower boy stepped on to one of the seven paths that led off from the fountain, radiating out like spokes from the hub of a wheel.

Tamus hurried after him. He was keen to get to the Mercury Tower. He felt sure the Exarp would remember him. After all it hadn't been that long since he was last there. That would stop the sniggers, when the Mars novices found out that he was exactly who he said he was! But as they drew closer to the yellow Mercury Tower, he couldn't stop a little voice of doubt whispering in his head. When was it he had been here? All his memories were jumbled up together with no sort of time frame around them, so that the picture of his old grandmother singing to the bees felt as recent as his visit to the Towers. The only marker he had to cling to, was the fact that he hadn't been small when he had been here. He glanced at the boy walking at his side, who stood several inches taller than him. It must have been recently. He was sure he remembered being quite grown up.

From a distance, the Towers had looked splendid, soaring spires of gleaming stone, but now he was closer, he could see that all was not quite as it had appeared. The facade of the yellow Mercury Tower was criss-crossed with cracks like a spider's web woven through the stonework, and in several places stones had obviously come loose and been replaced very shoddily. Even he would have made a better job of it than that! Very strange. He had no memory of this dilapidation last time.

The Mars boys stood back once they reached the wooden door to the Tower and Tamus felt a sudden stab of fear. The Mercury Guardian had a reputation for a sharp tongue, he remembered, and that was not a small thing in Yezirah, where sharp tongues seemed to be the norm. He glanced back at the waiting boys.

"Go on," one of them prompted him. "Knock."

Tamus turned back to the door. He had no choice if he wanted to get his memory back. He raised his hand, but before he got the chance to lift the knocker, the door swung open. A poker thin man stood before him, the yellow stripes in his long iron-grey hair and beard matching the yellow of his robe.

"Yes?" The man barked the word impatiently.

"I... er..." Tamus stammered.

"What do you want?" The man let out an irascible snort. "Speak." The Mars novices had melted away, leaving him standing alone.

"I've come to see the Exarp," he stated, trying not to let his voice shake.

"Well now you've seen him!" The man turned on his heels, about to slam the door.

"No! Wait, please!" He didn't understand. This man wasn't the Exarp. The Exarp was dark, with deep amber eyes, and far younger. The man standing in the doorway could possibly have had darker hair once, long ago, but his eyes were a pale, buttery-yellow and had surely never been deep amber.

"I didn't realize. When I was here before, I met the old Exarp." That must be the explanation. "I came with the Wardens, from the Temple of the Azoth."

The Mercury Guardian turned slowly back to face him. "The Temple of the Azoth?" he repeated, each word heavy with incredulity.

"Yes. I was in the Saturn Tower though that time," he added hastily. "You probably never saw me. The Ruach stayed here, in this Tower."

Silence met his statement.

"Where did you hear that word?" The Exarp finally spoke, his voice smooth and deceptively soft, but his gaze hard as steel.

Tamus swallowed nervously. He didn't understand. "What... what word?"

The yellow eyes bored into his own with alarming intensity and he turned his head quickly away as an inexplicable memory surfaced, a memory of peculiar flat, dead eyes holding him transfixed. But before he had a chance to even try to recall where he had seen those eyes, the Mercury Guardian grabbed his arm and pulled him in through the doorway and swung the door firmly shut behind him.

"Follow me!" His tone left no room for argument as he strode across the wide, flagstoned hallway towards the foot of a spiral staircase. Tamus hurried after him.

He barely had time to take in the yellow painted walls, hung with rather shabby looking tapestries depicting what looked like star charts.

For an old man, the Exarp moved remarkably quickly. Up they went, seven storeys in total, passing by doors leading off to hidden rooms. The smell of lavender wafted out from one of these and accompanied them up the remainder of the steps. Tamus could hear voices beyond another, sounding further off than he expected. But as they climbed still higher, he remembered something else about the Towers. They were much bigger inside than they appeared from the outside, or at least the lower levels were. He relaxed a little as the memory fell into place. They were conical in shape, rather like the hats the Wardens sometimes wore, with the novices' living quarters and the kitchens on the lowest level and the Guardian's chamber at the apex. Air magic – making things appear to the eye very different from their reality. It was something that Dar was particularly keen on but Tamus had always thought a bit dishonest. It wasn't like the illusions of Water magic or Moon magic, reflecting hidden realms. As far as he could see, the deceptive appearance of the Towers was created simply to show off, entirely for ostentatious display – rather like Bale Castle... He stopped mid-thought. Bale Castle? The memory made no sense to him whatsoever.

"Come on, come on!" The Exarp had reached the top of the staircase and was holding open the door to his chamber.

The room Tamus stepped into was a peculiar mix of familiar and unfamiliar. There were more star charts, something he recalled was named an astrolabe, countless jars of herbs and vials of liquids, and shelves and shelves of books. But the telescope that so closely resembled one that had pride of place in the study of his own Teacher, the Ruach, lay in several pieces on the floor and the chair that the yellow-eyed man indicated to for him to sit on, was inexplicably shabby and threadbare. He sat down quickly, trying to hide his confusion. This wasn't how things were meant to be in the Realm. In his memory, it had all been so beautiful and perfect. Far too perfect for a novice as clumsy as himself!

The Exarp took a seat facing him. "So." He paused as his eyes ran over the boy sitting opposite. "I repeat my question. Where did you hear that word?"

"Do... do you mean Ruach?" It was the only word that he had used that he could possibly see as being in any way unusual.

The Exarp gave him a scathing look. "There is absolutely no point in dissimulation. I am giving you one chance to explain yourself and one only."

Whatever dissimulation was, he had certainly not meant to do it! "No. I want to tell you everything. That's why I came here," he exclaimed. "I'll tell you it all – the Ruach... everything."

The Mercury Guardian leant back in his chair and gave Tamus an appraising look. "Go on."

"Well..." He wasn't sure where to begin but he remembered a phrase he had learnt somewhere about tracing things back to their origins to gain power over them. "I'll start at the beginning."

The Exarp sighed. "A good place to start, usually!"

But what was the beginning? Tamus frowned as he tried to recall as much about himself as he could. "My name is Tamus." That was a good start. At least he knew that much! "I am a novice in the Temple of the Azoth – not initiated yet. At least not in the Greater magic, but..." He was struggling. "I have been here before... and through all the Gateways, to Dayah and Bryah and Assyah and Azilut as well."

The man opposite was staring at him now with utter incredulity. "I... er... I came with the Ruach – the Air Priest." He stopped. Apart from odd snatches of memory associated with the Saturn Tower, he couldn't remember anything specific about his stay.

"It's my memory." He looked helplessly at the Mercury Guardian. "I can't remember any more – not clearly. I woke up this morning on the other side of the lake and to start with I didn't even know my own name. I haven't any idea how I got there." He trailed off.

A long silence followed this statement as the Exarp continued to stare in disbelief at him. Then slowly he leant forward, his eyes unblinking, boring into Tamus' own, holding him transfixed with a stare, which try as he might, Tamus could not break. He felt as if slender needle-like fingers were probing into his mind, reaching into his thoughts. He winced, not from pain but from revulsion at a sensation like fingernails scraping across slate. But then the needles stopped, as suddenly as if they had bumped into a solid wall. The Exarp started back in surprise, momentarily losing his focus and Tamus was able to blink and break the grip in which his mind had been held.

The Exarp took a few seconds to regain his composure.

"Fascinating!" he exclaimed finally.

"What?" Tamus was alarmed.

"It seems that you are telling the truth." The yellow-eyed man paused. "This is however, impossible." He frowned. "You believe what you have told me. And it sits in your head as a memory, not a delusion. But there is a block. Someone has locked your true memory behind a barrier, the like of which I have not encountered before."

"It must be a test!" Tamus could see no other reasonable explanation. "One set by my teachers."

"No, no." The Exarp cut him short. "You have not understood what I am telling you. It is impossible that what you believe is true." He looked pensively at him before continuing. "We have here, in this Tower, ancient books which tell of these things: the Temple of the Azoth, the Priests and Priestesses of the Elements, the Ruach even. But these are forbidden books. They contain secrets that are only for the Guardians of the Rainbow Guild to know. For they speak also of the Fall of the Temple, the wrath of the great Lord of Fire and the pulling down of the Moon. And it is in their pages that the keys to the Sword of Truth lie."

"I don't understand." Tamus felt a knot of fear tightening round his stomach. "What do you mean, the Fall of the Temple?"

"It is gone." The Exarp spoke gently. "Many, many aeons ago. The last of the Wardens came through the ancient Gateway carrying with him the Sword of Truth, rescued from the ashes of the Temple. He was the last. Many brave adventurers have stepped into the Gateway since then, hoping to find answers. None has ever returned."

Somewhere deep in Tamus' memory this struck a chord. He had heard this before, he realized.

"The Gateway is now taboo and so feared by most, that even the Wandering Tribes out on the Plains, who have little learning but much appetite for adventure, avoid it." He paused again. "So what you somehow believe to be your reality, cannot be."

None of this made sense to Tamus. He could remember the temple clearly. It wasn't a dream. "But how could I know these things if they are so secret, if I'm not telling the truth and it's not real?"

"That, my boy, is what I intend to find out." The Exarp sounded quite excited at the prospect now.

Tamus, however, wasn't sure he liked the way those yellow eyes were peering at him, as though he was a bizarre object to be experimented with.

But then the Exarp spotted his bag for the first time. "What is in your bag?" he asked.

"Just stuff. Nothing that I can remember anything about." He emptied the contents on to the table.

The Exarp homed in on the little black book like a cat pouncing on a mouse.

"What is this?" He opened the first page with undisguised excitement.

"It's nothing," Tamus began. "It's only..." He stopped. That was strange. The page the Exarp was holding open was blank. He was sure that was the page on which the poem had been written, the poem that began *"Welcome reader, enter in!'*

The Exarp frowned. "There is something most peculiar about this book." He turned over the page. The next one was also blank. And the next. But he didn't give up. He turned another two. "Hah!" The Mercury Guardian let out a cry of triumph. There were words on the page! Tamus leant forward for a better look. It wasn't much – the single word Air at the top and just one sentence.

"The pure heart of the Cup Bearer recognizes the Truth."

But then, just as he was thinking that that was it, the page below began to fill with strings of letters and numbers. They made no sense to him and looked like nonsense, gobbledygook. But the Mercury Guardian clearly thought otherwise. His breathing was shallow and fast, the hand that held the book, trembling.

"This is it!" He looked up with eyes that shone with a feverish intensity. "This is it! The key! The key to the Sword of Truth!"

Chapter 16

Arin woke early. From where he was lying, he could just make out the faintest pale mauve sliver of dawn rising over the hill beyond the copse. It felt strange to be the first one awake, as though he alone was sharing a special secret with the Earth, seeing and hearing things that were for his eyes and ears only. He gazed up through the shadowy, rustling canopy of leaves above. 'Whispering Trees,' Enlali had called them.

It was a dream that had woken him. Usually it was the Moon who ruled his dreams, with the full moon bringing nights full of visions, but last night there had barely been any moon visible. But she was still there. He had sensed her dark face, the Queen of Illusion, ever present in his dream – a dream which had involved Owen, as had many before, even before he and Raya had actually met him on the beach. But in this dream, Owen was in a dark place, a place of pain and confusion, a realm of nightmares.

He sat up and yawned. He would warn Owen about what he had seen. Experience had taught him that it was wise to heed his dreams. But when he glanced across to where Owen had been lying, the space was empty. He must be up already, he told himself, trying to push the unwelcome memory of the Protean Oracle from his mind. A few minutes later, however, when Owen had still not returned, he began to feel uneasy. It wasn't as if there were many places he could have gone. The copse was small, hardly a place that you could get lost in, and it seemed unlikely that he would have wandered off into the fields beyond in the darkness.

He leant over and woke Raya with a poke to her shoulder. "Raya!" he whispered. "Wake up."

"What?" For a few moments she was confused, bleary-eyed and

still half asleep, but when she saw Arin's worried face, she was instantly wide awake. "What's wrong?" She sat up, her voice tense with alarm. "Owen. He's gone."

Raya looked round. "He... he's probably just..." She hesitated. "How long have you been awake?"

"Long enough." His eyes met his sister's. "He shouldn't go off. Not after that Mirror Island stuff."

By now both Finn and Enlali were awake.

"What's all the noise about?" Enlali was less than pleased at being woken so early.

"It's Owen," Arin explained. "He's gone."

"Gone?" He shook his head. "Oh, he'll be around somewhere. There's nothing going to have crept into the camp last night and taken him – not without disturbing the horses."

"Owen!" Finn called out his name. But the only response was the whinnying of a horse. He was clearly nowhere within earshot.

"Then he's gone off exploring somewhere." Enlali stopped suddenly, grabbed the bag which lay beside him and hurriedly checked inside it. "Hmm," he grunted with relief. "At least he's not a thief."

"His bag!" Finn exclaimed. "Owen's bag – that's gone too!"

"See!" Enlali got to his feet. "He's gone of his own accord. If he'd been carried off by a roc or something, it would hardly have taken his bag!"

A roc – Arin remembered what Raya had said out on the Plain about gigantic birds. Was that what Enlali was referring to? But whatever a roc was, Enlali was right. Owen must surely have gone of his own free will to have taken his bag, and in that case he would probably return eventually. They would just have to wait.

Enlali, however, had other ideas. "As we're all up so early, we might just as well get on our way. I've lost too much time already."

"But... we can't go." Raya said. "What about Owen?"

"What about him?" Enlali whistled to his horses. "He must have had a reason for leaving. Maybe your friend has secrets you don't know... wants to get to the Towers before you perhaps." He looked sharply at Raya. "Do you know you can trust him?"

"Yes!" Finn broke in angrily. "He wouldn't keep a secret from us."

"Hmm..." Enlali looked unconvinced. "Unless of course..." he trailed off.

"Unless what?" Finn demanded.

"The Caves." Enlali gave a sigh. "He wouldn't be that stupid, would he?"

The Caves! Arin felt a surge of hope. Owen hadn't said anything more when Enlali had mentioned the Wind Masters, but now that he thought back, he was sure that a flash of excitement had crossed his face.

"What if he has gone there?"

Enlali shook his head. "If he's still there now, he's dead."

"What?" Raya gasped.

"The Wind Masters will be back by now. If they found him in one of the caves near the Wind Bags, they would have killed him." Enlali sounded callously matter-of-fact. "That's how it is."

"He's not dead," Arin retorted. "I... I would know."

He would know, wouldn't he? He had a dream link with Owen, not like the one he had with Raya, but a connection all the same. Surely if Owen had been killed, he would have seen it in a dream.

Enlali gave him a sceptical look, then with a shrug, turned back to his horses.

"We're going to stay and look for him." Finn too refused to believe that Owen was dead.

Enlali stopped in his tracks. "No," he said sharply.

"What do you mean 'no'?" Raya demanded.

"Look," Enlali changed his tone. "If you're right and he's alive, then he's going somewhere, isn't he? You told me you were going to the Towers. Well, that's where I'm going too. We can go faster on the horses than he can on foot, and we'll catch him up."

"If Arin says he's alive, he's alive," Raya said defensively.

"Well then, it's up to you of course, but I would think your best chance of finding your friend again is to go to the place you know he'll make for as well."

Finn nodded slowly. "He might be right." He exchanged a glance with Raya. "We do know that's where Owen will head for."

They didn't really have much choice. Without Owen, what were they going to do? Even if they found their way back to the Gateway and puzzled out how to get through it back to the lighthouse in Owen's world, what then? Without Owen and the key, the Gateways to their own worlds were locked. They had to find him. But as they set off back across the hillside with Enlali's horses, finding Owen wasn't Arin's only worry. Was he right? Was Owen definitely still alive? The dream that had woken him, the dream of darkness, fear and confusion, tormented him. What if it hadn't been a premonition? What if it had been like a skrying and he had been seeing what Owen was actually seeing last night, as he was killed?

Riding at walking pace was easy enough, but Arin sincerely hoped there would be no need for anything faster. Without a saddle, it all felt very precarious and the bruises from the previous day's ride were very tender. They stopped briefly as the Caves of the Winds came into view. He had expected something more than the simple dark holes that peppered the rocky escarpment ahead like pock marks. There was no sign of anyone living there and more importantly, no sign of Owen.

"We should go a bit closer, in case Owen's there." Arin drew his horse towards Finn. "You could do that invisibility spell. There are trees here – Wood energy." He spoke in a low voice, making sure Enlali was well out of earshot. "That way you could go into the caves."

But his plan was quickly dashed. "Come on!" Enlali beckoned to them. "We shouldn't stay here too long, or they'll smell us. Even after last night some of them will be awake guarding the Wind Bags." He turned his horse away from the cliff. "This is close enough. And I can tell you, for certain, your friend isn't there now."

Finn pulled a rueful face as they headed away from the caves. "It was a good idea," he said quietly to Arin, "but I don't know how long it would work here. It wore off in Owen's world really quickly, and there aren't any trees up there." He glanced back at the cliff. "And it doesn't hide smells," he added.

Raya had dropped back from the main herd of horses to join them. "It'll be all right," she said, not sounding terribly convinced. "Why would he lie to us? It doesn't make any difference to him if we stay and look for Owen or not, does it?"

"No..." Arin couldn't think of a reason. "It's just a bit strange, that's all, that yesterday when we said we were going to the Towers, he didn't say anything about going there."

Finn nodded. "Yes, especially if what the Butterfly people said is true about the Towers being attacked."

They rode on in silence. It was, to put it mildly, a bit strange, but then Owen's disappearance was strange too. And one thing Arin did feel sure of was that Enlali knew nothing about that. He had been genuinely worried when he checked in his bag to see if Owen had stolen anything; not the behaviour of someone who had been involved in his disappearance.

Any hopes they had held of catching up with Owen, were fading as time went on. Even at a walk, the horses moved faster than he could have done on foot, and by the time they stopped at a stream to water the horses and fill up their flasks, there was little chance left that they would find him.

Enlali tried his best to keep their spirits up. "It just means he didn't take this route, that's all. This isn't the only path to the Towers. And I've been thinking about those caves. As I understand it, if the Wind Masters had found him, they would have blasted him out of the cliff, so we should have seen him lying on the ground below."

Arin frowned. Yet another new piece of information from Enlali. He was beginning to wonder whether he was just making it all up as he went along.

"Those caves – you keep saying how Owen would have been killed if the Wind Masters found him, but you never said why you thought he would have gone there." Raya tried to sound calm, but Arin could hear the sudden excitement in her voice.

Enlali looked puzzled. "What do you mean? For the Winds of course! He would hardly have been the first fool to think he could ride one."

"And that's the only reason?" Raya persisted.

"What other reason could there be?" Enlali was suddenly interested.

"I don't know," Raya said hastily. "What I meant was ... well ... if he did go there to ride a Wind, how do you know he didn't do it?"

Enlali snorted with derision. "A child? Ride a Wind? It takes years – years and years of training. Ridiculous!"

But it wasn't ridiculous. Arin thought back to that look he had seen cross Owen's face at the mention of riding Winds. There was a lot they didn't know about Owen, and Finn was wrong that he wouldn't keep secrets from his friends. Finn might believe that he told them everything, but Arin had sensed things troubling him that he knew he wasn't sharing with them, and had seen an Owen in his dreams that he barely recognized – Tamus perhaps, he thought grimly.

"That's what he's done!" Raya said once they were under way again, and she was sure Enlali could no longer hear her. "I couldn't understand before why he would sneak off without telling us, but I bet he wanted to show off ... like with Eggo."

Arin wasn't sure that she was right about the reason, but he nodded in agreement. "I think you're right."

"And Enlali doesn't know Owen," Raya continued. "We've all seen him do stuff before – magic."

"Yes," Finn agreed. "So he could be at the Towers already – flown there!"

A huge cloud had suddenly lifted for Finn and Raya. This must be the answer and they were doing the right thing making for the Towers. Only Arin remained uneasy. He didn't trust Enlali, and try as he might, he couldn't get that dream out of his head.

They rode on through the day, following a track across gently rolling countryside. Arin knew he should have enjoyed it. The air was warm, the sun bright, even the occasional woodland that the track passed through was light and airy – very different from the dark, coniferous forests on the slopes of Mount Meru. Several times now they had spotted huge albatross-like birds soaring high overhead, their cries like those of a hawk, high and plaintive, carrying on the wind. Whether or not they were the rocs Enlali had mentioned, Arin had no idea.

The grey-cloaked man was riding out in front and appeared to have decided that there had been enough talking. Arin wasn't sorry. He didn't trust Raya not to say something she shouldn't. She and Finn were once again comparing the merits of Dayah and Bryah by the sounds of it, so he deliberately dropped back, not wanting to get caught up in a pointless argument. He didn't want reminding of Bryah either. He and Raya had always talked of adventures when they were younger, of sailing out to the Arivala Isles, exploring the western Reaches, but it was different having an adventure away from Bryah, in a Realm where Water energy felt so weak, where there wasn't even the hint of salt in the air, or the distant roar of the ocean. And if they were stuck here forever... He tried to push the thought from his mind, but in vain. Owen had told them the tale of Oolugh, trapped by the Wall of Blackness in Dayah. And Oolugh was a Singer, part of the Great Choir. He and Raya were just simple Delfans...

"We should just make it by nightfall." Enlali eventually spoke when they stopped to ford a stream. "Any slower than this though and it'll be a hungry night."

A look of alarm crossed Finn's face. "We can go quicker," he said.

Enlali laughed. "Yes, but we don't want you falling off again. And I'm not galloping the horses on this sort of ground. I want to get you all there in one piece. I..." He stopped.

"What? What is it?" Raya asked.

"Shh!" Enlali held one finger to his lips and tilted his head to one side, reminding Arin of the Butterfly Tribe.

At first, he could hear nothing unusual, just the gurgling of the water in the stream, the snorting of horses and the trill of birdsong from a nearby copse; but then he noticed a very faint hum, a little like the hum in the background in Owen's world, only deeper.

"What is it?" Raya repeated her question in a whisper.

"I think... hope... it's hornets." Enlali didn't sound at all certain. "My ear isn't good enough to tell the pitch."

"You mean like musical pitch?" Arin asked tentatively.

"Yes, of course. You do ask some bizarre questions," he said as he began to rummage in his bag. "Oh, Orion's tail! Why did I forget that wretched fork this time? Typical!"

He must mean a tuning fork, Arin thought. Moon Singers refused to have anything to do with them, seeing them as crude tools for common singers. A Moon Singer had to have absolutely perfect pitch and all the tuning forks he had ever heard had a tiny flaw in them, imperceptible to the average ear, but enough to corrupt any Moon magic.

"It's an '*Ah*.'" He knew he risked more questions from Enlali by speaking up, but it was clearly important.

"Are you sure?" Enlali's attention was all on Arin. "Absolutely certain?"

"Yes." Arin nodded. He was absolutely certain. The note that was humming through the air was a deep bass '*Ah*.'

Enlali clapped his hand together. "That's what I thought!

Hornets!" He let out a sigh of relief. "Right! On we go!" He whistled to the waiting horses and without any more explanation set off up the path ahead.

"What was all that about?" Finn looked utterly bewildered.

Arin shook his head. "Don't know. I should think we'll find out soon enough though."

He was right. The path led them up a grassy slope beyond which lay the source of the humming. He felt a degree of trepidation as his horse duly followed the rest of the herd over the ridge. Hornets. He had only seen a few in his life, when Eridu had been moored in the far south of Bryah, one particularly hot summer, and he remembered them as giant wasps. He wasn't overly fond of wasps at the best of times and the hornets filled him with an instinctive revulsion and fear. He couldn't understand why Enlali was so relieved that the hum came from hornets! As he drew closer to the top of the slope, he braced himself. But nothing could have prepared him for the sight that met his eyes. The track led down between what he realized must be trees – but they were barely recognizable. Vast conical structures clung to the trunks and hung from the branches, creations of such beauty that for a moment all thoughts of hornets were driven from his mind. He was mesmerized by the swirling patterns, the intricate tracery of mauves and yellows, palest blues, soft dusky pinks. It was like looking at the corals beneath the Great Ocean, only a paler, hazier version, more subtle and soft, as though they were reflected in a cloudy mirror.

Ahead of him, Finn let out a gasp of amazement. "Wow! I never realized they built nests this big! How...?" He stopped mid-sentence as a dark shape emerged from amongst the nests, a shape that was flying directly towards them. Now Arin remembered the hornets, remembered exactly what it was that had created the beautiful nests. Only something didn't make sense. His brain struggled to comprehend what he was seeing. How was it possible to see the hornet from this distance? It must be a strange, optical illusion, he told himself. But as the hornet approached, he realized it was no illusion. An icy, paralysing terror gripped hold of him. The hornet was the size of a small bird.

"Oh... whoa!" Even Raya, who normally laughed at her brother's wasp phobia, was shocked.

"Come on!" Enlali called back to them, apparently oblivious to the vast hornet that was flying straight towards him. "They're hornets not wasps! Beautiful creatures. They won't hurt us. They never attack people – not unless we attack the nests." He wheeled his horse round and set off down the track.

"He's right." Finn could see Arin's terror. "They're the same in Dayah, only much smaller," he added, as the monstrous hornet buzzed past within a couple of metres of his horse. "See! It's not interested in us." He tried to sound calm and matter-of-fact about it, but even with his knowledge of the nice nature of hornets he looked relieved that it had gone.

Arin looked with horror at the route ahead. It wound between the trees, surrounded on both sides by nests.

"There must be another way," he began, but as he spoke Enlali let out another long whistle and all the horses moved forward as one. For a moment he thought about jumping to the ground, sliding off the back of his moving horse, but as he saw Finn and Raya riding confidently on, he gritted his teeth. It was always him who had the phobias, not Raya – heights, wasps... This time he would not hold them all up like he had on the awful climb down the cliff in Bryah! He took a firm grip of his horse's mane, leant forward and closed his eyes. He would just pretend he was somewhere else, riding a seahorse perhaps across the Reef. Try as he might though, he couldn't block out the deep resonant hum which was growing louder by the second.

"Zzzzzzzzzzzzz." The buzzing surrounded him on all sides.

"I'm a Moon Singer, the Arch Moon Singer!" He said the words silently to himself over and over again, as he tried to recall the details of the vision the Protean Oracle had shown him. The Arch Moon Singer wouldn't be afraid of any insect!

It seemed to go on and on and on. "Zzzzzzzzzzzz." His head was filled with the humming as though the hornets were now on the inside of his skull. He gripped his horse's mane even tighter, suddenly aware of how much trust he was putting on her to carry him through. She seemed calm, unaffected by the buzzing, and gradually he too began to relax. He let one hand slide down on to her neck and felt warmth through her glossy coat. The pounding of his heart slowed, the hornets' drone moved back outside his head, and he opened his eyes. On both sides of the track hung row after row of nests, some

147

dangling like great fat stalactites from the wide-spreading branches of almost invisibles trees, others growing out from the trunks like huge carbuncles. They were beautiful, he had to admit, the intricate patterning and delicate swirling colours even more stunning in close-up. A hornet was crawling lazily out from one he was approaching, but strangely he no longer felt fear. He stroked his horse's neck again and a wave of calmness washed over him. And then they were out, moving along the grassy track with the city of hornets receding into a gentle background hum. Arin looked back over his shoulder, not quite able to believe what had happened. He felt almost sorry now, wished he could have spent a little longer taking in the beauty of the nests!

"Are you alright?" Raya drew up alongside him.

He nodded. "It was fine." He left it at that, rather enjoying her flabbergasted expression.

They rode on across the gently rolling countryside, heading ever further to the east. Far off in the north, a chain of snow-capped mountains guarded the horizon, mountains that reminded Arin of those he had seen in Assyah. Maybe they were in Assyah. He thought back to what Owen had told him about the Realm, about the different Lands. He had told them about the earthenware pot he had seen in Dayah, with scenes from Bryah painted on it; related the tales of Oolugh and the Eddra about travelling between the Lands. And hadn't his own father told stories of sailing far up the Great River, far inland to the edge of an endless forest? Not that he had believed his father. Arin tried to push the memory away. Finn talked sometimes about his family, trapped somewhere in the Wall of blackness, the Void as Owen called it, but as far as Arin was concerned, the only family he had was Raya. His father had done nothing but mock him for his love of music and singing, jeering at his desire to become a Moon Singer, and when he had failed to return from his last fishing trip to the pearl beds of Anamos, Arin had secretly been relieved. He and Raya managed just fine without him.

He focused back on the track ahead. The rest of the horses had almost vanished from sight as he had been idling along gazing at the mountains. He gave his horse a gentle nudge with his heels and bumped his way awkwardly towards the next rise over which his companions had ridden. Although he no longer thought he was about to fall off, he still couldn't get the hang of trotting. But as he reached the summit his horse slowed. Just beyond, Raya and Finn had stopped and were gazing down with awestruck expressions to the valley far below, a wide, verdant valley through which a broad river meandered, a valley in the centre of which stood something impossibly beautiful. Thin spires and columns of glistening crystalline rock soared skywards from the valley floor, like the stems of flowers made of light, stems so slender and delicate and reaching so high that it seemed to Arin that they should snap under the slightest breath of wind. And as the sunlight danced off the surface of the crystal, it splintered into countless rainbows that arced down to the ground far below.

The Towers! This had to be the Towers!

Chapter 17

"That's got to be the Towers." Raya echoed her brother's thought. "Wow... I never imagined..." She trailed off, lost for words.

"Come on!" Enlali called back to them. "We've still got a good couple of hours' ride before we get there. It's further than it looks."

He was right. They quickly reached the foot of the hills and set off across the valley, but half an hour later the crystal towers still looked just as far away.

"Like Moon Island," Raya said to Arin under her breath. But it wasn't really like the island where they had found the Water Sath, Arin thought to himself. That magic was familiar to him. Whatever was at work here was something he couldn't sense at all. A nasty thought suddenly occurred to him. Without Owen, none of them could detect Fire magic either. They would have no warning of the presence of a Baarash.

But he soon forgot his concerns. It was impossible to feel anything other than excitement and wonder as slowly they drew closer to the shimmering rainbow arcs that danced off the gleaming spires and columns. The pinnacles looked as though they might almost touch the sky, or at the very least the Moon. Arin squinted up into the cloudless late afternoon sky. Imagine if he could go up to the top of one of them and sing to the Moon from so close. But then a wave of nausea hit him as the spire he was gazing up at seemed to lurch towards him. He snapped his eyes shut and took a deep breath. It was bad enough climbing a ship's mast; he would never get up beyond the first few metres of one of the towers!

The rainbow light that reflected off the crystal as great arcs high up, blurred into a haze of colours down nearer the ground, a haze into which a few minutes later they were riding.

"It's like a field of rainbows!" Even the normally down-to-earth Finn was feeling poetic.

"No, a sea of rainbows!" Raya laughed out loud as the light rippled across her fair hair, turning it first blue, then violet, then red.

The track followed the course of the river now, meandering gently towards the spires. Arin felt a surge of relief at the familiar sight of water. For all their beauty, there was something entirely alien about the towers of crystal. It was getting increasingly hard to see more than a few metres in front of his horse's nose now. The hazy light seemed strangely thick and opaque, and he was glad that the horses, or at least Enlali, knew the way. Even the soaring columns were blurring in the kaleidoscope of colours that from this angle appeared to be cascading from them in a waterfall of light. He rubbed his eyes. The heavy red light in particular was beginning to give him a headache.

Ahead of him, the horses came to a halt.

"What is it?" Raya's voice sounded muffled and crackly, as though the light was distorting it. There was no reply, but as Arin drew up alongside her, he could see why they had stopped. Just a few metres in front of them was a wall of solid, dense redness. Enlali however, was unperturbed.

"Right." He pulled a little box out of his bag and peered into it. "Here we are!" He drew out something Arin couldn't see, held his hand up in front of him and shook it.

'Clong.' A deep resonant note rang out. A bell! Like the ones they used at sea to cast circles. 'Clong.' It sounded again and a moment later the red wall began to dissipate as though it was smoke being blown away by bellows. Ahead the path lay clear, a path that led across bright sunlit fields towards the gleaming spires beyond.

The horses followed Enlali through the remaining wisps of red mist into the dazzling sunshine. Arin glanced back over his shoulder. The red smoke had vanished, but in its place stood a solid green wall – a wall which seemed to merge far above with the blue of the sky, as though the horizon had tilted at a right angle. It didn't look like something you could simply walk straight through. But as they rode away from it, the dense green began to fade, until a couple of minutes later all he could see was the rainbow haze at ground level and the arcs sweeping up high overhead again.

He turned his attention back towards the towers. All that had been visible before were the columns of crystal soaring skywards, but now that they were on the other side of the rainbows, he could see that there was a lot more. The towers reached up from amongst low lying walls of milky white stone, above which yellow and violet streamers fluttered in the breeze, streamers not unlike those that had decorated the camp of the Butterfly Tribe.

"We leave the horses here," Enlali called back as he dismounted.

Arin slid off his horse only to find his legs buckling beneath him. He groaned as he righted himself. He was thankful that there wasn't far to walk to reach the outer wall. His legs were so stiff that he felt as if he was walking like a sailor on land for the first time in months.

A pair of creamy-white painted gates curved up, like the necks of two swans, from the stone wall, barring their entry to what lay beyond, but they had barely gone a few metres on foot before one of them swung wide open.

"Ha! Enlali!" A tall, thin man strode towards them: a man dressed in vivid yellow and violet robes that shimmered like fine silk in the sunlight. "Beautiful horses! Wonderful! Where did you..." He stopped mid-sentence as he caught sight of the three children standing amongst the horses.

"Well now, those are funny looking horses!" He looked curiously at the strangers.

"Found them up near the Caves of the Winds," Enlali replied.

"And brought them here?" The other man sounded puzzled.

"He didn't bring us!" Raya spoke up, not best pleased with being discussed as though she couldn't speak for herself. "We just travelled together. We were coming to the Towers anyway."

The man's eyebrows shot up in surprise. "What are you talking about?"

But Enlali interrupted quickly. "I'll explain." He shot the man a warning look. "Come on!" He beckoned to Arin, Raya and Finn. "Let's get cleaned up and get something to eat. It's been a longer trip than I expected, and you all look pretty hungry too." With that he set off towards the gate.

Arin watched as Enlali walked close beside the other man bowing his head to speak in an undertone. What was it he didn't want them to hear? And why had the tall man been so surprised by Raya's statement? But there was little chance to contemplate these questions. Moments later they were inside the wall and the gate was closing behind them. Given his fascination with Moon magic, Arin of all people should have been used to illusion by now, but stepping through the gate he felt as though he had just fallen through one of the Gateways into yet another Realm.

Before him spread terraces of luxuriant gardens, interwoven with cascading watercourses. A path inlaid with mosaic patterns of yellow and violet, led directly ahead, passing between banks of heavily scented flowers that he didn't recognize. From the other side of the outer wall it had appeared as though the area inside was quite small, and that the crystal spires stood closely packed inside the ring of milky-white stone, but now he stood on the inside, he could see that this was an illusion. He felt uneasy not being able to sense the magic at work. He could hear the water around him, the cascades, the gushing fountains, and that at least provided something familiar to focus on, but there was no Water magic involved. He felt suddenly very small and helpless. He and Raya didn't belong here and nor did Finn. It had been different in Assyah, with Owen there. Owen seemed to belong everywhere, in every Realm and Arin felt somehow special with Owen around; everything seemed possible because they were with the 'Chosen One'. The words of the Protean Oracle came back to him. Without Owen, he, Raya and Finn were just three children, powerless, lost.

A moment later, however, his fears were forgotten. He had heard a mewing cry from the next terrace, high and piercing like a hawk, but now as he reached the top of a flight of steps, the garden which lay beyond, previously hidden behind yet another wall, came into view and he saw the source of the mewing. Peacocks! Birds he had seen painted on vases back in Bryah but never in real life. Or at least he thought they were peacocks, as whilst those painted birds had been bedecked with feathers of blue, green and purple, these were pure, dazzling white. Beside him Raya let out a gasp of amazement. One of the birds shook its tail and the bright sunlight shivered through the feathers.

"Aren't they beautiful!?" Raya reached out her hand to try to touch one, but it danced away from her.

Enlali and his friend were so deep in conversation that they were halfway across the terrace before they noticed that the three children were no longer right behind them.

"Hey!" Enlali called back. "Come on. You'll have plenty of time to look around tomorrow."

His friend looked pleased at their expressions. "The peacocks." He smiled as they made their way across to join the two men. "You must have heard of them." Blank faces met his statement. "Surely you have! Even out on the Plains you must know about the Peacocks of Paralda." He raised incredulous eyebrows.

"Er... yes... of course," Raya said hastily. "The Peacocks. Of course."

For a moment there was an awkward silence, but then a voice rang out from the other side of the garden.

"Enlali! You're back! And late. I was beginning to think one of those Winds had got you, or a roc."

A middle-aged woman with fair hair and yellow eyes came towards them. She looked so like Enlali that if it hadn't been for the age difference, they could have been twins. "You don't look like you've been eating properly." She tutted with disapproval.

"Hello, mother." Enlali didn't sound exactly delighted to see her. Beside him, his friend tried unsuccessfully to stifle a snort of laughter.

"Well, I don't know what you're laughing at Eurani," the woman exclaimed. "You could do with fattening up yourself if you want to find a wife! You look more like Stork Tribe than a Paraldan!" She paused as her gaze settled upon Arin, Raya and Finn. "And who are these little chicks then?" Her tone softened.

"Adventurers," Enlali replied, with a wry smile. "I found them up near the Caves of the Winds. Lost."

"We weren't exactly lost," Raya broke in defensively. "We knew where we were going."

"Yes." Enlali looked uncomfortable. "Anyway, you're here now. And..." he glanced quickly at Eurani, "as I've got stuff to sort out with Eurani about the horses, perhaps... well, if you take them and give them something to eat, I'll be back soon and I'll explain everything then."

His mother frowned. "Hmm... I don't know what you're up to Enlali, but I hope it's nothing silly!" She turned to Arin, Raya and Finn. "You come along with me then and you can tell me all about this adventure." She addressed them as though they were little children.

"Thank you." Arin gave his sister a warning glance. He didn't want her saying any more about what they were doing in Yezirah. At least a meal gave him a bit of time to think. Something was very wrong. He had sensed that Enlali was hiding something from them even before their arrival, and now he was certain of it. Raya and Finn may not have noticed a word that had slipped out twice in the conversations of the last few minutes, but Arin had – the word *Paralda*: a word he recalled hearing first from Grandma Saiki. The Palace of Paralda; she had spoken of it as the enemy of the Guardians in the Towers. And if Eurani was a Paraldan and the Peacocks were the Peacocks of Paralda, then there was only one logical explanation.

Fortunately there was little chance of anyone putting their foot in it as they followed Enlali's mother across a series of walled courtyards, linked by more mosaic paths.

"You can call me Auntie," she began. "Auntie Gemina. Now tell me your names."

"I'm Finn." Finn took the lead. "And this is Arin and Raya."

"Well it's very nice to meet you. Goodness knows what your parents must be thinking; little ones like you out all alone on the Plain! I worry myself silly every time Enlali goes off after the horses. It's so dangerous! Only the other day my sister was telling me about those giant fleas that attacked the Mayfly Tribe one night when they were sleeping and ate them all. Not one survived!"

Arin wondered how anyone knew what had happened if no one survived but said nothing. And so the conversation continued. Gemina had a seemingly endless supply of tales about the dangers that lay beyond the walls, all heard from her sister or a neighbour, or a similarly reliable source, and before long he had stopped listening. It all meant nothing to him, and he had no idea whether there was any truth in the stories or whether they were like Raya's wilder tales.

The courtyards were bordered by low-lying white stone houses with pointed conical roofs. All looked identical to one another as did each courtyard, with a single tree in the centre from which hung long cylindrical wind chimes. He wondered how anyone could recognise their own house. There wasn't even anything like a pod sign hanging above the door. Once again, it was all far bigger inside than out. The crystal spires seemed to grow no closer as they followed Gemina through the maze of courtyards and he began to think that maybe they too were an illusion.

"Here we are." Gemina had stopped in front of one of the houses. "Home." She opened the unremarkable white door.

"Do you think they ever pick the wrong one?" Raya whispered.

Arin had expected to at least find something less uniform inside the house, something a little more like the higgledy-piggledy chaos in his and Raya's home on Eridu but instead was faced with a house so immaculate and impersonal that he could hardly believe anyone actually lived there.

"I think Raki should visit this place!" Finn said under his breath.

The room that they had entered was almost empty. With the exception of a predictably white slab of stone hanging suspended in the centre and six very uncomfortable looking stools, there was no other furniture, and the only decoration was a peculiar fan-shaped display of yellow and violet feathers on one wall. Despite having no window the room was surprisingly light. The conical ceiling had looked to be made of the same stone as the walls from the outside, but from inside looked more like the clearest quartz crystal, and the light streamed in as though the room was open to the sky.

Gemina beckoned to them to follow her through another door. "I do hope Enlali doesn't stay out too late," she tutted. "He'll miss dinner and have to go to bed hungry if he does!" She stepped into the hallway that led from the first room, a hallway which unsurprisingly was far too long to be contained inside the little round house.

"Here we are." She opened a door into another large room, empty but for a long trough of water running along one wall. Now, you wash your hands and faces like good children, and I'll find you some nice clean clothes to wear. Then we can go and have something ever so nice to eat and you can tell me all about your big adventure."

"Argh!" Raya growled, once Gemina had shut the door behind her. "Does she think we're five or something? Good little children! Huh! Wait till I tell her..."

"No." Arin interrupted her. "We can't say anything."

"But what about Owen?" Finn said. "If he's already here..."

"He isn't," Arin said grimly.

"You can't know that," Raya retorted.

"Yes, I can, because this isn't where he's going."

"What?" Finn was confused.

"This isn't the Towers."

A stunned silence met his statement.

"You heard them earlier, talking about those Peacocks – the Peacocks of Paralda, and Gemina said Eurani was a Paraldan," Arin explained. "Well, that was who Grandma Saiki said was the enemy of the Towers – the Palace of Paralda, and even if that Prince has already attacked the Towers and won, I can't see why their Peacocks would be here."

"You're saying this is the Palace of Paralda," Finn said slowly.

Arin nodded.

"But Enlali said he was going to the Towers. Why would he lie to us? It doesn't make sense." Confusion was written across his face.

"I know," Arin agreed, "it doesn't. But I'm sure I'm right." He stopped as the door opened and Gemina reappeared bearing three identical pale-yellow tunics.

"When you've changed, leave those things in here," she gestured with undisguised distaste at their clothes as she pulled a small knob on the wall and a previously invisible basket slid smoothly out into the room. "Then we'll get some food in those hungry tummies of yours."

"Thank you." Raya put on her sweetest smile as she took the tunics. "We'll be ever so quick. Yummy food! Goodie! Oh... how pretty!" She held up one of the tunics. "I'll feel like a princess in a palace!" She twirled round holding it up against her body as though dancing.

Gemina beamed with pleasure. "Well you are in a palace now my dear, so a princess you shall be!"

"We've got to think fast," Finn said, once Gemina had left them alone. "It sounds like you're right Arin, so... er..." He trailed off.

"We need to escape," Raya finished his sentence.

"Yes..." Arin wasn't entirely convinced. "But we don't actually have anything to escape from really. I mean, we're not prisoners or anything and maybe if we find out why Enlali lied to us, we might find out something useful, something about that Sword of Truth."

"I wish Owen was here." Finn sighed. "He would know what to do."

There was a long, heavy silence.

"I suppose we might as well stay here tonight," Raya said eventually. "We just play stupid, which with *Auntie Gemina* shouldn't be too hard!" she added wryly.

This was the plan they had to go with in the end. No one was entirely happy with it, but they didn't have time to come up with anything better. They had taken too long to change and Gemina reappeared at the door with a frown on her face. "What *have* you been up to?" she exclaimed as she herded them out of the bathroom and along the hallway on to an open-ended verandah upon which stood a table and two long benches. Beyond lay yet another wide courtyard, bordered by several identical verandahs and tables all occupied by yellow-robed Aevyans, whilst in the centre stood what Arin assumed to be a kitchen, judging by the smells emanating from it. Gemina patted one of the benches.

"Now, we'll leave a space for Enlali," she said half to herself, "but there's room for three more." She hurried off across the courtyard and was back only a few moments later, accompanied by two women and a boy of about their own age. The boy scowled as Gemina sat him next to Raya.

"You all make friends while the grown-ups get the food." Gemina beamed round at them.

"What's your name?" Finn, as the oldest, decided to take charge.

"Pashani." The boy continued to scowl.

Finn introduced himself, Raya and Arin, but Pashani just shrugged and grunted.

"So... er... you know Enlali?" Finn tried to start a conversation.

"Obviously." Pashani rolled his eyes as though Finn was an idiot.

"We met him out near the Caves of the Winds," Raya joined in.

Pashani snorted in disbelief. "That's such a lie!"

"No, it's not!" Raya was indignant. "His mother, Gemina, she'll tell you it's not."

Pashani frowned, his interest pricked despite himself. "So what were you doing there? What Tribe are you?"

"Butterfly," Raya said instantly. "We were on our way to the Chrysalis Fields." She paused. "You don't know what they are, do you?"

"Of course I know!" Pashani retorted. "They're where the chrysalises grow for the Butterfly babies. You're not the only ones who do that! It's nothing special. The Dragonflies and Mayflies have Pupa

Fields." He shook his head. "We know everything here in Paralda."

"What, even more than the Towers?" Arin ventured.

"Hah!" Pashani snorted. "They may think they're so clever, but our new Queen knows exactly what they're up to. She knows what the Singing Head means, and soon when our warriors attack, we'll have the Sword, not them. They can't win, not with her leading us. She's the greatest Queen there's ever been."

Unfortunately the conversation was abruptly interrupted by the return of Gemina and her friends, bearing heavily laden bowls of food.

"Soup." Gemina lifted the top from a tureen of pale green liquid. "Chervil, alfalfa and dill."

The meal wasn't what Arin would have chosen, but he thought he was hungry enough to eat almost anything. He and Finn left it to Raya to spin their audience a story. Now she knew not to reveal anything of their true quest, he was confident in her ability to tell a tale.

Arin's attention wandered off to the other tables set around the courtyard. As with the Butterfly Tribe, there seemed to be a lot of children and older adults, but very few of Enlali's age. Was this something to do with the preparation for the attack on the Towers perhaps? If only there was someone they could trust, like Urso in Assyah, or even Moshi; someone who they could question with no fear of betrayal. Ever since they had returned through the Gateway from Assyah to find Owen's world in chaos, it had felt to him as though they were walking on quicksand. Even Darius, the one person Owen now seemed sure of, made him feel edgy, for some reason.

"Hey! It's the Fool!" Pashani shouted out so suddenly that Arin nearly jumped out of his skin. "Here, catch!" He aimed a fruit stone at a painfully thin, smiling boy with long, curly, fair hair, who had just walked into the courtyard. Unlike the other Paraldans, he wore a tatty black jerkin, decorated with leaf and flower patterns in shades of red, green, yellow and blue.

Across the courtyard another boy joined in.

"Foolboy! Just say please and you can have this." He held up a bread roll. Someone else laughed and hurled an empty marrow skin at the boy.

"Get out of here!" This time it was one of the adult women, but her words were almost drowned out by a chorus of mocking hoots from around the courtyard.

"He looks half-starved," Raya said, her eyes wide with pity. As if to prove her right, the boy approached one of the tables with his hands held out before him like a cup. But instead of giving him food, the young boy he had chosen threw his glass of water over the skinny beggar. A roar of laughter greeted this, but still the fair-haired boy smiled.

Raya had had enough. Suddenly all the memories of Eridu and the bullies who had picked on Arin, rushed to the surface. "Stop it!" she yelled at the top of her voice, and ignoring Finn and Arin's alarmed expressions, she grabbed an armful of bread rolls and fruit, marched across the courtyard and handed them to the boy. "Here. For you." She glared defiantly round at the crowd, who were gaping at her in sudden stunned silence. "Bullies!" she shouted. "Mean, horrible bullies!"

Chapter 18

Gemina was not at all pleased when Raya returned to the table after her outburst.

"What will people think?" She was bright red with embarrassment.

"I don't care!" Raya said defiantly. "Why were you all being so horrible to him?" She turned away to hide the tears that were pricking her eyes.

"Yes. Why? He looked like he was really hungry, and you've got all this food." Finn jumped to Raya's defence.

The fair-haired boy had disappeared. He had accepted Raya's gift of food with wide eyes, then given her a beam of total delight, before running from the courtyard.

Pashani snorted with derision. "So what? He's a fool. He can go and eat with the horses..."

Gemina interrupted, her tone a little softer when she saw Raya's distress. "You weren't to know, but that... boy..." she seemed reluctant to use the word, as though the beggar boy didn't deserve the name, "he *is* a fool. He doesn't speak." She waited for a reaction from Raya, but when she got none, she continued with a pitying expression on her face. "Dear me, you really don't understand, do you? I suppose it's all different out there on the Plain."

Highly disapproving glances were being directed at Raya from all sides of the courtyard.

"It's not nice!" Gemina spelt it out. "He's not like us. He should have been cast out by now. I don't know how he keeps getting back in." She gave Raya a pained look. "No one is saying he should be killed," she added quickly, "but we don't want him here, and feeding him will only encourage him to stay."

Raya was totally bewildered. "I don't understand. Do you mean he is dangerous?"

"No. But it's just not very nice, someone like him. We don't like that sort of thing here." Gemina's mouth was set in a hard line.

Arin gave Raya a kick under the table and threw her a warning look. She had already drawn enough unwelcome attention to them, and he knew his sister only too well. Now was not the time for her to throw herself into a battle. A cool head was needed. Fortunately, for once, Raya took the hint and said no more.

The rest of the meal was rather subdued, with the visitors excluded from further conversation. Pashani had very deliberately edged along the bench away from Raya, as though she carried a contagious disease and Gemina appeared very relieved once the meal was over. She shepherded her three guests back into the house with apologetic smiles to her friends.

"Goodness knows what people will be thinking of me now!" She tutted as she closed the door to the verandah. "It'll be all round Paralda by tomorrow. And I don't know what's become of Enlali. He knows what time we eat, and he knows I was expecting him."

Arin was relieved at the change of topic, and more relieved still when Gemina led them to a bedroom furnished with two three-tiered bunk beds.

"This is where Enlali and his brothers and sisters used to sleep when they were little like you," she beamed.

"Do they live here with you too, the brothers and sisters?" Raya asked, curiosity getting the better of her.

"No, no. They're all dead," Gemina said, in such a matter-of- fact way that at first Arin thought he must have misheard.

"Oh... er... I'm sorry," Raya trailed off lamely.

"Yes, well, life is full of sorrow," Gemina replied blithely, as she opened the door of a wardrobe. "Night clothes in here. And you know the way to the bathroom. I expect you're all ever so tired after such a big adventure, so you be good children and don't stay up late chattering, or you'll be grumpy tomorrow. And tomorrow's a big day!"

"They probably chose to die rather than live with Gemina," Raya said weakly, in an attempt to lighten the atmosphere once they were alone.

"That's awful." Finn looked quite upset.

162

"I didn't mean…" Raya began.

"No, not you. I mean, if it's true and they are all dead." He looked with distaste at the wardrobe of clothes.

"She didn't seem exactly sad," Raya said with a frown. "They're weird people here. I don't think I like Yezirah much. Assyah was far better."

"Hmm." Arin thought of the last night they had spent in the dungeon pit in Arktos. "I wonder what she meant about tomorrow being a big day."

Arin was woken the next morning by voices. For a moment he was confused. Daylight was pouring in from directly overhead, as though he was lying out in the open, but then as he glanced to the side, he saw Raya on the top bunk opposite him.

"We're trying to work out what to do," she said, noticing that he had woken.

He yawned. "So what's the plan?" He asked the question without any great expectation that they had one.

"We haven't decided yet," she replied.

Arin was relieved to find Enlali sitting out on the verandah. They had decided to postpone any decision on escape, but the prospect of a day with Gemina was very unappealing.

"I gather you met that Fool-boy last night," Enlali said as he tucked into a bowl of soup.

"They were all bullying him." Raya was instantly on the defensive.

"That's not really what it was," Enlali tried to explain. "They just don't want him around – like er… like scringa birds. You know, you leave out some food accidentally and the next morning there's a scringa bird screeching away until you give it more – and then another and then another, and no matter how many times you chase them away they keep coming back."

Arin had no idea what a scringa bird was, but he got the idea. "Maybe like a Solochi," he said to Raya under his breath, though he couldn't really see what harm the boy had been doing.

"He's not like a Cracked Brain," Enlali continued. "Is that what you thought?"

"Yes," Arin interjected quickly before Raya had a chance to speak.

"Ah! Now I understand," Enlali said. "No, no. That boy, he's just a fool. He can't speak. There's nothing special about him. Whoever his tribe is must have cast him out and I can't think why he imagines we should want him around."

Fortunately, at that moment Gemina emerged from the central kitchen, bearing a large tureen of soup and the conversation came to a halt. Despite his determination to keep a cool head, a deep anger was beginning to well up in Arin.

"No," Raya hissed at him, their roles suddenly reversed, and her own anger temporarily forgotten.

Arin clenched his fists and bit his lip. It rarely happened that he got angry, but when he did, it was like a huge tidal wave of rage.

"Here we are!" Gemina beamed at them as she set the tureen down on the table. "A second breakfast for naughty Enlali. I knew you'd be a hungry boy, staying out all night like that!" She tutted in disapproval.

Arin still found it hard to believe what she had told them the previous night; hard to believe that she was someone carrying round such a weight of sorrow. But then he was finding it very hard to understand the Aevyans, full stop.

"Today you are going to have a real treat!" Enlali said, ignoring his mother's comment.

That got Arin's attention. He had been wondering ever since she had left them the previous night, what Gemina had meant about 'a big day'.

"I'm going to take you up to meet the Vizier," Enlali continued. "Right up to the top of one of the... er... towers."

"This isn't the Towers, is it?" Finn blurted out suddenly. "Not *the* Towers where Owen is going."

Enlali did at least have the grace to look a little embarrassed. "Well, no... no, it's not. But you didn't really want to be going there."

"Yes, we did." Finn glared at the older man. "Why did you lie to us?"

"Look, you would have died out there with those Winds if I hadn't rescued you," Enlali replied. "I'm your friend." He hesitated a moment. "It was for your own good. You'll understand once you've seen the Vizier. He'll explain it all."

Finn didn't look convinced, but it was clear that Enlali was saying no more on the subject.

"There's something not right about all this," Arin whispered to Finn when Enlali left the table. But there wasn't much they could do about it. Even if they ran, they had no idea how to get out of the maze of courtyards, and they would surely be caught within minutes. It looked like they would just have to go along with Enlali's 'real treat.'

As they set off through the courtyards towards the crystal spires, Arin couldn't help but feel a touch of excitement. Enlali wasn't behaving as though he was leading them to their doom, even pointing out noteworthy sights along the way.

"The crystal pools," he announced, as the mosaic path let them past a series of peculiar, steaming ponds. Arin wrinkled his nose as a smell not unlike seagull droppings assailed his nostrils. Enlali stopped beside one, above which a pale-yellow fog hung. "These are where we grow the crystal feathers. For flying," he added when that got no response.

"Flying?" Raya's eyes were wide as saucers.

"Yes," Enlali smiled. "How would you like that? No need for all those years learning how to ride a Wind. Just please the Prince and he might let you have a go."

Raya stared in disbelief at the pond. "What, I could fly? Like a bird?"

"Well of course!" Enlali gave her a funny look. "Where...?" He stopped. "Never mind." He shook his head. "Yes, you could fly like a bird. But they all belong to the Prince, and he'll only let you fly if you give him something in return."

Arin and Finn exchanged a glance. Was this what it was about then? Did Enlali think they had something that the Prince might want?

The optical illusion that had made the crystal spires appear constantly distant, was no longer present and the thin needles now towered impossibly high overhead. Arin felt dizzy just looking up at them. A couple of minutes later they were standing at the foot of the closest one, before an open doorway. He looked warily at the opening. The tower looked barely any wider than the span of his arms, but he knew by now that here in Yezirah this was probably an illusion. What he didn't like the look of however, one little bit, was the height of the structure. This was the Air Realm after all! As he feared, Enlali strode

165

through the doorway.

"Oh no!" Arin groaned. "Please say we're not going up there!"

But of course they were. Initially, however, his fears were forgotten. The doorway led into a wide hall illuminated from floor to ceiling with dots of light – dots which once the door had shut behind him, he recognized as stars and planets. He gazed down towards the representation of the Moon, which lay below his feet.

"That's right!" He turned to Raya. "That's exactly right. The size she is now." He stared wide-eyed at the slender crescent. "And the Balance!" He pointed to a constellation on the wall in front of him. "That's right too."

Enlali was waiting for them on the opposite side of the hall. "Of course it's right." He beckoned them over. "The Vizier is hardly likely to have a mistake in his Astroplan, is he?!"

Arin expected to find a staircase, or worse, rungs or a ladder, on the other side of the door that Enlali held open, but instead there was simply a small crystal walled room. He stepped inside, puzzled. There appeared to be no other way out. The door shut behind them.

"So... er... what is this place?" Raya didn't look happy at being shut in the little room.

Enlali held up one finger. "We're going up – up there, to meet the Vizier."

Raya frowned, no clearer than she had been before, but before she had a chance to speak, the door slid open again. Arin blinked in surprise. The hall with the Astroplan had vanished. In its place was a large glass-domed room.

"In you go." Enlali nodded towards the open doorway.

Arin followed Raya and Finn into the room. From the doorway, which opened out of a central pillar of crystal, all he could see beyond the dome of glass was a vast blue expanse of sky. But as he stepped further into the room, across a floor of glittering yellow and mauve mosaics, he caught a glimpse of the green line of the horizon far, far below. A wave of giddiness rushed over him and he couldn't take another step.

"Come in."

Arin heard a sharp voice, but his eyes were fixed firmly on the floor just in front of his feet.

"What is wrong with that boy?" The voice spoke again.

"His name is Arin," Raya said. "And nothing's wrong with him. He just doesn't like heights, that's all."

There was a long silence. Arin tried desperately to get control of his panic. This was silly. He was inside a solid building. Safe. He wasn't about to fall over the edge.

"He doesn't like heights?" The man eventually spoke, his voice incredulous.

"No." Arin managed to speak for himself. "I get dizzy. I'm sorry."

"Harrumph," the man snorted. "Ridiculous."

A moment later a soft bell-like note rang out and Arin was aware of a subtle change in the light around him. He glanced quickly up and then let out a sigh of relief. The walls were now thankfully opaque, as though made of quartz crystal.

He looked across now for the first time at the man who had been speaking, a man clad in a violet robe with a golden-yellow sash. He had long, waist-length grey hair, pale yellow eyes and darker skin than any Aevyan he had yet met – at least in Yezirah, Arin realized with a start. Because he had met an Aevyan with skin just that colour, one who resembled this man to such a degree that they must surely be related – Professor Vishnami!

Raya and Finn had clearly noticed this resemblance too, judging by their wide-eyed expressions.

"Better?" The man sounded distinctly scornful.

"Yes. Thank you." Arin felt a mixture of shame and anger. It wasn't his fault that he hated heights and back in Bryah it was hardly uncommon. But this man was looking at him as if he was some sort of freak. At least now though, he was able to take a better look at the room around him, and despite himself he was interested. Unlike Gemina's house, the room was anything but bare. Intricately wrought cases of what he knew from Owen to be books, stood against one 'wall', whilst free-standing tables and cabinets held peculiar looking contraptions that sparked with pulses of light. But in pride of place stood a great crystal pyramid from which light flooded in a rainbow of hues.

"The Sonogramme." The man noticed him staring at the pyramid, walked up to it and struck it deftly with a slender black rod. A chord rang out so pure and clear that the hairs on Arin's back stood on end. "Music," the man continued. "Aural light heard through the prism

167

of the ear." He struck it again at a different point and more notes sounded, rippling out from the crystal in waves. "It is attuned to the Music of the Spheres."

Arin gazed at it utterly spellbound. He had never seen anything so wonderful. He waited expectantly for the man to strike it again, but instead he laid down the black rod.

"I am the Vizier of Paralda." He paused, waiting for some sort of reaction.

Arin glanced at Finn, wondering if the Sylvan boy had any more idea what the correct response was to this than he had. But Finn just shrugged.

"We know. Enlali said he was bringing us to meet the Vizier, so it's not a surprise that you're him."

Arin winced. He was used to Raya speaking without thinking, but not Finn. Getting off on the wrong foot with this Vizier did not seem like a good idea.

The Vizier himself, however, let out a laugh. "Hah! Indeed. That would be a correct statement under such a circumstance." He paused. "Come over here and sit down." He indicated a long narrow benchlike seat opposite which he placed his own large, elaborately decorated chair.

"Now," he scanned his visitors once they were seated. "Enlali tells me that you wish to go to the Towers."

Enlali, who had remained standing in the background, looked a little sheepish.

"Would you like to explain to me why this is?" Even the Vizier's manner of speaking was uncannily like Vishnami's. "Well?" He leant in towards them. "Any of you?" He narrowed his eyes.

"We think our friend has gone there," Finn said finally.

"Yes. So I gather," the Vizier sighed. "But perhaps you could enlighten me as to why you were going there in the first place. Why is your friend going there?"

"We wanted to... er... find the Sword of Truth," Finn said somewhat hesitantly.

There was a long silence before the Vizier spoke again. "What do you know of the Sword of Truth?"

"Um... well..." Finn was floundering.

"We know that the Guardians might have found it." Raya helped him out. "And the Singing Head has been singing about it for a while." She tried to recall exactly what Grandma Saiki had said, "We thought we could get it and bring it back here, for the Prince."

Arin was impressed. She had strung together the bits of information they had heard, to come up with what sounded to him like a convincing story. The Vizier, however, looked sceptical.

"You thought you would recover the Sword... for the Prince?!" He raised his eyebrows in scorn.

Raya nodded.

"Really?! And how were you going to do that?"

Not for the first time, Arin wished Owen was with them. He seemed to find the right answers when they were needed. However, before Raya had a chance to come up with any sort of reply, the violet-robed man was on his feet. "Stay there," he commanded as Finn began to get up from the uncomfortable seat.

"Right." The Vizier turned over a disc shaped object that lay on one of the tables. "Now we can do this properly."

That didn't sound good. Arin glanced at Raya and saw the same alarm in her eyes that he knew must be in his own.

"You." He beckoned to Arin. "Come over here."

"Me?" Arin was panic-stricken. He was hopeless at coming up with stories and even worse at telling lies!

"Yes. You." The Vizier's tone softened slightly. "Don't look so worried. It doesn't hurt."

What didn't hurt? Arin felt even worse as slowly he stood up and walked across the room towards the table. He was aware of Finn and Raya watching helplessly from the bench behind him. What he found lying before him on the table didn't fill him with confidence. It was a mirror: a circular, silver-rimmed mirror, something he was very familiar with back in Bryah. Moon magic made much use of mirrors, and it should have been a welcome sight, but there was something very peculiar about this particular mirror. He stared down at his reflection and for a moment the mirror of the Protean Oracle flashed into his mind. But there was no Water magic at work here. He shivered. This was all wrong. Every mirror surely held some Water magic. How could it be a mirror otherwise? But when he tried again to sense the rippling, reflective currents of water, he still felt nothing.

"Now, tell me why you were going to the Towers." The Vizier's voice abruptly interrupted his thoughts.

"We were looking for the Sword of Truth," he began slowly. He was sure that there was at least an element of truth here.

"Continue." The Vizier was staring at the mirror as he spoke.

"Um... we... um..."

"Why did you think the Sword of Truth was there?" The Vizier prompted him.

"Oh... because we heard it was... or it might be anyway." Also true.

"And who told you this?"

Arin hesitated a moment. He didn't want to get the Butterfly Tribe in trouble. But then hadn't they assumed everyone knew, so it was hardly a secret. "Some people in the Butterfly Tribe."

The Vizier leant eagerly over the mirror, then straightened up, a look of disappointment on his face. "I see." He paused. "You are not Butterfly Tribe."

"No," Arin replied.

"So which tribe are you?"

Arin's heart sank like a stone. Whatever else he told the Vizier, he knew that he couldn't reveal who they really were.

"We're Mayfly Tribe." He plucked from the air the name that he had heard Gemina use.

Instantly the mirror clouded over.

"Hmm." The Vizier formed his fingers into a steeple. "A lie. Perhaps you would like to try again."

Arin would not like to try again! He looked round to Raya and Finn for help, but in vain.

"Well? I'm waiting." The Vizier sighed heavily.

"We're not from any tribe you would know," Arin said slowly. The mirror remained clear.

"That makes no sense." The violet-robed man frowned in bewilderment. "I know of all the tribes." He stared intently at Arin. "Let's try a different question, shall we? What was your intention in seeking the Sword?"

"To give it to the Prince," Arin said, relieved at least that the questioning had changed direction. Predictably the mirror clouded over.

"No. That was not your intention." A note of annoyance had crept into the Vizier's voice. "Enough." He turned the mirror back over.

"I have given you the chance to be honest with me, but you have chosen to lie. You now leave me no other option." He strode over to the Sonogramme and picked up the black rod he had used to strike it.

"What are you doing?" Raya was on her feet.

"Sit down." The Vizier's voice was sharp as the crack of a whip. Raya hesitated a moment and Enlali stepped forward.

"Do as you are told," he said. "He's not going to be hurt."

Finn pulled Raya back down. They had little choice but to obey, trapped up at the top of the tower of crystal – and Enlali's sword suddenly looked very sharp. The Vizier raised the rod slowly to Arin's temple, then closed his eyes. Arin waited with trepidation but felt only a gentle prodding sensation. He didn't understand what the Vizier was trying to do. But then he felt it again, a stronger poke, like a finger pushing at the inside of his head. And in an instant he knew what was happening. It was like a Zadi casting his hook into your mind to fish for memories. He took a deep breath, focused all his energy into the water inside his head and sent the most powerful wave of Water energy that he could muster out along the black rod.

"Argh!" The Vizier leapt back, dropping his rod in his shock.

Arin tensed, anticipating anger, but instead, once the Vizier had regained his composure, he looked intrigued.

"Well, well!" he exclaimed. "How fascinating!" He stared at Arin with undisguised curiosity. "Someone... or something, has been at work in your head. Someone with most extraordinary powers!" He looked over at Raya and Finn. "Hmm..." He paused a moment, then appeared to make up his mind about something. "I assume you have all been affected. Bring them back here this evening." He turned to Enlali. "The aspects are right for mind washing." He smiled at Arin. "No need to worry. I shall wash out whatever has been put into your mind." He picked up a bulbous glass vessel from the table. "I shall distil it into here and find the answer. Have no doubt of that. And then I shall replace your 'wrong-thinking' with the correct formula."

Arin's head was reeling as Enlali led them back to the doorway in the central pillar. Clearly the visit was at an end for now. The Vizier was already engrossed in a large hide-bound book that he had pulled out from one of the highest shelves, leafing eagerly through the pages, and didn't even look up as they left his room.

"There! I knew it would turn out well in the end!" Enlali

exclaimed. "I told you it was for your own good."

But Arin couldn't see how having his mind washed out and his thoughts replaced by the Vizier's 'correct formula' was in any way for his own good. And judging by the expressions on the faces of Raya and Finn beside him, they felt the same. Enlali however, was now in a very cheerful mood and had even begun to hum a song to himself as he led them back out of the hall of the Astroplan into the wide square. A moment later though he stopped.

"Oh... oh..." he stammered, lost for words. Arin looked up, momentarily distracted from his worry about the mind washing. Approaching them from the direction of the next tower was a tall woman, clad in deep purple, followed by a retinue of attendants.

"The Queen! The Queen!" Enlali's voice was a squeak. "Quickly! Kneel!" He threw himself theatrically to the ground.

Arin, Raya and Finn all hesitated, but then Arin took the lead and fell to his knees. They were in enough trouble as it was without offending a Queen! Enlali had his head bowed, staring at the ground and Arin duly copied his stance, but as the Queen swept by within a few metres of them, he couldn't resist taking a quick peek. His blood ran cold. One glance was all he had needed, one glance to see the flat, dead eyes and the skin stretched unnaturally taut across the angular cheekbones of the Queen of Yezirah!

Chapter 19

Arin fixed his eyes firmly on the ground in front of him, his head bent as low as he could. "Don't look at us. Don't see us," he repeated over and over in his head, willing the Queen of Yezirah to pass by without noticing them. He didn't dare warn Raya and Finn. Any sound risked getting her attention. He held his breath. It was only when he heard Finn let out his own breath next to him that he glanced up. She had gone! Cold beads of sweat ran down the back of his neck. He might not be able to feel Fire energy like Owen could, but he had seen enough Fire Spirits to know one when he saw one.

"I know," Finn said quietly, before he had a chance to ask the question.

Fortunately Enlali was too excited to notice anything odd in the behaviour of his three charges.

"That was the Queen!" He sounded awestruck. "Queen Azaka!"

"Wow!" Arin realized that a reaction was called for. "I... er... I never thought we would get the chance to see her."

"No! You're very lucky. She rarely comes out of the inner palace," Enlali said. "What luck! The Queen herself!"

Arin thought back to what Owen had told him about Baarashes and his own experiences on Scorpion Island and with their captor on Mount Meru. Baarashes had no shadow. It was one thing fooling a crew of gullible Delfans or blending into a crowd in Assyah and Owen's world, quite another when you were the Queen and all eyes were on you.

"Can I ask you a question?" he asked carefully as Enlali led them back past the crystal ponds and into the maze of courtyards. "Is it er... bad manners to look at the Queen?"

Enlali let out a gasp of horror. "What?! Of course – unless you are given specific permission to do so, which for you three is highly unlikely!"

"I wish I knew more about her," Raya sighed, quite convincingly. And that was all it took. Enlali was more than happy to tell them all about the wonderful Queen. "The Singing Head prophesied her arrival," he explained. "It sang of the coming of the Chosen One, from far off Realms. The One who is chosen to find the Sword."

Raya could barely contain her excitement. "The Chosen One?"

"Yes. It was just after it began to sing that she appeared at the Palace. The Prince, he... um..." Enlali hesitated as he tried to find a diplomatic way of putting it. "Well, he hadn't been very well after the Battle of the Balance."

Raya nodded. Clearly they were meant to know what this was.

"But after she arrived, his recovery was remarkable!" Enlali sounded quite emotional for an Aevyan. "She is so knowledgeable, so wise, so perceptive. Her mind is like the sharpest of blades," he gushed. "If it wasn't for those Guardians and their wrong-thinking..." He trailed off. "That is why I brought you here. It was obvious that you were not who you claimed to be, that you have secrets."

Raya opened her mouth to protest, but he continued. "No, no. I see now, after what happened up there," he nodded back towards the Vizier's Tower, "that you are just tools of whoever it is that is really after the Sword." He smiled patronizingly at her. "But if you hold the key to what they are up to in the Towers, then we must know. There have always been stories, legends, that connect the Guardians to the Sword, and prophecies that speak of the Sword sleeping in the arms of the Guardians. And now she says the time is at hand. It may even be that they have found the Sword. But it is our Queen who is the Chosen One, not them. If they hold the Sword of Truth..." He shuddered. "Unthinkable! They do not have the interests of Yezirah at heart, only their own. Imagine the Rainbow Guild holding the key to all knowledge, the Ultimate Truth!" He shook his head. "Queen Azaka has seen the truth. She says they will see Yezirah destroyed. The Land will fall beneath the Sword and the Realm will be laid waste under their reign of terror."

Arin thought of Owen's world. 'Laid waste' was a good phrase, but it was not the Guardians who planned this fate for the Air Realm.

"So, you see why it is I had to lie to you, why I had to bring you

174

here," he continued. "If there was any chance that you might know something that could help us. Because there's not much time now. Only two days before the stars are in the most auspicious position for the expedition."

Arin didn't understand what he meant, but Raya responded instantly.

"You mean the attack on the Towers?"

Enlali nodded. "Don't tell mother – though I'm sure she will have heard from someone already. I'll be going, and there's a good chance I won't be coming back. I'm in the front lines this time." He sounded very matter of fact about it.

"But..." Arin wasn't quite sure how to phrase his next question. "Your mother, she said your brothers and sisters had... er..." he trailed off. It seemed hard to believe that Enlali as the last living child, would be sent into battle. Certainly in Bryah there was a tradition of always keeping at least one child safe at home if the others sailed off across the Reef searching for adventure – survival of the Pod-line.

But Enlali simply nodded. "Yes. They fought their battles and now it is my turn." He spoke more gently now. "We are on the side of right, the side of justice and truth. You will understand all this later when your minds have been washed, cleansed of whatever poison has been planted in them. You will think correctly." He smiled encouragingly. "Don't worry! It really won't hurt."

Arin tried his hardest to smile back through gritted teeth. It may not hurt, but he had absolutely no intention of having his mind washed! Now that they had seen the Vizier, and more importantly learnt about the Queen, there was only one possible course of action open to them: escape, and as soon as possible – certainly before their appointment with the Vizier that evening.

Arin assumed that Enlali was leading them back to Gemina's house, but whatever he had been planning, the Aevyan man changed his mind when he heard the sound of music starting up from somewhere beyond the maze of courtyards.

"This way!" He hurried along the mosaic path towards an archway of pale, honey-coloured stone. Despite everything, Arin felt a stab of excitement. The music was a fast, intoxicating melee of strings, pipes and drums, and he couldn't help but be drawn in by the insistent beat and the peculiar, discordant melodies. The path led out into the terraced gardens that they had crossed the previous day. The music was coming from the next level down and Enlali was so keen to get to its source that he seemed temporarily to have forgotten them as he strode on ahead. For a brief moment Arin considered running. He looked around the garden they were in. Beyond the beds of herbs that lined the path, stretched banks of shrubs and yet further out to both his left and right, he could see what looked like fruit trees. If they were able to reach those, could they find enough cover to hide from any pursuers until they found a way out?

But Enlali had noticed his hesitation. "Come on!" he called back. "You don't want to miss this!"

He was right. When Arin reached the gate at the top of the steps down to the next terrace, his eyes widened in wonder at the sight before him. In the centre of an immaculate swathe of green lawn, was what he took at first to be a huge swirling wheel of colour. He watched transfixed as the spokes of the wheel seemed to weave in and out of one another as the wheel spun, in a dizzying kaleidoscope of rainbow colours, whirling in perfect time to the rapid drumbeat. But then, just for a few moments, the music slowed and the wheel slowed with it. Suddenly he realized what it was he was looking at: people! The wheel was made up of dancers spinning round and round, trailing vivid, shimmering scarves in their wake. And then they were off again, faster and faster.

"They're people!" Finn exclaimed beside him. "Like that circle dance in Arktos!"

The 'Extraordinary Evocation'. It *was* similar, Arin realized. But whilst in Assyah it had been directed down into the Earth – 'waking the gnomes' as Urso had put it, here, even without any sensitivity to Air magic, he could see that the dancers were sending spirals of colour upwards towards the sky – the Air. He wondered if everyone was about to go into a trance as they had in the Earth Realm.

However, when he descended the steps to join the watching crowd around the edges of the lawn, he could see none of the same exhilaration in the faces. They looked like they were enjoying the spectacle, but no more than that. In Assyah everyone had been drawn into the dance, with the exception of himself, Raya and Finn. Here, there was a gulf between the audience and the dancers.

"What are they doing?" Raya asked Enlali, struggling to be heard above a crescendo of strings.

"Calling to the Sylphs," he replied, "for their aid in our battle." He sighed. "It's a dangerous thing to do. They can change sides simply because the wind changes direction. And even if they don't, they very quickly lose interest. But the Rainbow Guild will be doing the same thing, calling to the Sylphs for their support, so we have to present our counterargument. And ultimately they will come down on our side. The Queen is the Chosen One and no matter what lies the Guardians spin, the Sylphs will always know the truth, won't they?"

"You mean they, the Sylphs that is, might er... come here now?" Finn didn't sound very happy about the idea, but fortunately at that moment the volume of the music rose, and Enlali didn't catch his question.

"You enjoy yourselves." Enlali had to shout to make himself heard. "There'll be jousting and cloud hopping later this morning – and food," he added. "I have things to do but you should stay and enjoy the entertainment. I'll find you later, don't worry." And with that he was off, heading back up towards the Palace.

Arin couldn't quite believe their luck. He looked round, expecting Eurani or Gemina to appear, or at least to find someone with a sword hovering close by. But the crowd showed no interest in them. All attention was focused on the whirling dancers.

He turned to Raya and Finn who looked equally disbelieving. "It can't be this easy, can it?" he said.

"Well I'm not waiting around to find out!" Raya scanned the row of trees that hid the terrace below from view.

"Hang on." He put his hand on his sister's arm to stop her. "This could be a test. He might be hiding just beyond the gate up there," he nodded towards the higher level, "waiting to see if we try to run. I think we should just act as though we're watching the dancers, just until we're sure."

Raya wasn't very keen on the idea but had to admit that it did seem unlikely that Enlali would let them escape as easily as that. But after about ten minutes, when the dance showed no sign of stopping any time soon, Finn suggested that they might reconsider.

"I don't think it would look suspicious – even if we are being watched. Not now. I mean it's all very pretty," he glanced across at the wheel of dancers which had once again briefly slowed their pace," but he can't expect us to just stand here all day."

This time Arin agreed. "No. And at least we might find out whether someone is watching us." Though even as he spoke, he realized that this might not be true. What if their guard was invisible, like Professor Vishnami spying on Owen in his sleep? But they had little choice. They had to escape before the evening.

They tried to look as casual as possible as they edged away from the crowd. At least the pale yellow Paraldan tunics that Gemina had provided helped them to blend in a bit. Finn led the way, crossing the lawn towards a rose-draped archway and a path which wound away from the revelry of the dancers and, more importantly, appeared to head away from the direction of the Palace. A couple of minutes later they stood at the top the steps leading to the next terrace down.

"No one has followed us," Raya said, scanning the garden behind them with her keen eyes.

Arin decided against mentioning his 'Professor Vishnami' concern. It didn't change the fact that they had to try to escape.

It took them longer to reach the outer wall of the gardens going in this direction, than it had when they arrived. Enlali had led them along a path which had cut directly across the terraces, whereas they now seemed to be following the 'scenic route' on paths that wound circuitously down. They were however, at least going down and when finally Arin heard the cry of a peacock, he let out a sigh of relief. The Peacocks of Paralda! They were in the first garden that they had entered the previous day. He caught sight of a flash of white darting between the hedges off to his left. Strange... He didn't recall the peacocks moving very fast yesterday. But a few moments later it reappeared on the path ahead of them. And it was no peacock! Instead he found his way barred by a small white dog.

"A dog." Finn stated the obvious when he saw it. "That's what that is."

"Of course it's a dog!" Raya gave him a scathing look. "It's not a dragon, is it?"

"Hello." Raya took a few steps tentatively towards the dog and reached out her hand.

"Be careful!" Arin warned her. Dogs were creatures of the Moon after all, and not always what they appeared to be. But the little white dog didn't look dangerous. He wagged his tail as Raya approached, in wide, friendly sweeps. However, just as she got within reach of him, the dog turned and ran off back behind the hedges.

"I think he's a puppy." Raya gazed after him. "I wonder why he's out here on his own."

Ahead of them now, Arin noticed a slight coloured tinge to the light. He was right, this was the last of the terraces. A couple of minutes later they reached the gates in the outer wall and as Finn pushed them open, the rainbows that arced down from the crystal towers came into view. Arin glanced behind him, half expecting Enlali to emerge from behind a tree, but there was no one in sight. From above, he could still hear the frenzied music of the dance, the drum beat urging the dancers on ever faster. The grassy meadows beyond the wall appeared a haven of calm by contrast.

Enlali's horses were grazing contentedly beside the river, untroubled by the music. Or were they Enlali's horses? Arin glanced up towards the sun, as a thought struck him. "This isn't the gate we came in through, is it?"

"What do you mean?" Finn asked, puzzled. "It looks like it to me."

"But it can't be," he replied. "I'm sure we came in from the west. I remember because when we got here the sun was behind us, reflecting back off the towers. It was late afternoon, wasn't it? So the sun was going down in the west."

"Yes!" Raya chimed in. "It was. I was dazzled by it reflecting off all the white stone."

Finn was impressed. "I never noticed."

"It's sailing," Arin explained. "You always check your bearing – without even realizing you're doing it usually."

"This gate is facing north." Finn didn't want to be totally outdone.

"Yes. So that river isn't the same one we followed in. That one was flowing east-west. And those may not be Enlali's horses either."

Arin couldn't see 'his' horse amongst them, though that wasn't necessarily proof that he was right.

"So which way do we go?" Raya asked.

Arin frowned. He wasn't used to being asked to make decisions.

"Well, we know that the Towers were east of where we were, but from here..." he trailed off.

"I think we should just get as far away from here as we can, as quickly as we can." Finn glanced back at the crystal spires. "Once we're clear of here, then we can think about how to find those Towers and Owen."

It sounded as good an idea as any to Arin, but he still wasn't convinced that someone wasn't watching them, and as they set out across the meadow he felt less and less comfortable. There were small copses of trees close to the riverbank that provided some cover, but otherwise they were very exposed. Anyone looking down from the gate to the terraces would have been able to see the three figures making their way across the open field.

The light from the rainbow arcs was getting 'thicker', just as it had done coming the other way the day before, only this time it had a green hue to it. A nasty thought suddenly popped into Arin's mind, and a knot of fear twisted in his stomach, a knot which tightened as the greenness grew ever more solid. And then a few moments later his fear was confirmed.

Raya, who had been out in front stopped, picked up a small stone and threw it at the solid wall of green just in front of her. It dropped to the ground as if it had hit a wall of stone.

"Oh no!" She turned back to Arin and Finn. "I didn't think it would work this way. I mean, I can see why you want to stop enemies getting in, but..." she trailed off.

It was now clear why Enlali had been so unconcerned about them escaping. They stood staring helplessly at the green wall.

"Do you think there's a way round it?" Finn suggested with little hope in his voice.

Arin shook his head. "Why would there be?"

"I wish Owen was here," Finn said. "He would think of something."

But Owen wasn't there, and it seemed very unlikely that any form of Wood or Water magic was going to help them get through the wall.

Arin glanced back towards the clearer air in the direction of the Palace.

"Whoa!" He nearly jumped out of his skin. Sitting calmly only a few metres behind them was the small white dog, and standing smiling at his side, the boy who Raya had helped the night before, the 'Fool.' Arin was dumbfounded. Where had he come from? He was sure no one had been there a moment earlier.

"Have you been following us?" Finn asked accusingly.

But the boy just tilted his head to one side like the Butterfly children had done, and continued smiling.

"Hello!" Raya smiled back at him, ignoring Finn's glare of disapproval. "Is that your dog?"

The boy nodded, his smile getting even broader. He beckoned to the dog, and it jumped up straight into his arms. He held it out towards her.

"Hello, dog!" She moved across to scratch the dog's head. "He likes me!" She beamed as the dog gave her hand a big lick.

"Yes, but that's not going to help us get out of here, is it?" Finn frowned.

"We'll have to go back." Arin could think of only one possible solution. "Enlali used that bell to clear the wall, didn't he?"

"Yes, but I don't see how we can get hold of it," Finn interrupted. "Even if we can find Enlali he's hardly going to give it to us just like that. If we had longer, if we could get it while he was sleeping... but we don't."

"I know." He waited for Finn to finish before continuing. "But maybe his isn't the only bell. Enlali can't be the only person who comes in and out of..." He stopped suddenly mid-sentence, his mouth gaping in disbelief.

The Fool-boy had once again tilted his head bird-like to one side, and was still holding the dog under one arm, but now in his free hand, held out before him, was a small bell.

"Hey!" Raya gasped in amazement. "A bell! You've got a bell!"

"It might be just a normal bell," Finn began. But before he could say any more the boy gave it one shake, and a deep, resonant note rang out. Instantly the green wall began to fade and thin out, evaporating like a cloud burning away under the sun.

For a moment no one moved, but then Finn was off, racing across the grass ahead, running as fast as he could away from Paralda, the Vizier and the Baarash Queen. And now Arin ran too. Ahead of him he could see Finn getting further away. Raya too was outpacing him. A white streak darted past. The little dog! Only when he thought his lungs were about to burst, did he finally slow down. He glanced back over his shoulder. A heavy red haze hung in the air and the crystal spires looked reassuringly distant.

"Thank you," he said to the boy, once he had got enough breath back to speak. He felt ashamed of how unwelcoming he had been before. "Thank you," he repeated. "I hope... er... you're not going to get into trouble, if they find out you helped us..."

The boy shook his head and then with a grin spun into an impressive series of somersaults and cartwheels across the grass. Despite everything Arin found himself smiling.

"I can do that too!" Raya laughed and performed her own cartwheel.

"Children!" Finn sighed, trying to sound far too grown-up for such things, but there was something contagious about the boy's innocent enthusiasm.

"So where now?" Arin asked once everyone was back the right way up.

Silence met his question.

"Follow the river?" Raya suggested. At least that way they were close to water.

Finn agreed. "Yes. We need to find the way to the Towers, so we need to find someone to ask. People always live near rivers... unless..." He turned to the yellow-haired boy. "Do you know how to get to the Towers?" But the boy just looked blankly back at him.

Before long the red haze had cleared completely and when Arin looked back all he could see was the needles of crystal and the rainbow arcs. Thin wispy strands of cloud drifted high overhead, carried on a soft breeze, and for the first time since Owen's disappearance, he began to relax. The little white dog ran on ahead, stirring up clouds of iridescent butterflies from the meadow flowers.

"Almost as pretty as the butterflies in Dayah!" Finn commented.

For once Raya didn't respond with her usual reply that Bryah was even better. They walked on, following a track along the riverbank, which meandered through small copses and across gently undulating meadows until finally, when Arin looked back, he could no longer see the spires of Paralda. From far off he heard a long round note, like a horn. He wondered whether that was indeed what it was, or if it was an animal or bird that he hadn't come across before. There was a whale in Bryah that had a mating call a little like it. A few minutes later he heard it again, and this time it was definitely closer.

"What's that horn noise do you think?" Raya asked gazing back in the direction it came from.

"It sounds like a hunting horn," Finn replied. "Hunters use them in Dayah." He stopped as the horn sounded again. "They're coming in our direction. I wonder what they're hunting."

A horrible thought suddenly struck Arin. "What if it's us?"

"Us?" For a moment Raya was confused, then she realized what Arin was saying. "You mean they're coming after us?"

"But how would they know we're gone?" Finn didn't want to believe it. "Enlali said he'd find us this evening, didn't he?"

"Are you sure that's what he said?" Arin didn't recall Enlali having specified when he would be returning to find them.

Again the horn trumpeted a long, strident note. A wave of fear hit him. If the Paraldans were coming they would be on horses. He looked desperately around. There was nothing offering any form of cover except for a small copse in the distance.

"Those trees." Finn had the same idea as Arin. He didn't need to say any more.

Again they ran. Arin willed his legs to go faster as Finn, Raya and the Fool-boy all sped off ahead of him, but in vain. Behind him now, he could hear another sound – dogs, their barks high and excited. He focused on the ground ahead. He mustn't trip, he mustn't fall. Briefly he glanced up. The copse still looked a long way away – too far away. He heard shouts now joining the barking, very close on their trail. His breath came in ragged gasps as panic seized hold of him. He couldn't carry on much longer. Whether he collapsed first, or the dogs caught him, it didn't make any difference now. And then he tripped. He clawed at the ground, pushing himself up, only to find Raya, Finn and the Fool-boy in front of him, all stopped still. For a moment he couldn't understand what had happened, but then he saw it. Something that didn't make sense, something that had surely not been there before. Instead of the grassy meadow and distant copse, ahead of them was a precipitous cliff edge, jutting out into midair above a sea of clouds. His head spun and he scrambled back. Behind him the baying dogs and riders were nearly upon them. They were trapped. He looked up and saw the same awful realization on the faces of Raya and Finn.

The Fool-boy however, was smiling as always. He didn't even look out of breath after the run! He beamed round at all of them, then turned, and followed faithfully by his little dog, stepped straight out over the edge of the cliff and was gone.

Arin let out a cry of horror, but then suddenly a voice rang out in his head, a soft, musical boy's voice. "Leap!" Just the one word.

"Come on then!" Raya had heard the same voice. "Let's do it!" Without waiting for a reply she took a step back then ran, and with a shriek leapt out over the cliff.

Arin couldn't move. He was paralysed by shock. This couldn't be real.

"There they are!" A man's voice called out.

Finn grabbed Arin's arm and pulled him to his feet.

"Leap!" He repeated the single word, then together they ran. Arin heard himself scream, felt the air torn from his lungs as he fell. Then nothing.

Chapter 20

'The pure heart of the Cup Bearer recognizes the Truth'. Once the Exarp had seen those words he had hurried Tamus out of his chamber, leaving him in the care of one of the Mercury novices, a bright-eyed boy called Aeoli. He led Tamus down through the tower, talking so fast about what each room was for, that he had struggled to keep up. Laboratories, libraries, studies – there had been so many that it had all just begun to go in one ear and out of the other. Except for one, which for reasons he couldn't fathom, had struck him as vitally important: the laboratory for the Study of the Void, Aeoli had called it. He had gone on to talk at length about the nature of nothingness, about numbers less than zero and things which had just sounded like nonsense to Tamus. But the phrase '*The Void*' had stood out. Somewhere deep in those lost memories of his was something about the Void.

"What is the Void?" he asked when Aeoli paused for breath.

"The Void?" Aeoli looked surprised. "Is that something else you've forgotten?"

Tamus frowned. How was he meant to know if he had forgotten it? It was a ridiculous question, but then the whole situation was ridiculous really.

"I suppose so," he sighed.

"Well... it's... We don't really know what it is," Aeoli admitted. "There are parts of Yezirah, in the north, south and west, that aren't there anymore."

Tamus nodded slowly. There was definitely something familiar about this.

"On old maps you can see them and even quite recently people used to travel beyond the Plain in the west to a great forest and north to the Lands beyond the Mountains. But now there's nothing there."

"Nothing?" Tamus didn't see how there could be 'nothing.'

"Yes. It's like a black wall of nothingness. There are Inquirers who have been up quite close to it to try to find out what it is, but it's too dangerous to get too near. A whole team got swallowed up by it only last month." He paused as he opened the door to the refectory where breakfast was waiting. "It moves, you see," he continued once they were sitting down with plates of salad before them – an odd breakfast choice in Tamus' view.

"It's been moving forward for many years, eating into the land bit by bit, but the last year or so it's been moving much faster – exponentially!"

Tamus didn't know what that meant, but he got the gist. "So... eventually..."

"Yes," Aeoli nodded. "Eventually Yezirah will be gone. This is why we have to find the Sword. All the diviners see the same prophecy now. It's the Sword of Truth that can save Yezirah, and only the Sword. And the Singing Head at Paralda says it's close to being found and that the Towers is where the key lies."

So that was why the Exarp had been so excited about his book! *The pure heart of the Cup Bearer recognizes the Truth.'* That was the phrase that had appeared before all the mysterious letters and numbers had filled the page. And the Mercury Tower Guardian thought that the key to finding the Sword of Truth lay in his book!

Aeoli led him into a large, airy room where other novices were seated at a long table, all so engrossed in discussion that no one paid any heed to their arrival.

"But that's the essence of imperfection," a small, beaky nosed girl was saying adamantly. "It's all down to the numbers being unbalanced. The vibrations are all wrong."

Tamus sighed inwardly. He remembered this about the Mercury Tower now. Everyone was frighteningly clever – too clever. He found his attention drifting to the peeling and faded paintwork on the walls. Not surprising really, given how impractical Aevyans were as a whole, and the Mercury novices in particular. He wondered how they had ever built the Towers in the first place. Air magic was all well and good for creating the illusion, but surely some good solid

Earth magic had been woven into the original structure. And then he realized what must have happened. The Void! Aeoli had spoken of the great Forest beyond the Plain to the west. That was Dayah! He felt a great wave of relief as the memories came back. The Earth magic would have been wrought by Boryads from Assyah to the north. And if the Void had now cut off all the Realms from one another, that would explain the state of the Towers.

His thoughts were cut short as the door swung open and an older woman, clad in yellow like the Exarp, entered the room. "Ah! The boy with no memory!" She peered curiously at him. "The Exarp seems most interested in you."

Tamus shifted uncomfortably as she scrutinized him.

"I gather you are to visit the Saturn Tower tomorrow morning."

His heart dropped like a stone. "I didn't know that."

The woman looked at him with a degree of sympathy. "Well, you do want to recover your memory, I assume. We are working on a potion here in the Mercury Tower, but it may take some time. I gather it is no ordinary affliction." She paused, thoughtfully. "The Exarp is insistent that you must regain your memory as swiftly as possible, and since Krona is so adept at removing blocks, he feels we may have to yield to her in this case."

"That doesn't sound good," Aeoli whispered to him as they took their seats. "Saturn Tower! You wouldn't catch me going there."

The lesson for the novices that day was as incomprehensible to him as he had expected. They were working on the creation of something that moved faster than thought, something necessary for combat in the Dream-Lands. "Not that we're allowed to go anywhere near dreamwalking yet," Aeoli muttered under his breath. "I wish sometimes we could actually *do* something not just learn about it."

But Tamus was only half listening. He couldn't get the thought of the Saturn Tower out of his head. He remembered it well from his previous visit – the Tower of Ghosts it had been nicknamed, a place where the novices learnt death magic, hexes and binding rites. He frowned as another memory popped into his head; a memory linked to a binding rite. Eggo. The word floated into his consciousness, but it made no sense to him. The black tower was however also the place that specialized in the removal of blocks. "It is all the same thing," his teacher had told him. "The one is simply a reflection of the other on a different plane. You must learn the Lesser Art before you can progress to the Greater." Tamus had been quite happy not to progress. He had no interest in death magic or working with 'The Bridges,' as the Adepts of the Greater Art were called. He remembered his joy at leaving the Saturn Tower, and his determination not to go back.

"My next journey will be to Dayah," he had sworn when he stepped back through the Gateway. But there his memory stopped. When had that been? Had he been back to Dayah? It was as though chunks of his memory were intact, but they were floating around in midair, unattached to anything else. And were they really his memories anyway? If the Exarp was right, all these memories must have been placed in his head, and none of it had really happened to him at all. It was all so confusing.

His upcoming visit to the Saturn Tower was the subject of much discussion over dinner.

"If I had to choose another tower, it would be the Sun Tower," a girl sitting opposite him commented. "I heard that they were working on cloud ladders and that one of them would be allowed to attend the harvesting of the cloud nectar."

"Yes! Definitely NOT the Saturn Tower!" another novice exclaimed, throwing him a sympathetic look. "I was late back from gathering night herbs a few weeks ago and I nearly bumped into Krona herself!" There was a unison gasp of horror. "I ran so fast I think I'd have beaten the wind in a race that night."

Tamus wanted to ask what was so scary about Krona but bit his tongue. He suspected he wouldn't like the answer. When he had stayed in the tower before, had he met the Guardian? He didn't remember her, but that was no guarantee of anything. He tried to ignore the speculation as to what it would feel like having a block removed by Krona – very unpleasant seemed to be the general opinion.

"You're unlucky," Aeoli commiserated with him. "The Exarp would normally be able to find a potion for sure, but I suppose he hasn't got time because of this problem with the Ill-Wind."

"What problem?" This phrase rang a bell.

"Oh, some idiot let an Ill-Wind out of one of the Wind Bags, up at the Caverns of the Winds. The Wind Masters need a new net to catch it in. It's mutated into a funny shape and if they don't catch it quickly there'll be a plague down on the Plain." He sounded quite cheerful at the prospect. "They always come to us, to the Mercury Tower. If it wasn't for us, Yezirah would be crawling with Germ Spirits!"

Tamus barely managed to touch his food. He had been fearful enough of the Saturn Tower before, but by the time the Mercury novices had all told him their opinions of it and the awful tales they had heard about Krona, he couldn't think of anywhere he would less like to visit, let alone be subjected to Krona's mind block removal magic! Anyway, he reasoned to himself, bits of his memory had come back. Perhaps if he returned to see the Exarp in a few days' time, he might have had a chance to make that potion Aeoli had spoken of. However, he knew that Aeoli was wrong about the Ill-Wind being the reason that the Exarp was sending him to the Saturn Tower. The Mercury Guardian was intent on him regaining his memory as quickly as possible, whatever it took, so that he could cast light upon the mysterious book. He frowned with concentration as he tried desperately to recall something – anything – about it. Who had given it to him? When? Where?

He gazed up through the leafy canopy watching a tiny silver ball hovering like a hummingbird above the branches. The sun was strong even in the shade of the oak tree, and the scent of honeysuckle hung heavily in the air. He rolled over on the wooden platform of his tree house so that he could see the garden below. The picnic table was half laid for lunch. He could see a big, covered jug that he knew would contain one of Nana's cordials, and felt suddenly very thirsty. From beyond the lavender bushes he caught sight of a movement, and a moment later Nana emerged with a laden basket of freshly picked fruit and vegetables.

"Hello Nana!" A deep voice boomed out from the direction of the Mill. Captain Sigursson!

"Thought Owen might like to come out sailing this afternoon," the big man called out. "I'm taking the boat out round Berry Head. There's a pod of dolphins out there."

'CLONG.'

Tamus woke with a start.

'CLONG.'

He stared in total incomprehension at his surroundings. He was in one of four bunk beds in a large, circular room. From the bed next to him a boy groaned.

"It can't be time to get up already."

'CLONG.' It was a bell, he realized – a bell summoning them to breakfast. A vague memory surfaced of a breakfast bell ringing somewhere else... or was he thinking of an alarm clock? Conflicting memories spun round in his head as he struggled to make sense of anything.

"Hey, Tamus!" A head peered down from the bunk above him, and then a pair of legs swung down over the side. "We get up now." A friendly-faced boy jumped down to the ground beside his bed. "You don't want to be late! There'll be no food left."

The Towers! That's where he was. The events of the previous day came flooding back to him. But as he pulled on his Mercury Tower tunic, he couldn't get the strange dream out of his head. Nana, Captain Sigursson, Owen... There was something familiar about them, something that niggled at the edge of his memory, just out of reach.

A faint spark of hope lit up inside him as he made his way up the staircase of the Mercury Tower. Maybe the Exarp had found a potion that would work. Maybe he had solved the riddle in the book, and there was time to wait whilst he worked on a cure for him.

But his hopes were swiftly dashed when he reached the Exarp's study. "Come in!" The words rang out before he had a chance to knock.

"I don't suppose you have remembered any more since yesterday." The man stroked his beard as he spoke.

He started to shake his head, then stopped. "Not about the book," he admitted, glancing across at the Exarp's desk where it lay open, "but my memory is coming back – bits of it, about back home and the Temple and everything."

"No, no!" The Exarp interrupted him impatiently. "That is not your memory. What you think you are remembering is a projection – an image or series of images placed there by someone." He looked thoughtfully at Tamus. "What is so intriguing is the fact that this is almost certainly not the work of the Palace. Their mind-washing arts are far too crude to have wrought a block like this." He picked up the little book from his desk. "There is also magic in this book of a nature entirely unfamiliar to me, magic that is not Air magic, I suspect. It is for this reason that I have also concluded that none of my fellow Guardians is involved, that it is not a decoy to throw me off the scent of the Sword."

"But why would they want to throw you off the scent? I thought you were on the same side." Tamus was confused. Surely if what Aeoli had told him was correct, they wanted the Sword in order to save Yezirah from the Void.

"Yes, yes, of course we are!" the Exarp replied hastily. "There is just... er... healthy competition between the towers. It is for this reason that I shall be keeping this book very securely guarded here in my tower. Clearly Krona will learn of its existence once the memory block is removed. This cannot be avoided." He frowned. "I shall be summoning all the Guardians here this evening to present the book and my solution to the riddle, or for us to combine our minds in the unlikely event that even after the de-blocking I have not reached a conclusion. The book will, however, remain under my guardianship." He looked very sternly at Tamus. "Keep this in mind. Krona may well attempt to get hold of it herself once she hears of it, but it is in the Mercury Tower that it rightfully belongs and in the Mercury Tower it shall stay."

Tamus nodded mutely. There seemed little point in protesting that the book was actually his. He obviously wasn't to have any say in what happened to it.

"The block removal... it... it's not dangerous, is it?" he asked tentatively.

"Dangerous?" The Exarp was surprised by the question. "In what sense?"

"Well... Could it go wrong?"

The Exarp frowned. "I suppose, in theory, of course it could go wrong. One never knows exactly what one is dealing with with mind blocks. In the case of a simple straight-line block, there is rarely any damage caused. In this case, it is more complex. As far as I can see the block appears to be in the form of interlinked hexagons, a structure that I have never seen before."

"And if it does go wrong?" He didn't like the sound of this.

The Exarp shook his head. "I have no idea. Theoretically it could result in the mind collapsing in on itself or..." He stopped. "There is no point in idle speculation. If it does go wrong, we just have to find the solution to the riddle by another means. Rest assured that the combined minds of the Rainbow Guild will meet this challenge and the Sword will be found!"

And me? Tamus thought miserably. What about me? It was clear that his welfare was irrelevant in all of this.

He followed the Exarp back down the spiral stairway of the Mercury Tower with a heavy sense of impending doom. Any ideas that he had had in the beginning that this was some sort of test, were long gone. It had been a mistake to come here. When he had awoken beside the lake he should have turned away from the Towers and tried instead to find the Gateway back to his own world, the normal safe world where he had friends like Finn, Arin and Raya. The names popped into his head, but only the names, no faces, nothing else about them.

He barely noticed his surroundings as they followed the path to the dark, ominous looking Tower. The temperature seemed to have dropped by several degrees and he shivered as an unseasonal gust of cold air whipped past. The Exarp raised his hand and knocked on the dark wood door – the door of death, Tamus thought grimly.

Even the Mercury Guardian looked a little apprehensive, as slowly the door swung open to reveal a black-robed figure, whose face was hidden by a dark hood. No words were spoken, but none were needed for him to know who this was. The Exarp's tense and formal bow was enough to make it clear that this was Krona herself. He followed the two Guardians silently across the dimly lit hall into another room illuminated by black candles, in the centre of which hung a pendulum made of a dull grey metal that looked like lead. Krona stopped and turning to face him, lowered her hood to reveal skin of alabaster white, surprisingly unlined, but so paper thin that it was almost transparent – like looking at a skull, he thought with an involuntary shudder. Her hair was as colourless as her skin, her lips a dark, bloodless thin line, and if it hadn't been for the gleam in her pale-yellow eyes, he would have thought he was looking at a corpse.

The pendulum swung slowly, tracing an arc through the air. Tock.

Tock. Tock. Still no one spoke. A memory jumped into his head of another old woman, a crone in tattered rags, sitting on a throne of white crystal in an icy cold, grey room.

"Er-hm." Tamus jumped as the Exarp cleared his throat. "I require a few words with you in private My Lady, before the de-blocking commences."

Krona gave a curt nod but remained silent as she turned away.

"Wait here," the Exarp instructed him, before following Krona through a doorway on the far side of the room.

He heaved a sigh of relief once the door had shut behind them. He had felt as though those yellow eyes were cutting straight into the deepest part of him, seeing secret, hidden things that he had no awareness of, and though he knew his stay of execution was only a brief one, he was grateful for it. For the first time, he noticed a heavy, sweet smell in the air, like overripe, rotting fruit and then a moment later he caught a glimpse of a grey, filmy shadow darting silently across the hall beyond. The memory of the old lady on the crystal throne came back to him again, followed by one of him running, gripped by fear, across a room of glittering black stones, pursued by dark silhouettes that slithered across the walls. And suddenly he knew that he must not let Krona get inside his head to see these memories, and in the same moment he realized what he had to do, though it solved nothing.

Chapter 21

Arin opened his eyes. A long white nose was peering down at him, a nose that belonged to a dog... the dog who had run off the cliff! Slowly he sat up, his mind struggling to get a grip on what had happened.

"Are we dead?" he heard Raya ask from behind him.

"I'm not dead," Finn replied. "Hey! Look! An Eddradi!"

Arin turned round just in time to catch a glimpse of a little silver ball darting behind the trunk of an apple tree.

Tentatively he tried out his arms and legs. Everything seemed to be working, and better still he didn't appear to have sustained even a bruise in his plunge from the cliff. But then as he looked around, he could see no sign of a cliff anyway. Instead he was sitting in the middle of an orchard, an orchard that hummed with the sound of bees busy gathering nectar in the warm sunlight. The scent of roses and honeysuckle drifted lazily through the fruit trees and as he took in a deep breath, he realized that there was something different about the air from everywhere else he had been in Yezirah – softer, was the only word he could find to describe it. He wondered if they had fallen through a wormhole as they had done in the cave of the Sath in Bryah and ended up in Dayah. The orchard was certainly very like Finn's descriptions of his home. But the Sylvan boy shook his head at the suggestion.

"No. Fruit trees do grow together back home. We have fruit herds to make sure they stay close and to stop things like Eddleshi stealing them." He stopped as he saw Arin and Raya's looks of incomprehension. "They don't grow like this though, without other trees. Dayah is all forest. This is more like the orchard at Owen's house – Nana's orchard," he added.

It hadn't looked much like this place the last time they had seen it, Arin thought sadly, remembering the chaotic tangle of upturned trees and fallen branches which had greeted them on their return from Assyah.

A wood pigeon cooed softly from the branches of the tree nearest him. He looked up through the dappled sunlight dancing in the leaves, to see two birds side by side on the branch, their feathers shimmering with the rose-grey iridescence of pearls.

"This place reminds me of somewhere," Raya said, "somewhere back home."

Arin nodded. He would have been hard-pressed to explain what the connection was between the orchard and the Water Realm, but for the first time since arriving in Yezirah, he felt safe, as though he were indeed at home in Eridu.

Finn nodded in agreement. "Yes. It feels like Dayah is just behind me... sort of."

That was exactly it! Arin had the distinct impression that if he turned round right now he would find a sparkling turquoise sea spread out before him, with sea horses galloping through the foamy surf. He couldn't resist turning to look, but instead of the ocean, standing just a few feet away smiling happily at them, was the Fool-boy from Paralda. He could have sworn he hadn't been there a moment earlier.

"What happened?" he began, but the boy had already launched into a series of cartwheels and somersaults, and was tumbling his way heedlessly across the orchard away from them.

"Come on!" Raya said. "He wants us to go with him."

Arin wasn't about to argue with her. Raya had been right from the outset about the boy who had just saved them, if not from death, from the mind-washing – which might well have been worse!

Everywhere he looked the air was alive with bees – bees that seemed to be heading in the same direction as them, following the Fool-boy through the orchard, between trees that he knew bore fruit, but couldn't put names to. Finn would know what they were. But before he had a chance to ask him, another sound joined the humming of the bees – the sound of a voice singing a song which sounded vaguely familiar to him. He hurried after the fair-haired boy, who had just vaulted a low honey-coloured wall that separated the orchard from a flower garden. Not that it had been necessary to leap over the wall;

195

there was a perfectly good gateway standing wide open just a few metres away, through which the little white dog now ran.

Once again, he had no idea what the plants were, but the colours were so vivid, the scents so strong, that he felt quite dizzy. It was like looking down into the corals of the Reef, but undiluted by water, and unlike the gardens of Paralda, so carefully and neatly laid out, this garden seemed untouched by human hand. There was a vibrant, wild, uncontrolled exuberance about it that made him want to run and jump like the Fool-boy ahead of him.

The singing was getting gradually louder as they followed a narrow, grassy track through the sea of flowers. He craned his neck to try to catch sight of the singer, but in vain. She was somewhere to his left but hidden from sight by clouds of towering violet-hued plants with bell-shaped petals and enormous golden flowers that looked like little suns. That was it! He realized suddenly why it was that the singing sounded familiar. It was like the songs of the Moon Singers, only in a bright, clear key. The sort of song a Moon Singer would sing if he had instead been a Sunsinger – not that there was such a thing of course.

The path continued on, winding in slowly tightening coils, ever closer to the source of the song. A cloud of butterflies wafted up from the flowers as the path turned in sharply. For a moment he could see nothing but a kaleidoscopic whirl of colours, as velvety wings fluttered lightly across his face, but as they parted, clearing like evaporating mist before him, he saw the singer for the first time. Standing beside a stone-edged pool was a woman with long honey-coloured hair, honey-coloured skin, amber eyes, and clad in a long filmy robe of deepest-tawny gold. She stopped singing, and for a moment all the other sounds of the garden also ceased, the birdsong stilled, the hum of the bees muted in a deep silence. Then her face broke into a smile.

"Welcome to the Garden of the Seed!" She spoke in a soft, mellifluous voice and instantly the spell was broken, all sound returned and the life of the garden recommenced.

The Fool-boy ran forward and kneeling beside the pool cupped his hands and drank deeply, heedless of the hundreds of bees that were doing the same, dipping into the water for the briefest of drinks before buzzing swiftly off towards the flowers.

"I am Mellonia." She beckoned to the three children. "Come, drink your fill."

Finn was the first to move, showing none of his usual suspicion about 'enchantresses.' He stepped towards the edge of the pond, then hesitated, warily eyeing the bees that skimmed the surface. Mellonia laughed, a light silvery laugh that was somehow not what Arin had expected, and picked up two cups that he hadn't noticed before, one silver and one gold. Then without dipping it into the pool, she poured a clear liquid from the silver cup into the gold. Arin blinked in surprise. The golden cup was not below the silver, but across at a diagonal angle. The 'water' should have poured straight on to the ground, but instead it ran in an impossible slanting stream through the air into the golden receptacle.

"Here." She held out the cup to Finn. The Sylvan boy looked surprised, but accepted the cup without question, lifted it to his lips and drank.

"Mmm! It tastes like honey!" he exclaimed with delight as he drained the last drop.

Mellonia nodded. "Good!" She looked pleased. "And for you too." She beckoned to Raya and Arin.

Arin watched as once again the golden cup was filled and Raya drank with obvious relish. Then finally it was his turn. The silver cup seemed to contain an endless supply of the clear liquid and he was reminded of Moshi and his Bowl of Plenty. He took the golden cup and raised it to his lips. The liquid inside gleamed like gold in the sunlight, no longer the clear watery substance that it had been when it poured from the silver cup. Finn was right! It did taste like honey. But it seemed to him now as though the honey he had tasted before was a pale, dilute imitation of this, even the Moon-harvested honey from the Arivala Isles that he and Raya had once sneaked a taste of when they were young, honey that he was sure their father had stolen. He drained the cup and handed it back to Mellonia.

"Thank you."

The Fool-boy meanwhile had finished drinking from the pool. He jumped to his feet, ran across to the flowers, picked a single white rose and presented it to Mellonia with a beam of delight. Then with one shy glance towards Raya, he turned and ran off back down the path they had come along, his little dog hot on his heels.

"He is gone now," Mellonia said as she saw Raya gaze after him. "He comes and goes. If he wants to be with you, he will be."

Arin was sure he had heard exactly that phrase somewhere before. "You shall stay with me tonight. You are the guests of the bees here in this, their garden. I have food, good food waiting for you and a safe bed for the night, where you may sleep the sleep of the seed dormant in the earth."

Good food! He suddenly realized how hungry he was.

They followed Mellonia back along the spiral path to the garden wall, but this time instead of opening on to an orchard, the gateway led out into a wild-flower meadow.

"It's just like Dayah!" Finn exclaimed approvingly. "The paths move back home as well. That's how it should be." But his words were almost drowned out by the crescendo of humming coming from across the meadow.

"The hives," Mellonia called back to them.

So that was what hives looked like. Arin was surprised by the dome-shaped structures. They looked from this distance as though they were simply made of a rich, golden-brown earth. He had expected something more like the fabulous hornets' nests they had encountered with Enlali.

The hives were set in a wide circle surrounding a single tall grey stone, a stone which reminded Arin of the Guardian Stone in the Temple of the Navel.

Mellonia stopped to wait for them. "You have never seen hives before?" she asked, noticing his expression.

"I have," Finn broke in quickly. "But not quite like that. The stone... it looks like another stone I saw once." Arin was obviously not alone in thinking it looked familiar.

"Ah," Mellonia smiled. "Yes. That is the Great Axle Stone. It connects the Worlds and transmits the life-giving breath of Yezirah through the web lines."

"Like in the Temple of the Navel in Assyah!" Raya exclaimed.

"You are in the Garden of the Seed here," Mellonia replied. She paused as though about to say something more, but then turned away and set off again across the meadow.

Mellonia's house looked to all intents and purposes like a large version of the beehives – perfectly round, with a domed roof and walls of hexagonal stone of the same golden hue as the earth that coated the hives. The only major difference as far as Arin could see, was the presence of windows and a door. The impression was, if anything, reinforced once they got inside. The walls gleamed with a golden warmth and the scent of honey mixed with apple-wood smoke infused the air.

Finn was delighted by the house, nodding with approval at the flowers hanging drying from the beams and the large, heavily laden baskets of fruit standing to one side of the central table.

"This is how a house should be!" He echoed his earlier comment about the moving paths.

Arin wasn't about to contradict him. Although it didn't really feel like a proper house, being fixed firmly to the ground, the rounded windows reminded him of the portholes of their own home in Eridu and when Mellonia brought out a big tub of salt and set it in the middle of the table, a wave of happiness washed over him.

Mellonia had been right. The food was good! There was freshly caught fish with sletti, mossground cakes and a pie that Finn recognized as elder root, orumber and squout, all washed down with a delicious honey drink not unlike the one Mellonia had offered them earlier in the golden cup. A perfect meal. Evening seemed to have fallen very fast. He had lost all track of time since they had fled Paralda. It certainly didn't feel as though the whole afternoon could have sped by, but as Mellonia led them to the bedroom he was struggling to stay awake. He barely registered the odd hexagon-shaped beds linked one into the next as though in a honeycomb. All he really noticed was the soft looking pillow and warm downy cover waiting for him.

Tamus fell to the ground, finally running out of breath. The bee hadn't made it easy for him! He wasn't sure what it was that had made him follow her, but when he had made the decision to run, to flee from the Towers, the appearance of the bee had felt reassuring. It had been one of the first strong memories to come back to him after all, talking to the bees in Grandma's orchard. She had told him the bees were his friends, that he could always trust the bees with any problem. He tried to remember what she had looked like as he got his breath back, and a brief image of a woman with long, black hair and dark eyes, flashed into his mind. But then another memory rose to the surface, one of a tiny old lady with a coppery face, like an old walnut, and a shock of white hair. Nana! The name came to him. He frowned. There was nothing unusual about having two grandmothers, but... 'Nana' – he repeated the name out loud. There was something important he ought to remember about Nana, something seriously important.

He got to his feet. Maybe walking would help jog his memory. He wasn't sure how far he had run, how much distance he had put between himself and Krona, but when he turned to look behind him, there was no sign of the Towers. The bee had led him across meadows and through woodland away from the lake that he had come around the previous day and he had no idea where he was. Not that it would have made much difference if he did. His 'plan' had only gone as far as running. What he did next hadn't come into it. The narrow, rutted track that he was on led down over gently sloping fields into a valley. It looked well-trodden, and for a moment he wondered whether he would be wiser to cut across country into the cover of the woods that he could see in the distance. But he wasn't really in danger, was he? The Rainbow Guild didn't leave their towers. The surrounding gardens and land provided more than sufficient food and no self-respecting Adept would abase him or herself by mingling with 'common' Aevyans outside their gates, except in an extreme emergency; even then he suspected it would be the novices who were sent out. Surely his flight wouldn't count as an emergency! Even so, he began to walk a little faster.

He had been following the path along the floor of the valley for about half an hour, accompanied by a gently murmuring little stream, when he became aware of the hum of bees once again. He smiled. It felt like a good sign. He began to hum too, a tune that floated up from somewhere in his foggy memory. The sweet scent of roses and honeysuckle drifted through the air, carried on a light, warm breeze. It all felt so very different from the Towers, he thought, almost like Dayah... He ducked, just in time to avoid a bee flying directly across in front of his face. The humming was louder now and seemed to be coming from just beyond the next bend in the meandering valley, the direction in which the bee was flying.

As he walked on the scent of flowers grew stronger. A garden out here seemed unlikely, but a moment later he found himself standing in front of a wall of honey coloured stone, beyond which lay an orchard. He stopped, uncertain what to do. He could see a wooden gate just a few metres further on, a gate which stood invitingly open. Could he risk going in? What if the orchard was connected to the Towers? The wall did look remarkably similar to the one that encircled the apothecary gardens. But then he caught a glimpse of something out of the corner of his eye: a tiny silver ball darting between the branches of an apple tree. An Eddradi! His mind was made up and with a sense of enormous relief, he headed for the gate.

He knew he was right the moment he set foot in the orchard. A wave of happiness washed over him and for the first time since he had woken beside the lake, the continual background panic that had been gnawing at him disappeared. He felt safe, as though he had come home. It would be all right now he thought. His memory would come back, and everything would return to normal. He smiled to himself as he walked through the orchard, following the path of the bees. Nana had been right. You could always trust the bees with any problem.

"Owen!"

Tamus nearly jumped out of his skin as a voice rang out from across the orchard.

"Owen!" A boy with long dark hair was running towards him, followed by two more children, a boy and girl with blond hair.

He stopped in his tracks, confused. He had no idea who they were.

"Owen! How did you get here?" The first boy spoke. They all seemed delighted to see him.

"No, no," he shook his head, rather unnerved by their enthusiasm. "Sorry, you've made a mistake. I'm not who you think I am.

Chapter 22

There was a long silence as the three strangers stared at him in disbelief. Then finally the girl spoke.

"Do you really not recognize us?"

Tamus shook his head. "No." But as he spoke, he realised how meaningless his denial was. His memory was still so befuddled that it was possible he knew them – except for one thing: surely if they really knew him, they would have known his name. But the name they had used did ring a bell.

"What did you call me?" he asked slowly.

"Owen!" the girl exclaimed. "It's your name."

Tamus frowned. He had heard the name before, but it seemed to him that it had been in a dream.

"No. It's not," he began, but the first boy interrupted before he could say any more.

"Well, what is your name then?"

He hesitated. Would it be better to lie?

"Tamus," he said finally. A false name wasn't going to save him if the Guardians did decide to hunt him down.

The reaction of the three children was instant.

"Tamus?!" the girl cried out. "No, Owen, it *is* you. Tamus is dead. He's just in your head, not real, not you."

"It's true." The blond boy spoke for the first time. "Look, do you have a pouch hanging round your neck?"

"Ye... es," he replied warily.

"Right. Well inside it is a key."

Tamus was dumbfounded. "How do you know...?" he began.

"A key with stripes of red, blue, green, yellow and violet," the boy continued. "I'm right, aren't I?" he added when Tamus didn't reply.

Tamus pulled out his pouch from under his tunic and wordlessly drew out the key. Strangely it felt warm, and the violet stripe was gleaming with a peculiar glow that he hadn't noticed before.

"See! You *are* Owen," the girl said. "I think maybe you're under a spell – an enchantment or something."

"Owen." Tamus repeated the name slowly.

"Do you have a book with you?" the blond boy asked, his voice suddenly tense.

"Yes... no..." He sighed. This was all too confusing. "Please... can you just tell me about Owen and maybe then it might help me remember."

However, as he followed the three children through the orchard into a flower garden, it became clear that it wouldn't be so simple. His companions introduced themselves with the vaguely familiar names of Finn, Arin and Raya, but try as he might he could get no further than a sense that he had heard the names somewhere before.

They sat down on a bench beneath an arch of honeysuckle.

"It helps the memory," Finn said, looking at the trailing tendrils and creamy white flowers. "This too." He handed him a sprig of rosemary that he had picked on the way. Then taking it in turns, Finn, Arin and Raya told him about a house called the Old Mill, about a world that meant nothing to him. Only the mention of the name Nana stirred a memory. But then he wasn't sure if he was mixing her up with the Nana of the bees who he had recalled earlier. It all seemed hopeless until Arin spoke of the Sath.

"Oh!" he broke in. "I remember the Sath! And the Azoth, in the Temple back home, with the Wardens."

"No." Arin shook his head. "That's Tamus' memory, not yours."

It was no good. Whatever they tried, he just came up against an impenetrable wall in his memory. It wasn't like something he had forgotten, something that had left a ghostly imprint behind it so that he was aware that it had once been there. The Owen stories that he was hearing seemed so far removed from him that if it weren't for the key, he would have found it almost impossible to believe, despite knowing his memory was affected.

One other thing however, convinced him that his companions were telling the truth – a dream. It came back to him as Finn spoke of a treehouse. The dream from which he had woken in the Towers, the dream in which he had heard the name Owen.

"Hello! You must be Owen."

He jumped as a voice spoke from behind the bench, a warm, melodious voice.

"Mellonia!" Finn was on his feet, smiling broadly.

He turned to see a woman with skin and hair the colour of honey. At first, he thought she was only a few years older than him, but as she drew closer and he looked into her deep amber eyes, he saw something very ancient gazing out at him. An Enchantress? She reminded him of the High Priestess of the Earth Element back home. Strange, since this was the Air Realm.

"This *is* Owen," Raya said. "Only he doesn't know he's Owen!"

Mellonia reached down and took his hand. "I see."

"You do?" He was taken aback. It certainly wasn't the reaction he had expected.

Mellonia nodded. "Yes." She smiled warmly. "You would like your memory back now."

It was said as a statement rather than a question and he nodded, temporarily speechless.

"Come with me!" Mellonia kept hold of his hand as if he was a small child.

Obediently he got to his feet and walked with her along the path back through the flower garden. Despite his 'Enchantress' thought, there was something so reassuring about the hand holding his own, that he felt nothing but trust. He was aware of the bees around him, humming contentedly, a constant, steady drone. He was aware too of the sweet scent of honeysuckle and roses and the warmth of the sun on his face, but beyond that everything seemed a bit blurry, as though the world beyond had drifted off somewhere else far away, irrelevant to him now.

The next thing he was clearly aware of was sitting down on a wooden chair with carved arms, inside a room that glowed with a warm golden light. He could smell honey, and a deep resinous odour mingling with beeswax. Mellonia handed him a cup and without hesitation he lifted it to his lips and drank. Mead... no, something more like mead and smah mixed together with what he could only describe as an 'orchardy' taste. He drained the cup and leant back in the chair. The honey-coloured liquid slid down his throat slowly, warming him from the inside – like one of Nana's cordials. The thought floated into his head, meaningless without any attached memories, but he now felt too relaxed to worry.

"Close your eyes." Mellonia spoke softly, and with a smile of contentment he did as he was told. Then suddenly he felt a sharp stabbing pain in the middle of his forehead, and everything faded away.

The boy opened his eyes slowly. Around him all was dark. He waited, calmly, unafraid. This wasn't the darkness of a nightmare. It was a warm, safe darkness. He could hear a deep, low humming, a humming that seemed to begin inside his head and then spread out in ripples into the darkness beyond. Then gradually he became aware of light. Very slowly, as the humming spiralled down through him, the darkness took on a deep amber glow. He couldn't move, but it didn't feel to him at that moment as though he had a body to move anyway. Later, when he tried to explain to his friends what had happened, he skipped over this bit. There weren't words in his vocabulary to describe the sensation. The closest he could come was that the golden, amber light that rippled with rhythmic waves of humming, was now inside him, and instead of looking out through his eyes at it, he was looking in.

And then in an instant, in a flash of utter clarity, his memory came rushing back. His mother, Olafssey, his father's voice, Devon, Nana, the key, the book, his friends, the Sath, and the bad stuff too: the Fire Lord, Sir Dennis, the earthquake-stricken Mill. He was Owen again – Owen Shepherd! Only something had changed… He waited a moment longer, aware now that he was seated in a chair, aware of Mellonia softly humming a tune close by. But he wasn't quite ready to face the world again. Because whilst Owen might be back, Tamus hadn't gone.

Tentatively he reached for one of Tamus' memories – an innocuous one: playing in the boat with Dar. And it was there, clear as crystal, no longer the isolated snatch of a dream-like recollection that it had been before. Magic? He concentrated on the Tamus memory again, choosing a hard one: Air magic. It came to him easily – the memory of how to levitate an object. He focused back on to Owen and the Tamus 'door' in his head shut. But though the door was shut, he now had the key, and he was not at all sure he liked this. There were things behind that door that he knew he didn't want to see.

He opened his eyes.

"I'm back. I'm Owen again!" He decided not to mention the new Tamus development.

"Welcome back Owen!"

All other problems were forgotten for the moment as his friends came over to re-greet him. Raya gave him a big hug.

"I'm so glad that Tamus has gone!"

He wriggled away, embarrassed. It was easier when Raya was being horrible to him.

"Do you think Tamus would go that funny red colour?" Finn asked with a grin.

"Have another drink." Mellonia held the cup out to him once more.

He hesitated. "But I'm better now."

"Yes." Mellonia nodded. "It's just to balance you. That's all. Otherwise you'll find yourself a little giddy for a few days."

A few days! He didn't like the sound of that. He gulped down the honey liquid. It tasted slightly different this time, as though one of the sharper, spicier tones had been replaced with something a bit like sherbet. He set the cup down feeling no different from before.

"Good." Mellonia smiled. "Now, I must be getting on. The bees are waiting. I'll see you all a bit later with some new honey."

The moment the door closed behind her, the room erupted with noise, everyone speaking at once.

"Stop!" Owen took control. "Look, why don't you go first as there's three of you?" It wasn't the most logical of reasons, but his friends accepted it.

Raya as usual volunteered for the role of storyteller, and he listened without interruption until she got to the treachery of Enlali.

"But why save our lives if he thought we were his enemies?"

"He thought we might be spies," Arin explained. "And that we might know something about this Sword of Truth, something that could help Paralda."

Owen nodded slowly. Now that his own memories were back, he understood the terror that gripped Yezirah as the Void closed in on the Land, understood the desperate lengths that the Aevyans would go to to save the Air Realm. And they were right. There was an object that could do just that. Whether or not it was really a sword, he had no idea, though a quick check of his 'Tamus' memory was enough to tell him that it would make sense for the Sath of Air to be a sword.

Raya continued her tale, describing in colourful detail gossiping Gemina and the meanness towards the Fool-boy.

"He's here," Finn began, but she hushed him to silence, not wanting him to ruin her story.

The experience with the Vizier sounded uncannily like his own inquisition from the Exarp.

"I think it was because we're not 'Air,'" Arin interjected. "He thought someone had been doing stuff to our heads, but when I felt him sort of prodding... I er..." He hesitated, as he chose the right words. "I made a huge wave of Water energy go along the rod he was holding, and it worked."

Owen let out a laugh of relief. "Oh good! So it's not just me!"

"What?" Arin didn't understand.

"That's what I did when Professor Vishnami tried to get into my head," he explained, although he didn't admit that in his case it was Fire energy that he had used, not Water.

But his relief was short-lived when Raya got to the Paraldan Queen.

"You're sure?" He could hardly believe what he was hearing. It was one thing a Fire Spirit leading a cult in Dayah, quite another one being Queen. "I mean... you can't feel Fire energy, so you could be wrong."

"No." Arin shook his head adamantly. "She was definitely one of 'them'. We all saw her. And Enlali said how she almost never comes outside – well you wouldn't if you had no shadow, would you? Not if you were pretending to be a normal Aevyan."

And as Raya related what Enlali had said about Queen Azaka, the Singing Head and the Sword, any last doubts he may have had, vanished. He only half listened to the rest of the story, the escape from Paralda and reaching the Garden of the Seed, and though he made a mental note to thank the Fool-boy if they ever met, he heard nothing that seemed as relevant as the information about the Paraldan Queen.

When it came to his turn, he glossed over the Ill-Wind as best he could. "I thought it would help us," he explained rather lamely, "if I could fly... It would give us an advantage." None of his friends looked terribly convinced. "Anyway, it's good I did do it really, because if I hadn't, I'd have been in Paralda with you, not in the Towers and I wouldn't have found the Guardian." He decided to omit the dreamwalking episode. "That's when I lost my memory." He left it at that. It was bad enough that he had sneaked out alone to try to ride a Wind, let alone admitting to something even more stupid!

"And the book? Where is it?" Arin homed in on the critical point.

"Well... because I couldn't remember anything, I didn't know what it was."

"So what's happened to it?"

"Oh, it's OK," he said hurriedly, trying to reassure his friends. "But it's back there, at the Towers with the Mercury Guardian. And he *is* the Guardian," he added. "He read what was written on the Air page."

"What? What did it say?" Raya couldn't contain her excitement.

"It was mostly nonsense – or it looked like nonsense to me, anyway," he replied. "Just strings of numbers and letters all jumbled up. There was only one proper sentence, right at the beginning." He frowned as he tried to recall the exact words. "The heart... no... the pure heart of the Cup Bearer recognizes the Truth." Was that right? He closed his eyes as he cast his mind back to the Exarp's study. "Yes! That was it. *The pure heart of the Cup Bearer recognizes the Truth*' That was all. Then just nonsense."

Disappointment was written across his friends' faces. "Are you sure it was nonsense?" Arin asked.

He nodded. "Yes. Even the Exarp couldn't read it after staring at it for ages. It must be a code."

The rest of his story was a bit of an anticlimax. There had been no dramatic escape, no leaping over a cliff, just running after a bee.

"So that's it," he concluded. "The bee, my guide, led me here." He stopped. Why had it done that? Yes, he had recovered his memory by coming here, but that was surely not the role of the bee as his guide. He had always assumed before that the guides had one task and one task alone, guiding him to the Sath. For the first time he wondered if there was more to it than that. But before he had time to speculate any further, Mellonia returned, bearing a large jar of honey.

208

Owen felt inexplicably overcome with shyness as he sat down to eat. He had so many questions that he wanted to ask, but every time he plucked up the courage to speak, a hot wave of guilt swept over him. He was sure Mellonia knew what he had done, knew about the Ill-Wind, knew about the stupid attempt at dreamwalking. He glanced across the table and his eyes met hers.

"What's wrong?" She spoke softly and suddenly he was reminded of his mother. He bit his bottom lip and shook his head.

"Nothing." He was not going to cry in front of his friends, no matter what happened.

"Would you like to know a bit about the Garden of the Seed?" she asked, looking round to include his friends in the question.

"Yes please," Arin replied casting a quick glance at Owen. Raya and Finn might not have noticed, but he could see that something had upset him.

Mellonia smiled. "This is where the seeds were germinated in the beginning. Not in Dayah." Owen started in surprise at the word. How did Mellonia know of Dayah?

"We are in the east," she explained. "The Realm where the sun rises first, where spring is first born. Dayah is the living Spirit, the centre that holds all the other Realms together. Yezirah to the east, Bryah to the west, Assyah to the north," she paused a moment, "and Azilut to the south. Without Dayah our Lands would be but a hollow ring."

Owen was aware of a Tamus memory knocking very loudly on that door that he had shut, a lesson about the Azoth, and how it related to his own world. *'As above, so below'.*

"It is the bees who dance the dance of new life," Mellonia continued, "The lemniscate path."

The what? He was lost now.

"The bees." Mellonia saw his uncomprehending expression. "As they fly past from flower to flower, they carry pollen – the essence of life, concentrated sunlight. And as they land upon a new flower and pollinate it, so new life is born. They are the creatures of the All-Maker."

Again Owen started. That had been a phrase in his book: *'The All-Maker created the Guardians, elemental beings from the Realm of Spirits, to tend, nurture and love each Element.'*

And wasn't that what the Fire Lord was after – 'The power of the All-Maker?'

"Without bees…" Mellonia trailed off, shaking her head. "The bee does the will of the All-Maker, the flowers are pollinated, so then the plant-eaters may eat and live, and then the meat-eaters may eat and live. And here, this garden, is the Home of the Bees. It is here that the first breath of the All-Maker is born."

"There are bees in Dayah too!" Finn pointed out. He was still looking pleased by Mellonia's references to the importance of Dayah, even if he hadn't really understood what she was saying.

"Yes. There are bees in all the Realms. They are all one. Hive mind connects them all back to the source, back here to the Garden of the Seed."

Owen was suddenly reminded of what Arin had told him about dolphins having a twin in another world.

"Except for those who have been lost." Mellonia's voice was suddenly solemn.

"Lost?" He had a horrible suspicion he knew what she was going to say.

"The Void," she replied. "The place that is no-place. They enter there and are gone. And in those other Lands that lie beyond the Void, it grows ever harder for the bees there to stay connected to the life source, the hives. They tell me of sickness, of bees dying and not reborn, Lands abandoned by bees. And without bees there can be no life… not for long. The Land will die. The pattern of the All-Maker will be broken." She paused, lost in thought. "Here in Yezirah, they understand only that their Realm is shrinking," she continued after a moment. "The Rainbow Guild in their towers read the books that tell of other Lands, other ages, but they have lost true understanding. It has become a war of words, a war of ideas between the Towers and the Palace, as though clever arguments and swords can save Yezirah." She sighed. "The bees know the Truth. They hold the Truth within the heart of the hives and have done since…" She stopped. "Enough. These are not happy words. The Garden of the Seed is in essence a place of joy. And enjoy it you shall! Let us eat and talk of happier things!"

Finn, Raya and Arin needed no encouragement after their last meal with Mellonia, but Owen was sorry the conversation had come to an end. What had she meant about the bees knowing the truth? What truth? And why was the Sword called Truth? He suspected that in his 'Tamus memory' there was something that would help him understand this Air Element/Truth connection. But he was reluctant to dip too deeply into Tamus' thoughts. It felt as though behind the door that he had shut was a bottomless pool of Tamus memories, and having only just escaped from it, he didn't want to fall straight back in and never get out again!

"It will get easier," Mellonia said to him softly. "A bit like learning to swim." A pensive look crossed her face. "The bees never act for any reason other than the good of the hive. Your memory block was put there for this reason alone. I cannot explain any more than this." She paused a moment. "But now it is gone. And when a block is removed, it can feel a little like removing a dam in a river. But wait for the waters to calm, swim with the current, and all will be well."

He hoped she was right. At the moment, the Tamus memories felt more like a dangerous whirlpool.

Chapter 23

Owen woke late the next morning. A great wave of tiredness had hit him, and he had struggled to stay awake through the evening meal, despite it being one of the best he had ever eaten. He had barely been able to keep his eyes open long enough to make it to the bedroom and was asleep the moment his head touched the pillow.

The other three beds in the room were empty, but had the untidy look of having been slept in. He yawned. It had been a dreamless night – no Tamus or Owen memories intruding on his sleep. He knew he should get up. If even Arin was up, it was probably late! But lying in the soft bed, bathed in the warm golden light that filtered through the curtains, he felt as though he was in a cocoon of safety. Outside lay danger and problems: the Towers, the Paraldan Queen... He sighed. He had achieved nothing in Yezirah. Worse in fact. He still had no idea where the Sath was, but now both the Palace and the Towers would be after him and his friends. Queen Azaka had probably already worked out who they were, so the Fire Lord himself would know. And to make things even worse, he had lost the book. There was no way the Exarp was going to let him have it back, and breaking into the Mercury Tower to steal it was a hopeless idea; even if the Guardian hadn't realized how important it was, with an attack on the Towers imminent he was sure that there would be any number of magical defences in place.

He climbed slowly out of bed. Maybe something could be done with the three Sath he already had. Maybe somehow his world could be saved without the Air Sath. But even as he thought it, he knew how ridiculous the idea was – a world without Air.

He found his friends out in the garden with Mellonia and a small white dog.

"We've been helping with the bees," Finn said through a mouthful of pollen pellets.

"And the boy from Paralda is back – the one who saved us," Raya added for extra emphasis.

Everyone seemed so cheerful that despite himself, he felt his mood of gloom lift a little.

"There!" Raya laughed as a fair-haired boy ran past at full pelt, apparently chasing an invisible quarry along a zigzagging path.

"He is following a bee as she gathers nectar," Mellonia explained.

"Why?" Owen asked. It seemed an odd thing to do.

"Because it makes him happy to do so."

He watched the boy jumping deftly over clumps of flowers in his pursuit of the bee. He did certainly look happy. He was so focused on the bee that as he came running towards them, it looked as though he was going to hurtle headlong into Mellonia and send her flying. But at the last moment he skipped to one side and came to a standstill, then held out his cupped hands to her. With a smile, she picked up a silver cup from the table beside her and poured a clear liquid into his hands, a liquid which turned a rich golden colour, like the drink she had given Owen the previous afternoon.

As he watched the boy drink down the liquid, an incredible thought came into his head. *The pure heart of the* Cup Bearer *recognizes the Truth.* That was what the riddle in his book had said – the Cup Bearer. He had guessed back in the Mercury Tower, as he puzzled over this code, that it was some sort of astronomical reference – the water-carrier/cup-bearer sign, and that was as far as he had got. But what if he was wrong?

"Are you the Cup Bearer?" He blurted out the question, his heart in his mouth.

"Me?" Mellonia was momentarily surprised. "No." She shook her head.

It took him a moment to pick up the inference in her words.

"Not you... but... you know who is," he said slowly.

She gave him a long, pensive gaze before answering.

"They were known as the Children of the Rushings of the Air. They were wanderers between the Lands, attached to nothing and to no place. There was no falsehood in them, no deceit or illusion,

213

and their words were the truth, pure as the first breath of a new-born baby. Once they were loved and honoured here. Where they passed by, the people fed them, sharing what they had and seeking nothing in return."

This was ringing a bell in his memory – something to do with the Priests of the Elements perhaps...

"But times changed," she continued. "Welcome turned to hostility, and they were driven out of Yezirah."

"Driven out?" This didn't sound good. "But why?"

"The Aevyans' love for the Truth became clouded." She sighed. "Words became more important than the truth, cleverness more important than justice and fairness. And then innocence came to be seen as foolishness, and no one filled the cups of the Cup Bearers any longer."

His heart sank like a stone. When the riddle had been created, there must still have been Cup Bearers in Yezirah.

"Maybe all those nonsense letters and numbers need a Cup Bearer to read them," he said to his friends when Mellonia had left them. "When the Wardens wrote that riddle, they wouldn't have known that when the time came to read it, the Cup Bearers would be gone."

A long silence met his statement.

"That doesn't sound right," Arin said eventually. "Why would there be an extra person needed for Air? Surely there's enough protection with you needing the Guardian's help to read it."

"I don't know," he admitted. "Except..." A thought struck him. "There is a difference. The other Guardians – Beth, Nyxa, the Axle Stone – none of them was a 'person'. Maybe already, when they hid the Sath, they knew that the Guardians in the future might not be... er... perfect."

"What do you mean, perfect?" Arin asked, puzzled.

"Well, the Exarp – the Mercury Guardian – he wasn't interested in helping me. All he wanted was to get his own hands on the 'Sword' to make sure that he got the credit for it, not any of the other Tower Guardians. And I don't think they would ever let us take the Sath out of Yezirah if we did find it. I think they would use it to defeat the Palace and fight amongst themselves about which Tower it belonged to." He recalled the warning of old Io, the Yew Tree Spirit, about hiding the Wood Sath from the other Eddra. "It doesn't make any difference anyway. I can't see any way we can get the book back," he said with a sigh.

"So we wait here." Finn was more optimistic. "We stay with Mellonia and wait until they solve the riddle. After all, they're clever, aren't they? They should be able to solve it."

"And then work out how to get the Sath off them." Raya nodded her agreement.

But Owen knew it couldn't work like that. "They can't find it without me."

'*He alone is the one chosen.*' That was what the book had said. "I'm sure the magic protecting it means it has to be me who actually takes it, holds it. I think I'm going to have to go back to the Towers," he said gloomily.

But just as he was speaking, Mellonia reappeared.

"No." She had heard his last sentence. "You cannot go there now. The army of Paralda is on the move. They will have reached the Towers by nightfall. You must leave. Go back west, to the Great Plain. There you'll be safe."

"But I can't just go." He wasn't sure how much she had heard.

"Yes, you can," she said softly. "Remember what I said about swimming with the current?"

He didn't see how this was relevant but nodded. Perhaps the best thing was to try to get home, rescue Nana and come back with Darius to help them. He turned away from his friends and Mellonia, sure that the despair he felt must be showing in his eyes.

He hadn't realized that Mellonia had meant that they should leave that very morning, but when she emerged from the house a few minutes later, bearing a covered basket of food for them, it was clear that their stay in the Garden of the Seed was at an end.

"Sometimes things are far simpler than they appear," she said as she handed him the basket. "This was the first mistake of the Aevyans. They lost the ability to see the Truth, even if it was right under their noses all along. They fell in love with cleverness, with complicating things, in meaningless nets of words and numbers."

Words and numbers? He frowned. Had she read his mind? But before he could ask her what she meant, they were interrupted by the little white dog racing towards them in wildly spinning circles, as he chased his own tail, and a moment later the Fool-boy appeared, skipping across the grass with a bunch of red and white roses and lilies in his hand.

He came to a halt in front of Raya, then blushing shyly, held the flowers out to her.

"Thank you!" She too was now blushing as she accepted his gift.

And with one last beam of pure happiness, he turned away, launched himself into a cartwheel and ran off, disappearing into the orchard beyond.

"What?" Raya turned to her friends, a more familiar glare now on her face. "It's just because I was nice to him, and you weren't. You were horrid like the others. Stop grinning Arin. It makes you look like a monkey."

Despite everything, Owen couldn't help but smile himself. There was something contagious about the Fool-boy's enthusiastic happiness.

"You know, maybe it doesn't really matter that you don't have the book now," Arin said pensively, as they set off back down the valley, away from the Garden of the Seed. "I think I can pretty much remember that bit at the beginning about the Azoth and the key and all that stuff."

Owen was impressed. He was sure he had only read it to his friends a couple of times.

"And the Wood, Water and Earth riddles don't matter anymore," he continued. "So it's only Air."

"And Fire," Owen reminded him.

"Yes, but that's not going to have a page, is it? They didn't hide the Fire Sath."

He was right, Owen realized. There would be no riddle for the Fire Sath. The thought didn't make him feel an awful lot better, however. His hand drifted towards the pouch round his neck, where the tooth of Ayin Dragontooth lay. He was sorely tempted to take it out and see if it could help in any way, but perhaps it would be wiser to wait until his friends were sleeping.

They decided to stop for lunch beside the little stream that ran along the valley bottom.

"We can cut down here," Owen said, spotting what looked like a small animal track leading down through the gorse and brambles. A bee had just buzzed past his nose heading in that direction, and even though logic told him it was probably just any old bee and not his guide, it wouldn't do any harm following the track down. Had it not been for the bee, he would never have noticed the track, and never spotted a pile of black hair next to a bramble bush – a pile of black hair that suddenly moved.

He stopped. A pair of dark brown eyes was gazing up at him.

"What is it?" Raya came up behind him.

"It's OK." He squatted down, holding out the back of his hand to the dog. "I'm not going to hurt you." Gently he scratched his head. "Are you hungry?"

He certainly looked hungry, judging by how thin he was. He pulled a hunk of bread, butter and honey out of Mellonia's basket and offered it to him. It was gone in an instant.

"Poor boy, you're starving, aren't you?" He found some fish wrapped in leaves and that went down almost unchewed.

"Hey!" Raya protested. "Don't give him all our food!"

Owen got back to his feet. She was right. He didn't want to make the dog sick. "I wonder where he lives." He looked pensively at the black dog. "Maybe he's hurt or ill."

"Give him a few drops of this." Finn pulled a small phial of liquid out of his bag. "Made by my grandmother: old man's beard, star flower, touch-me-nots, rock rose and cherry plum – for emergencies. It's better in water, but it'll work with food too."

He took the little bottle, wondering just how many other useful potions Finn had brought with him from Dayah, and poured a few drops on to a mossground cake.

"No more food now," Owen said as the cake was gobbled down, "or you'll be sick." He gave him one last head scratch then turned back towards the little trail down to the stream. There was nothing else he could do. Even if the dog was hurt, he could hardly take him to the nearest vet!

But when he glanced back, the dog was no longer lying by the bramble bush. Instead she was only a couple of metres behind him, following him down the track.

"You can't come with me!" he began, but even as the words came out of his mouth, a little voice in his head said, 'Why not?'

"Maybe she's a guide, like Brock," Finn suggested.

Owen shook his head. There wouldn't be any more guides.

They sat down for lunch beside the river, the black dog settling happily at Owen's feet. He had expected him to beg from his friends when they too had food, but instead he remained with him.

"A fish!" Finn let out an exclamation and jumped to his feet as a silvery shape leapt through the air in the stream below. "Let's go and catch some. It's always best to have spare food. You never know..."

Owen looked at the now empty basket. It wasn't a bad idea, especially if they were going back out on to the Plain again. Arin and Raya were both keen to accompany him, but Owen decided to stay put with his new friend.

"I'm no good at fishing anyway," he said, glad of an excuse for a few minutes alone.

"Look after my flowers!" Raya laid the bunch of roses and lilies down beside him. Despite the impracticality of travelling with a bunch of flowers, she had wrapped a piece of wet cloth round the stems and insisted on bringing them with her.

"What are we going to do?" he asked the dog, once his friends were out of earshot. "I've made a mess of everything here."

The dog wriggled up to lay his head on his lap and sighed heavily.

"We need to find you a name." He reached down to scratch his tummy and the dog rolled over – straight on to Raya's flowers!

"Oh no!" He looked in dismay at the squashed mess. The dog wagged his tail and pawed at the flowers making the situation even worse. Hastily he began to gather them up. Maybe he could put the bunch back together and Raya wouldn't notice that they were squashed. But as he picked up the roses and lilies, he noticed a flower he hadn't spotted before, one which must have been hidden at the heart of the bunch – a flower with a spike of pale-violet, funnel shaped blooms. He recognised it from Nana's garden but couldn't recall its name. It was a strange flower for the Fool-boy to have included. It had something to do with remembrance, he thought. But then as he looked at the long, pointed leaves, the name came to him – 'Sword Lily' – that's what Nana had called it. And in an instant he understood! Mellonia's words rang in his ears as with a shaking hand he reached for his pouch, *'sometimes things are far simpler than they appear'!*

He pulled out the key – a key with one gleaming stripe standing out from the rest, a key that burnt his fingers as he touched it. And everything fell into place. He could see in his mind's eye the Fool-boy holding out his 'cupped' hands to receive Mellonia's gift of the drink. He was the Cup Bearer! And they had been in the 'Garden of the Seed' – weren't the Sath seeds? The Guardians in their towers could spend an eternity trying to decode the nonsense letters and numbers but to no avail. The 'Truth' had been right under their noses all along, only they couldn't see it.

His heart in his mouth, he picked up the Sword Lily. The violet flower heads were all open except for one, a tightly furled bud at the top of the stem. Carefully, he peeled back the petals. The Wood Sath had been hidden in Water, Water in Earth, Earth in Fire. And hidden in Wood... He drew out a slender, gleaming sliver of metal, like a bee sting – or a tiny sword! The Air Sath.

The man sat gazing out of the window of his study, out towards the distant horizon. His arm was itching. It often did these days. He glanced down at the thin white scar. Even after all these years it hadn't faded. The binding spell had been far stronger than he or his twin brother had realized. A shared destiny... He smiled to himself. He knew he could rely on Tamus.

Printed in Great Britain
by Amazon

43489904R00128